REUNITED WITH HER VISCOUNT PROTECTOR

Mary Brendan

MILLS & BOON

First Published in Great Britain 2019
by Mills & Boon, an imprint of HarperCollins*Publishers*
1 London Bridge Street, London, SE1 9GF

© 2019 Mary Brendan

ISBN: 978-0-263-26929-1

MIX
Paper from
responsible sources
FSC® C007454

Chapter One

‘You little scamp! Come back here!’

Mrs Fenton picked up her lavender skirts and chased the shrieking child on to the pathway. She soon caught up with him and hoisted him off his feet in a cuddle. ‘You are far too nimble for me. You win again, Master Bernard.’ She placed a kiss on his soft cheek.

‘Oh, stop it, Bernie. You will tire poor Auntie Dawn out and she won’t come again to play with you,’ the Countess of Houndsmere said, issuing a warning to her giggling son.

‘Of course I will come. I love our games, don’t I, Bernie?’ Dawn put the wriggling child back on to the flagstones.

After his game of chase, Master Bernard still had plenty of energy; his godmother, however, was holding the stitch in her side and fanning herself with a hand. The boy immediately dashed off to throw a ball across the emerald lawn for two wolfhound puppies to squabble over. Dawn strolled over to sit with her friend in the shade and have a well-earned rest.

A table and chairs had been set up under the dipping broad boughs of a magnificent plane tree in the grounds of a mansion in Grosvenor Square. Upon the table was the finest rose-patterned porcelain and a tray upon which reposed silverware for making tea. Two maids hovered close by. They attended to refreshments and to tilt parasols this way and that to ensure the ladies were shielded from any rogue sunbeams infiltrating the whispering greenery.

Dawn sat down next to the Countess, who was cooling her pink cheeks with a fan of ivory and lace. Leaning closer to her friend, Dawn benefited from some wafted air.

'You make me feel very old, Dawn. I wish I could still charge about like that,' Emma complained, whipping the fan to and fro with increased vigour.

'You can, my dear...just not while you are carrying a baby. And as I am the elder of us by two months, please never again mention our advancing years or I will feel quite miserable.' Dawn sat back comfortably, then took her friend's hand in hers, giving her a cheeky smile. 'Come, we are neither of us yet in our dotage, Em, at the grand age of twenty-nine.'

'I feel quite ancient sometimes, you know, when my back aches.' Emma shifted on the seat as her unborn child made its presence known by giving her a kick.

'When you are rocking your new babe you will forget you ever had these twinges.' Dawn sighed. 'I wish I could take my godson home with me. I love having Bernie's company. You are so lucky to have such a handsome son and another little one on the way.' She smoothed a hand over the small bump beneath her friend's silk gown. 'Girl or boy…what do you think?'

Emma cocked her head, a smile on her lips. 'I really don't mind as long as all fingers and toes are present.' She felt guilty now for having moaned about feeling uncomfortable. Indeed, she was fortunate to have her family: Dawn had miscarried a child and then been denied the chance of another when her husband had died in an accident a short while later.

The tea was poured and distributed and young Bernard rushed up to enjoy a glass of cordial and some biscuits. He sat on the grass at his mother's side, the faithful puppies stretched out at his feet.

'Don't feed them biscuits, dear,' his mama gently cautioned. 'Your papa will not like it if they get fat.' She added an aside for Dawn's hearing, 'He doesn't seem to mind me getting rounder, though.'

'I hope you are not going to boast about your handsome husband chasing you around your bedchamber every night.'

'Indeed, he does not,' Emma returned with a wink. 'I never run away...'

They chuckled and Dawn sipped her tea. The two women had known each other since childhood and had always shared their good and bad times with one another. A bit of unladylike chat was nothing new for them either. But wistfulness settled on Dawn whenever she dwelt on her friend's blissful happiness. She loved Emma too much to feel jealous. Besides, Emma had suffered her share of misfortune before the Earl of Houndsmere fell in love with her and put everything right for Emma's embattled family.

Dawn's own marriage had been different: a convenient match. When Thomas Fenton had proposed to her, he had been open and honest in his reasons for doing so. He was a widower and needed a wife to care for his teenage daughter and guide her into womanhood. Dawn had been equally honest when accepting him. Her father had remarried a woman with whom she rarely saw eye to eye. It had been the right time to move out from beneath Mr Sanders's roof and let the middle-aged newlyweds enjoy a harmonious atmosphere. Her bossy stepmother would have driven her to distraction. Nevertheless Julia was good for her father, keeping an eye on his health and his over-imbibing. So in a most timely fashion fate had intervened and provided a practical solution. A short while after Thomas proposed, Dawn had become Mrs Fenton.

No grand passion, but in her own way she had grown fond of her husband and of her stepdaughter. They would have continued to rub along tolerably well as a little family if he had stayed in London rather than travelling on treacherous roads to spend Christmas with his wife and daughter. The carriage had overturned on the way to their Essex retreat and Thomas had perished.

'Papa!' Bernard leapt to his feet and started to race across the grass towards the house as he noticed his father approaching along the path.

The Earl of Houndsmere swept his son into his arms, then carried on towards them. He bent to kiss his wife's flushed cheek.

'This is a nice surprise,' he said to Dawn.

'As it is to see you, Lance,' Dawn returned on a smile.

'Will you stay and dine? I have invited some friends to come later.'

'Oh, do have dinner with us, Dawn,' Emma pleaded before turning to her husband. 'Who have you asked?'

'My sister and brother-in-law and I believe Jack might put in an appearance, but then with Jack you never quite know...'

'Jack?' the Countess echoed on a frown. 'You don't mean Jack Valance?'

'I most certainly do.'

'But...is he back from his travels?' Emma exclaimed.

'His ship docked a few weeks ago. Valance is home to stay, having found his feet and his fortune. I'll be glad to settle down for a good long chat with him over a bottle of cognac this evening.' Lance deposited his wriggling son on the turf.

Emma turned a sparkling gaze on Dawn. 'Oh, you must remember Jack. He is Lance's best friend. Many years ago we went for a drive with him in Hyde Park and your stepmother came, too.'

'Yes, I do remember him,' Dawn said mildly. 'Thank you for the invitation, but I won't stay for dinner.'

The Earl abandoned the ladies to go with his

son, dragging on his hand to make him play chase. Lance dodged to and fro to escape the puppies and Bernard jumping up at him, leaving his wife to attempt to persuade her friend to dine with them later. Emma clasped Dawn's fingers, idle on the table.

'Why won't you stay?' Emma frowned. 'If you'd like to change, I have a gown for you to wear, or, if you'd sooner go home first to choose a dress, of course you're welcome to take a carriage.'

'I know…thank you…' Dawn said, patting her friend's hand to calm her anxiety. 'It is not that.'

'I know you don't have another dinner appointment,' Emma said bluntly.

'No…but…'

'But you don't want to see Jack again,' Emma guessed. 'I know that you like my sister and brother-in-law, so they're not putting you off staying to dine. Are you not quite over Jack?'

'Of course I am over him, my dear!' Dawn protested on a huff of a laugh.

'Of course you must be; you've since been married to a nice gentleman and five years have passed since you saw Jack Valance,' Emma said.

'Closer to six,' Dawn murmured.

'Aha! So you're not quite as over him as you'd have me believe, are you?'

'Will he bring his fiancée to meet you, do you think?' Dawn teased.

'Fiancée?' Emma echoed in disbelief.

'I already knew he'd returned. I heard some ladies gossiping about him when I was at the library earlier in the week. Apparently he has returned to marry a Miss Sarah Snow.'

'Why did you not say sooner?' Emma gasped.

'If I'd mentioned him, I knew you'd think what you *are* thinking.' Dawn shrugged. 'My liking him was all long ago. Honestly, Em, I am over him and have other, more important things on my mind. One of which is my stepdaughter. My letter to Eleanor is quite rudely overdue, as is my visit. I must immediately dash off a reply to her and get it in the post, then prepare for a trip.'

'So you're abandoning me and going off to Essex for a sojourn?' Emma teased in return.

'Only for a fortnight!' Dawn protested. 'It makes me feel quite ancient to mention my stepgranddaughter…and another child soon due. Lily is a little dear…up on her feet now. I love to take her presents. Would you like to come shopping tomorrow in Regent Street and help me choose some things for her?'

'I would love to…' Emma frowned regretfully. 'But walking round the shops will fag me out and I'll spoil your enjoyment.' She paused. 'I wonder whether Lance knows Jack's getting betrothed? If he does, why did he not say?' She shot her husband a glance just as he gave a hefty overarm throw, setting the puppies charging quite a distance after a large stick.

Dawn got to her feet. 'Men tend to put little store on these things, Em. If he does know of it, he probably hasn't thought to bring it up. I haven't seen a notice gazetted yet.' Dawn had been searching for one, too. As soon as she got home after hearing the gossip in the library she'd scoured the lists of announcements, but had seen none that mentioned Jack Valance. And then she'd scolded herself for having put herself to such trouble for a man who'd easily forgotten about her. 'Now, I should get along and let you prepare for your guests.'

'I wish you could stay a while longer...' Emma wheedled.

'I really must go. Polly will be grumpy if her efforts in the kitchen are spoiled.' Dawn clucked her tongue. 'She's not the best of cooks, poor girl. But she tries hard and can dress hair very nicely.' She chuckled at the memory of yesterday's burnt pie. But Polly was a treasure to her, loyal and versatile, and that was of great help when one could only afford to employ a single servant.

'Well, if you're not going to get a good dinner that's even more reason to stay,' Emma said archly. 'But... I understand.' She gave her friend a rueful look. 'If Jack brings his intended this evening, I'll be sure to let you know all about her.'

'And when I get back I will let you know all about my trip to Essex.' Dawn assisted her friend in rising from her chair. Linking arms, they set off at a slow stroll towards the house. Dawn raised a hand in farewell to the Earl. He had his son in his arms and was on his way across the lawn to the flag-edged pond to show the boy the goldfish. He shifted Bernie in his grip to return her a farewell salute.

'I've not heard of this Miss Sarah Snow or her family. Is she young...out this Season?' Still Emma seemed absorbed in knowing more about Jack Valance's plans.

'I believe she keeps to herself and hasn't been seen much. But she is pretty from what the ladies were saying. A redhead.' Dawn hugged Emma closer. 'She sounds like a wise young lady. Thank goodness we no longer have to attend those ghastly balls at Almack's. I feel quite sorry for those poor girls being criticised as though they were a herd of prime fillies.'

'I've asked Lance to bring me home some tattle, but he rarely does. He says it all passes over his head when he's in his club. Not that he goes there much. I expect he might go more often now that Jack is home. They've been friends since school, but have hardly seen one another in years.'

Dawn thought back on those years, wondering where the time had flown to. Yet much had happened in her life: she'd been married, widowed and now had a family, none of whom were her blood relatives. The only one of those left to her was her papa.

'Once my confinement is over *we* must sally forth and find out what the *beau monde* is up to,' Emma announced, interrupting her friend's pensiveness.

'The *beau monde* will be much as it always was, my dear,' Dawn returned. 'You will discover nothing much more than who put their last shilling on the turn of a card and lost an estate and which husband was found *in flagrante* with his chum's wife.'

'You are a dreadful cynic, Dawn,' Emma fondly chided.

'Am I? I don't mean to be. Perhaps life has made me grumpy.'

Emma hugged her friend. Indeed, Dawn had had some tough luck and words were of little comfort to somebody who had found contentment with a gentleman, if not love, and had settled for that consolation just to have it whipped away.

Chapter Two

The following morning Dawn was up early to post a letter to her stepdaughter, belatedly accepting Eleanor's invitation to visit. Her second child was soon due and Dawn guessed the expectant mother was becoming easily tired and would like some help looking after her boisterous little daughter.

The Reverend Peter Mansfield wasn't a fellow given to lending a hand to his wife. In fact, Dawn had had to bite her tongue when she was there last time. The couple employed just two servants: a maid and an elderly cook. When the maid had been laid up with raging toothache the vicar had allowed Eleanor—in the early stages of her pregnancy—to sweep out the grate rather than do it himself. At the time Eleanor had said she didn't mind, although Dawn had noticed a certain spark in her stepdaughter's eye. Dawn had rolled up her own sleeves to take over the task, while hoping her stepson-in-law might feel shamed into acting. He had, dropping to his knees with a martyred look. Dawn imagined there had been other, unwitnessed, times when Eleanor had been treated less than considerately.

But Dawn did her best to be amenable to Peter for his wife's sake. She had put off this visit by some weeks because she hadn't relished having his company. She had—quite validly—blamed the delay on the vagaries of the March winds making travelling hazardous. She gazed up at the clear azure sky. There was no such excuse to be had now the weather had turned unseasonably fine. But before it returned to normal for this time of the year she must make that trip or she might be caught out. Besides, she genuinely loved seeing Eleanor and Lily, so enduring the vicar's bombast was a price worth paying. And she'd only be out of town for a fortnight.

Dawn lived on the fringes of town in a modest town house on a leafy crescent. She walked on in the direction of Regent Street, intending to browse the shops for something nice to take with her to Essex for her little granddaughter.

Reaching her destination, she sought out a toy shop, browsing the counters and pondering on whether a spinning top would be too advanced for Lily and a rag doll too mundane. The girl was by no means a baby, but Dawn had little idea of the progress children made as they grew, having never been a mother herself. In the end she purchased just the doll, undecided about the top, and headed to the drapery to buy some pretty clothes. She was on the point of entering the premises when a sleek black curricle drew her attention as it pulled in to the kerb some distance away. Its arrival seemed to have caused a stir— she noticed that people had turned to observe the passengers. Idly, she tilted her head to get a better view of the driver.

Dawn stood quite still and, once she'd conquered her surprise, commenced wondering how she *had* recognised him. It had been years since she had seen or spoken to Jack Valance and he looked very different. His hair was no longer fair and cropped short, but a silvery tone and worn rather long. His face had lost its city pallor and was now bronzed by a foreign sun, but his height and breadth were familiar. As was the way he agilely leapt to the pavement to assist his companion to alight.

Dawn watched his strong dark hands; once she had felt those long fingers fastened on her, courteously helping her from a vehicle. There had been two occasions on which he'd invited her to take a drive with him. Before they'd parted for the final time he had crowded her behind an oak tree in Hyde Park to kiss her as soon as her chaperon's back was turned. During that snatched, thrilling episode Jack Valance had broken her heart. He wasn't in a position to court her, he'd told her. But he'd promised to come back as soon as he improved his prospects enough to take a wife. She'd not seen him again until this moment. Dawn focused on the young woman smiling coquettishly at him…to little response. He seemed more interested in ensuring the tiger had the reins of the fine pale-flanked Arabian in harness.

He hadn't recognised *her*, Dawn realised— his gaze had roamed her way and then travelled on. Rather than feeling piqued at being overlooked by a gentleman who once had told her she was beautiful, she was rather glad to be able to discreetly observe the couple from her vantage point in the shop doorway. With an amount of wryness she realised that if *that* was his future wife, then Sarah Snow wasn't the refined young lady she'd believed her to be! Neither was she a stunning redhead. But the blonde was pretty, if a touch gaudy in her fancy bonnet and diaphanous muslin gown of pale blue. Dawn imagined that Jack Valance was out shopping with a *chère amie*. And she wondered how his prospective betrothed might feel about that.

Hastily she entered the shop on realising the couple were heading towards her. She was sure they hadn't noticed her vulgarly staring at them—even so, she felt annoyed at herself for having done so. She forced herself to put him from her mind and to inspect small ribbon-trimmed bonnets and a lemon-hued dress that the draper assured her were all perfectly sized for a growing toddler.

Having made her purchases, Dawn headed towards the exit, keen to get home and wrap her gifts in colourful paper.

'Mrs Fenton?'

His voice hadn't changed even if his appearance had...but she'd been Miss Dawn Sanders when last they had spoken. So he knew she'd been married... Perhaps Emma had spoken about mutual acquaintances yesterday evening when they'd dined together. These thoughts whizzed through Dawn's mind as she slowly turned about with an admirable show of surprise at seeing him. In fact, she *was* a trifle alarmed as she'd not been conscious of him entering the shop, let alone approaching her.

'Why… Mr Valance. How are you, sir? I had heard that you'd returned from overseas.'

'I know. Your friend Emma said you were aware I was back. I have to say I'm disappointed that we didn't see one another yesterday evening. You declined to dine with us, I was told.' Jack's eyes discreetly studied her. The dark bonnet brim was shielding her complexion, but he knew that beneath it was a face of rare beauty. On first glance Dawn's features might appear rather severe, yet on finer appraisal were undoubtedly exquisite. Her green eyes were fringed by lengthy black lashes and topped by delicate brows that looked as soft as sable. Her nose was thin, her mouth asymmetrical with a lower lip that was fuller than the curving cupid's bow on top. She was petite, her smooth peachy cheek barely reached his shoulder, but her figure was generously curvaceous in all the right places. He hadn't forgotten a single thing about her in all those tormented years they'd been apart.

It might have been a long while since she had lain with her husband, or even been kissed, but Dawn could recognise the signs that a man found her attractive. She had seen the same smouldering intensity at the back of predatory gentlemen's eyes when they propositioned her. But none of those fellows had managed to neutralise a tense situation, or his lust, as it seemed this man could.

'You missed a fine dinner,' Jack said, patting his stomach. 'I'm still feeling the effect of too many courses.'

'Emma is a wonderful hostess, but I'm afraid I was too busy to attend. I have a trip to Essex to prepare for to see my family. I've had a lot of packing and shopping to do and so on.' Dawn indicated her parcels. Had she detected something in his tone? Subtle amusement because he believed she'd deliberately avoided him? She *had*, although she'd never admit to it.

'Well, no matter, when I saw you walking on Regent Street I hoped I'd have a chance to say hello.'

So he *had* been aware of her presence all along. Dawn felt her complexion starting to glow as she realised he'd probably observed her spying on him.

'You go to Essex bearing gifts.' His slate-grey eyes dropped to the parcels in her arms.

'Of course…but I have left choosing them to the last minute as usual.' Her eyes discreetly flitted over his shoulder, seeking a sign of his companion. The young woman was at a counter with a pile of merchandise mounting beside her. He, too, had been buying gifts, she imagined, even if he didn't get to choose them or decide what they cost. The blonde appeared to be too busy inspecting gloves to come and claim her beau.

But other people...women...were watching them. Indeed, Dawn understood why. His travels and the acquirement of riches had transformed him from an attractive gentleman to a devilishly handsome one. But it was more than good looks and expensive tailoring setting him apart from his younger self: he had an air of sophistication and distinction. Jack Valance had gone away years ago with his pockets to let and come back with a rather startling self-assurance. Yet Dawn had liked him as he was...modest and familiar. On the few occasions they had met she had marvelled at how at ease she felt with him after so short an acquaintance. He had amused yet excited her and on the day they parted she had felt upset enough to cry in private. But months and months had passed and she'd received not a single letter from him. Her hope that he intended to renew their acquaintance had withered; she recalled feeling foolish for having almost begged him to keep in touch because she liked him very much. And then Thomas had asked her to be his wife and a dilemma had been forced upon her: wait longer for Jack, or marry Thomas. The right decision it had been, too, to accept his proposal.

She might have been infatuated with Jack Valance for almost a year, loitering in the hallway with bated breath for the post every day, but to him she'd been just a passing fancy, soon forgotten.

'I believed your father still resided in Marylebone,' Jack remarked. 'Where in Essex do your family live?'

'My father and stepmother have now moved to Shropshire. I am going to visit my late husband's family in Essex.'

'I see. I was sorry to hear about your husband's accident. Emma told me you'd been widowed.'

'Yes…some time ago now.' Dawn dipped her head and stepped away. For some reason she didn't want his pity, or to speak about her short marriage to Thomas. 'It is nice to see you, sir, but I must get on. I haven't yet finished packing for my trip.'

'Where does your stepfamily live in Essex? I might know of it as I have a house there.'

She turned back. The demand in his question had made her bristle and feel tempted to tell him it was none of his business, but she didn't, although she was again reminded of how very different this gentleman was to the languid fellow she had known all those years ago. But she was determined not to appear flustered by his company. 'My stepdaughter and her husband live in Wivenhoe,' she said, then with a fleeting smile and a small bob she made for the exit, conscious of the weight of his hooded grey gaze on her back.

'Do slide up a bit and give the lady some room.' Mrs Broome's country brogue broke the quiet as she directed an order at her daughter seated beside her. Both mother and daughter were broad of beam and had left Dawn very little room, squashed as she was into the corner of the mail coach. But she was grateful that at least she had some air and a mist of sleety rain blowing on to her face from the open window.

'The weather's been warm for early spring recently. I'm glad it's back to normal now or we'd be sweating buckets,' the older woman cheerily announced while fidgeting on the seat.

Dawn murmured an agreement, the only passenger to politely respond. Indeed, the vagaries of the March weather had caught her out. The prematurely mild air of last week had now acquired a feel of frost that stung the cheeks. The roads that had been dry and dusty had been churned to a bog in places by coach wheels.

The tweedy farmer opposite jiggled his brows,

then closed his eyes, making clear he desired no conversation directed at him. The two thin young women seated either side of him turned their heads in opposite directions to gaze out of their respective windows into the gloomy afternoon. They looked to be servants, perhaps travelling from London to visit their families back home. Dawn used a hanky on her rain-spattered brow while hoping that the coaching inn would hove into view so they could all escape this cramped, musty environment. More than that, she wished she had the wherewithal to keep a small conveyance of her own so she wouldn't need to travel in such discomfort when visiting her stepfamily. Even when Thomas had been alive, the most the Fentons had possessed in the way of transport had been an ancient carriage that he had inherited from his father. His trusty contraption as he had called it had been his downfall. He had known it needed repairs. But his insurance business had been floundering beneath heavy shipping claims and purchasing new springs and axles had been last on his list of expenses.

At their country cottage they had kept a pony and trap to get around. Thomas had taught her to drive it so she could be independent when he was in town on business. The cottage and the pony and trap were gone now…luxuries she could no longer afford on her widow's pension.

The blast of a bugle curtailed Dawn's reflectiveness and made her offer up a prayer of thanks that they were approaching a watering hole. All the passengers stirred into life as they anticipated stretching their legs and partaking of some refreshment.

'I'll have a beef pie if they've got such a thing. My stomach's fair grumbling.' Mrs Broome gave Dawn a nudge. 'You'll be glad to get down and tuck into something, won't you, my dear?'

'Indeed, I will.' Dawn peered through the window as the coach passed beneath the swinging sign of the Cockerel Tavern into a busy courtyard. She'd no appetite for a pie; a snack would suffice. By nightfall she would reach her destination and hoped to have a good dinner waiting for her. Although the Reverend Peter Mansfield tended to parsimony, he usually provided a hearty evening meal as he always joined them at table then. Other than that, his work kept him abroad for most of the day…and that arrangement suited Dawn very well.

'What can I get for you then, ma'am?' The landlord hovered at Dawn's elbow.

'A pot of tea and a plate of buttered crumpets,

thank you, sir.' Having given her order, Dawn sat back in her chair and untied her bonnet strings while the fellow moved off to attend to other weary passengers. A log fire was blazing in the grate, spreading a cosy ambience throughout the low-beamed taproom. Dawn removed her hat and ran her fingers through a tumble of untidy chestnut curls in an attempt to neaten them.

Mrs Broome and her daughter joined Dawn, sitting down without a by your leave. Immediately the landlord reappeared with pencil and paper ready.

Having given her order for pies, Mrs Broome turned on her daughter an old-fashioned look. 'You can stop giving him the eye, miss!' She smacked the girl's hand, idle on the table-top. 'The sooner this one's wed, the better it'll be.' Mrs Broome rolled her eyes.

Dawn gave the blushing girl a glimmer of a smile. She was a pretty brunette of about fifteen and had been sliding sly glances through the window at a strapping stable lad toiling in the courtyard.

'So… I recall you said you're visiting relations, Mrs Fenton.' The older woman crossed her arms over her chest, hoping for a gossip.

'I am…' Dawn confirmed. 'I'll be glad to get

to journey's end and to my bed tonight. It's been a long day.'

Mrs Broome jiggled her aching shoulders. 'Indeed, it has. My bones are fair creaking. But I was determined to go to London to see my father laid to rest. So did his granddaughter, wanting to pay her last respects.' She frowned at her daughter who was still batting her eyelashes.

'Oh… I'm sorry to hear about your loss.'

'As I am to know about yours,' Mrs Broome said sympathetically. 'How long are you widowed, my dear? La…and you so young and pretty, too.'

'Oh…some years.' Dawn's lavender gown had given the game away that she was in the latter stage of mourning.

'Who are you visiting?' the girl piped up.

'Betty Broome! Mind your manners,' the girl's mother scolded. 'Inquisitive little thing,' she half-apologised before taking up where her daughter had left off. 'Local people, are they, these relations? Or are you travelling on further?'

'I'm going on to Wivenhoe…'

The Broomes' questions reminded Dawn of Jack Valance's interest in her family's whereabouts. Not that she needed much to prompt her to think of him. For the duration of the journey, with nothing to do for hours on end but gaze into drizzle, she had found it difficult to banish him from her thoughts. She had been going over their brief conversation in the drapery and rueing that she hadn't looked at her best that afternoon. It was too late now to wish she had dressed with more care when sallying forth to do her shopping. And why should it matter? Jack Valance was getting married. But Dawn knew why it mattered. She had seen desire in his eyes; once he had thought her beautiful and she was woman enough to hope he still did, fiancée or no fiancée. More than that, now they had met again and exchanged a few words, perhaps, just perhaps, he might rue not having kept in touch with her. He hadn't sought her out in the shop just to be polite. He wasn't indifferent to her, of that she was sure. She'd seen a spark of some emotion at the backs of his eyes…

'Do you know that vicar, my dear? The one who is staring at you?' Mrs Broome nudged Dawn to gain her attention, then jerked a nod at somebody outside.

Dawn gave a soft gasp of surprise. 'Indeed, I do know him. I am on my way to his house. It's my stepdaughter's husband.' She glanced at her companions. 'Please excuse me, I should go and speak to him.' She got up with an inaudible sigh. She had certainly not been expecting to see the Reverend Peter Mansfield until she reached Wivenhoe. And from the expression she'd glimpsed on her stepson-in-law's face she guessed he'd been equally taken aback to spot her. Donning her cloak, she hurried outside, tweaking forward her hood to protect her face from the sleet.

The fellow who had been talking to the vicar had disappeared and Peter had headed towards the tavern to meet her beneath the shelter of the porch. He was a dark-haired man of medium height and build who, despite being her stepson-in-law, was her senior by five years.

'Mrs Fenton...' Peter removed his hat, securing it beneath his arm. 'This is a nice surprise. I wasn't expecting to see you until this evening, at the vicarage.'

'I wasn't expecting to see you yet either.' She paused, sensing that his attitude was false and that this premature meeting was as unwelcome for him as it was for her. 'Have you business in the area, sir?'

'A clerical meeting...nothing too important. Now, I insist that I take you the rest of the way to Wivenhoe in my gig.'

Dawn hesitated in replying. Oddly, she knew she'd sooner make the rest of the journey squashed in the coach with the Broomes than have his company. But how to refuse without giving offence?

'My luggage is stowed on the coach. It will be a bit of a commotion to swap vehicles and only a few more hours of travel. It would be as well to carry on as I am...'

'I insist, ma'am. My wife will be glad of your company as soon as may be and happy to let you occupy the child so she might rest.' He patted her arm to quieten her. 'I shall speak to the coachman, never fear. Everything will soon be arranged.'

'Very well...' Dawn dipped her head in agreement, forcing a smile. She raised a hand to acknowledge her friends in the taproom. Mrs Broome was indicating with sign language that her crumpets had been placed on the table.

'I ordered something to eat...'

'Oh...go to it, ma'am,' the vicar urged solicitously. 'I will speak to your coach driver and have your bags transferred. I need no refreshment myself, but will wait for you.'

Chapter Three

⁂

'Oh, Eleanor! Why did you not write and let me know you have been poorly? I would have come far sooner to care for you.' Dawn felt a pang of guilt, wishing she had responded to her stepdaughter's letter promptly. But she had preferred to spend time with her friends in Mayfair than take up her invitation to visit her stepfamily in Essex.

Eleanor made a feeble gesture from the bed upon which she was resting. 'You have your own life to live in town, Mama. It is nothing too bad…just a little breathlessness making me feel giddy. The babe is probably lying in the wrong position, but will surely soon move and give me some relief.'

Dawn wasn't convinced about that. Her stepdaughter didn't look as though she were merely suffering discomfort, but a proper illness. Eleanor's complexion was greyish, yet spots of scarlet were on her cheekbones and a film of perspiration beaded her hairline.

Dawn wished she had some experience of childbirth to draw on. She hadn't been present at Lily's birth. After being advised of the happy news she had travelled to Essex a week later to see the new arrival. On that occasion Eleanor had looked quite perky, telling her that a midwife had attended her and all had gone as well as was to be expected. 'Have you been like this for a while? Might it be the baby coming early, do you think, my dear?' Dawn picked up a hanky from the nightstand and dipped it in the water jug, then cooled her stepdaughter's brow with it.

'I felt more myself last week. I doubt it is the baby.' Eleanor frowned. 'It is over a month too soon and the pain seems different.'

From the moment Dawn had entered the house and been advised by the vicar that his wife and child were napping and shouldn't be disturbed, Dawn had sensed something wasn't quite right. Peter had carried on to say, in a way that seemed to brook no refusal, that Dawn should also rest after her journey. He had ushered her up the stairs and carried her bags for her to deposit in the guest room. But she sensed he was being dictatorial rather than solicitous. Once she'd spotted him from her window, striding along the cinder path in the direction of the church, she had hurried to find her stepdaughter.

A first glimpse of Eleanor's ashen face and dishevelled appearance had made Dawn's heartbeat accelerate in alarm. Her stepdaughter might not be a beauty, but she was pretty enough and had always taken pains with her appearance. But it wasn't just her lack of grooming—the young woman had a look of sadness and defeat about her, too.

'Has Peter sent for the physician to attend you?'

'He says there is no need for the doctor to be summoned and that it is a natural ailment to be expected close to a woman's confinement. I don't recall feeling so feverish last time, though, Mama.'

Dawn picked up her granddaughter as she tried to climb on to the bed to lay beside her mother. She jigged Lily in her arms to quieten her as she grew fretful. 'I have some presents for you, young lady. But first you must promise to be good. Will you be?'

Lily solemnly nodded her head, becoming still. She was bright as a button and had remembered that her grandma brought her nice things from London when she visited.

'I'm so sorry I wasn't up to greet you,' Eleanor wiped a tear from the corner of an eye. 'What a feeble sort of woman I am turning into.'

'Don't say that! Of course you are not.' Dawn guessed that her stepdaughter was repeating criticism. It sounded like the sort of snappish remark Peter Mansfield might make.

He had been impatient with her earlier. At the Cockerel he had not waited outside while she finished her meal as he'd said he would. He had come to find her and made it clear he was ready to set on the road immediately now her luggage had been transferred to his gig. His bullying had been polite, but Dawn had felt under pressure nevertheless to say an immediate farewell to the Broomes and go with him.

Thereafter he had driven at reckless speed, bouncing over ruts on the road to Wivenhoe, with little conversation passing between them. That had suited Dawn. She found little to say to him at the best of times. Yet on that journey of almost an hour he hadn't once mentioned his wife other than to give a throwaway answer to Dawn's question of how her stepdaughter was. Eleanor at times felt a little under the weather, he'd said.

'I should get up now,' Eleanor said, struggling to rise on her elbows.

Dawn gently pressed her back down. 'You must rest. And, whatever Peter says, *I* think the physician should attend you,' she added firmly. 'Sometimes women have more of an intuition about these things than men do.' She gave Eleanor a smile of encouragement. Her stepdaughter was loyal to her husband, but he needed to be overruled on this. 'A professional opinion is needed. If Peter is right and I am wrong, then I shall feel so much better for having worried over nothing.' Dawn approached the door of the bedchamber with her granddaughter still in her arms. 'I saw Peter go out some time ago, but he might have returned. If he has, I shall speak to him about fetching the doctor. Would you like some tea…or something to eat, Eleanor?'

'I'm thirsty…some lemonade would be nice.' Eleanor put out her hand for her daughter. 'You can leave Lily with me. She will be good now she knows you have some treats for her.' She gave her little daughter a fond smile.

Dawn went quickly downstairs, hoping Peter had returned because she was determined to make the daft man see sense and immediately go in his gig to fetch the doctor. Or she would go herself into the village and find the fellow.

'Do you know if the vicar is due to return soon, Mrs Grove?' Dawn had looked into the downstairs rooms, and knocked on the door of Peter's study, but found no sign of him. She had headed to the kitchen in the hope of discovering his likely whereabouts from the cook. They had met before when Dawn had made previous visits, and Dawn had always thought her a pleasant woman.

'He'll probably be up at the church, Mrs Fenton, or he could have gone into Wivenhoe.' Mrs Grove carried on rolling out pastry. 'I expect you'd like some tea, wouldn't you, m'm, after your journey?' She wiped floury hands on her pinafore. 'I would've brought a tray up to your room, but master said as to leave you to rest after your journey.'

'I would like tea, thank you,' Dawn replied. 'And I'll take Mrs Mansfield a glass of lemonade.'

Enid Grove avoided Dawn's eyes at the mention of her mistress.

'For how long has my stepdaughter been feeling ill?'

'For *too* long,' Enid replied pithily. 'The poor lass needs a doctor looking at her.' She slipped a glance at Dawn from beneath her lashes. 'I'm that glad you've come, Mrs Fenton.'

'And so am I,' Dawn replied in a heartfelt way. 'Why has the doctor not examined her?'

'Why indeed! I told the master my feelings on it and was told in return to mind my own business.' Enid shook her head. ''Course polite fellows don't use those words, but I knew his meaning. I've done what I can for the poor lass, to ease her discomfort, but now that the day girl doesn't come I'm run off my feet trying to cook and clean and nursemaid the little 'un.' She sighed. 'I'm turned two score years and ten and that Miss Lily needs a young pair of legs to keep up with her.' Enid blew a defeated sigh. 'Truth of it is, m'm, I've had enough and shall soon give notice. I don't want to leave the mistress, but I'm feeling so fagged out that I might end up ill in bed myself and what help can I be to Mrs Mansfield then?'

Dawn had listened in amazement. None of the letters she'd received from her stepdaughter had hinted at a crisis. 'I had no idea that things had got so bad.' Dawn frowned. 'What on earth has happened since my last visit?'

'Not my place to say, m'm...' Mrs Grove turned away and busied herself with rattling the crockery and boiling the kettle.

'As things are serious I think you *must* speak up or how will I know what to do to help?' Dawn said bluntly.

'What is it you wish to know, Mrs Fenton?'

Dawn's stepson-in-law had come into the kitchen, unseen and unheard. She noticed at once that Mrs Grove looked nervous. The older woman turned away and busied herself with the tea things.

'There is so much that I wish to know, sir, that our conversation will be lengthy and better conducted upstairs,' Dawn answered firmly. His lips had grown thin. She hadn't pleased him with her outburst in front of his servant. But Dawn didn't care for coddling his ego. Eleanor and Lily were the only ones that mattered. 'I shall just take your wife her drink, then join you in your study, if that is convenient.'

'It is not,' he said on a sigh and gave her a smile that didn't quite reach his eyes. 'I am sorry to sound too busy to properly welcome you, but I'm due to meet a parishioner at the church. We can converse later on when we dine.' He would have left the kitchen, but Dawn stepped after him.

'Just a moment, sir. One important thing must be said now. Please fetch the doctor with you when you come back. Your wife is very ill.' She knew vicars led full lives administering to their flocks and had imagined that he must be too preoccupied to fully appreciate how sick Eleanor actually was. Dawn had hoped her concern might rub off on him, making him feel guilty and neglectful.

'My wife is young and strong and has had a baby before. She is used to the rigours of child-birth...unlike you, madam.'

His voice had been soft, almost gentle, but Dawn knew the remark had been intended to wound and remind her of her miscarriage. 'I might not be a mother, but I know well enough what a person in pain looks like. Eleanor should be examined by a doctor in case the babe is coming sooner than expected—'

'My wife needs no fussing over. She doesn't like that sort of thing.' His voice was slightly raised now. 'She was up yesterday and playing with her daughter. It is to be expected that there will be occasions when she feels tired as her time nears. She was like this before Lily was born.'

Mrs Grove gave a cough...or perhaps it was a snort, Dawn thought, on glimpsing the woman's angry profile. 'Nevertheless I insist that the doctor comes here today, to put all our minds at rest.' Dawn's voice was controlled but full of grit.

'As I have said, we shall talk later, Mrs Fenton.' Peter turned to the cook. 'Let me have my wife's drink. I shall take it to her. If she's left undisturbed for the rest of the afternoon, then I'm sure she will feel better and be able to get up at dinner time.' With a nod for Dawn he left the kitchen with the glass of lemonade Mrs Grove had thrust at him.

For a moment Dawn could only stare at the closed door, at a loss to know what on earth was wrong with the man for him to hold such a callous attitude. And why had he banned her from seeing her stepdaughter until dinner time? She knew that was what he had done. A weight settled in her stomach as she realised she had a battle on her hands. She wouldn't give up on getting Eleanor the help she needed and hoped to glean some information from the cook as to what had recently happened. 'Mrs Grove…' she said, but was halted by the woman putting a finger against her own lips. A few seconds later Dawn heard footsteps receding along the corridor.

Dawn felt a chill creep over her. So Peter had been loitering to eavesdrop and from the way Mrs Grove had reacted she guessed he had done so before. Perhaps when a conversation had been taking place with her mistress. Did the vicar spy on his wife?

Dawn had never liked him, but never before had she felt uneasy in his company, or in his house. Now she did. Having observed Mrs Grove's caginess, Dawn knew his servant felt the same misgiving as she did about the Reverend Peter Mansfield.

'Don't ask me questions about the master's business. I'll not gossip even if I have an answer to give.' Enid shook her greying head.

'Well, tell me this at least. You have had children, Mrs Grove. Is this a normal malaise for a woman in her condition? My stepdaughter looks so very ill.'

'Some women do have a hard time of it. But he's right about one thing: she's young and once she was healthy, too. To my mind, there's unhappiness in this house,' Enid whispered. 'And that can be as harmful as plague. But now that you're here, m'm, things will be better. I know the mistress will be taken care of and little Miss Lily, too. Mrs Mansfield must be that glad you've turned up at last to help her.'

Dawn winced at that hint at her tardiness. 'I wish Eleanor had put more in her letters. I would have come directly had I known she was ill.'

'He reads her letters…them that comes and them that goes.' Mrs Grove gave Dawn a significant glance.

Dawn started to question the woman, but Enid shook her head.

'I'm sorry, m'm, but I'm done with it all.' She looked sorrowful, but ploughed on. 'I'll leave your dinners on the stove before I go home, but I'll hand in me notice now you've arrived to take care of things.' She agitatedly resumed rolling pastry. 'I expect he'll find another cook quick enough. Plenty of women in the village want part-time work.'

Dawn had listened in astonishment. 'What has caused Eleanor's unhappiness?'

'*He's* the trouble she's got,' Mrs Grove muttered. 'And the trouble the vicar's got is to be found out there. Maybe the recently departed are playing on his mind.' The woman pointed towards the graveyard that lay to the east of the church. 'This warning I will give you and you'd best heed it: don't be venturing out after dark that way, Mrs Fenton, 'cos you don't know what you might meet.' With finality the woman turned her back and busied herself with cups and saucers. 'I'll bring a tray to your chamber when the tea's brewed. I must get on and get this pie in the oven. He likes his dinner on the dot. Six of the clock sharp.'

Dawn felt rather angry with the woman for talking such tosh. She knew that country folk could be superstitious and believed in gremlins and ghosts. But she didn't! And she wouldn't be taking heed of any warning. She believed the trouble in this house was most definitely of this world rather than the other.

Dawn could cook and clean…but why should she when the vicar was perfectly able to pay for a couple of servants? She knew she couldn't do everything herself any more than Mrs Grove could. 'Will you at least stay on until another cook is found and I will help with other tasks?'

'Very well… I'll do it for the mistress. I'll stay until she's back up on her feet and the new babe in the nursery. She's been good to me, has Mrs Mansfield,' Enid Grove said. 'God bless her.'

'You must tell your stepmama that you are simply feeling tired, my dear, and do not need the doctor to come. Mrs Fenton is fretting about your health.' The vicar gave his wife a smile. 'Now that you have rested in bed all afternoon you feel much better, don't you?'

'I do. My headache has gone,' Eleanor said and rearranged the cutlery in front of her.

'But, you don't look better…' Dawn fell silent, having noticed her stepdaughter's startled look. Eleanor didn't want her husband to be gainsaid.

'I am quite well, I assure you.' Eleanor picked up her soup spoon.

'We will say grace,' her husband reminded her before making a steeple of his fingers and closing his eyes. His wife rested her spoon on the bowl and copied him. Dawn simply bowed her head, glaring at pea soup.

Eleanor was still flushed and unsteady on her feet, needing to be escorted to the table by her husband. Earlier Dawn had gone to her step-daughter's room despite Peter's veiled demand that she stay away. She had tried the door, but it had been locked and when she'd softly called through the panels Lily had whimpered to be al-lowed to see her grandma. Eleanor had then ad-mitted she didn't have a key to open it up.

The knowledge that Peter had locked his wife in her room increased Dawn's feeling that something sinister was going on. But she wasn't frightened, as Mrs Grove appeared to be. She was angry and determined to protect Eleanor and Lily. She wasn't afraid of what was 'out there' as the cook termed it. But she knew there was a real danger from men who believed they knew what was best for their womenfolk when clearly they didn't.

The prayer at an end the vicar poured them all a glass of ruby wine as though he were the most solicitous and amiable of fellows.

Dawn noticed that Eleanor glanced her way several times with a look that seemed to silently beg her not to again raise the subject of her health. So Dawn decided she would not. She'd deal with the matter herself, with or without his assistance.

The moment the meal was over Peter excused himself saying he had to go back to the church for a meeting with the verger.

'Do you feel well enough to come into Wivenhoe with me tomorrow, Eleanor?' If the doctor could not be brought here, then Dawn would take her stepdaughter to his house.

'I can't face travelling. And Lily can be quite mischievous.'

'I expect she is bored being cooped up. She went to bed quite early.'

'Peter likes her to be kept to a routine. Mrs Grove settles her while we dine.'

About to tell her stepdaughter that the cook was on the point of quitting, Dawn thought better of it. She imagined Mrs Grove had already told her mistress she was unhappy…and so was Eleanor unhappy. Dawn sensed Eleanor would never admit to it, though. Peter Mansfield had warned his wife not to mention whatever secrets they had. Eleanor should be anticipating the arrival of her second child with joyousness as Dawn's friend Emma was. But there was no joy in this house.

'Shall we play cards?' Dawn suggested brightly.

Eleanor shook her head. 'I'm sorry to be such poor company, but I think I shall go and say goodnight to my daughter, then return to my room.'

'You're not poor company. Just being with you and Lily is a delight for me.' Dawn wished there was more truth in that statement. She had come to Essex in high spirits, but now felt utterly deflated. But she must stay cheery for Eleanor's sake. 'I'd like to say goodnight to Lily, if I may.'

'Of course… I'll call Mrs Grove in to clear things away.' Carefully Eleanor rose from the table, but before she reached the sideboard to ring the bell she tottered. Quickly she recovered her balance and clattered the brass implement.

'You're still feeling giddy?' Dawn had risen immediately and gone to her aid.

'I'll be fine by morning.'

'I very much hope you will. Your dress is very stylish,' Dawn said, wanting to boost her stepdaughter in some way. She fondled a blue-dimity sleeve. And your hair looks very pretty. She was encouraged to think that as Eleanor had presented herself looking neat at dinner, she was feeling better. She had declined Dawn's offer to lend a hand with buttons and curling tongs.

'I'll be off home when I'm done here, m'm.'

Mrs Grove had come into the room to start collecting the used crockery.

Dawn gave the woman a questioning glance.

'I'll see you in the morning, usual time, Mrs Mansfield,' the cook added before departing with a loaded tray.

'Will you retire early, Mama, or stay up after saying goodnight to Lily?'

'I think I'll play solitaire in the sitting room, just for a little while.' Dawn had found the cards in a bureau drawer in that room earlier and had whiled away an hour while waiting for dinner to be served. She glanced at the window. 'The sun has made an appearance at last.' She smiled wryly. 'Just before it is due to set.' Heavy cloud had covered the heavens for most of the day, but had parted to allow a narrow strip of blue to be visible. But still it was bitterly cold. 'Perhaps tomorrow, if it is fine, we could walk in the garden. Once I've unpacked my things I can give Lily her presents.'

'She'll like that. You are good to her and to me, Mama.'

They had been slowly walking the corridor towards the stairs, but Dawn suddenly halted and put an arm around her swaying stepdaughter. 'Hold on to me!'

Eleanor was no lightweight now she was big

with child, but Dawn managed to guide her to
a chair in the sitting room. She would have preferred to get her to her bedchamber, but knew she
would struggle to support her up the stairs. 'I'll
fetch Peter,' Dawn said determinedly. 'Enough
is enough. You are sick, my dear, and urgently
need a doctor's care. If he still refuses, I will
fetch the fellow myself!'

Eleanor put out a feeble hand as though to detain her, but Dawn ignored her, dashing out into
the corridor and then out of the house.

Picking up her skirts, she flew along the cinder path towards the church. It was about a quar-
ter of a mile distant and she arrived breathless,
but burst in through the heavy oaken doors, calling her stepson-in-law's name. The place seemed
deserted. Nothing stirred in the cold, eerie space
and the only sound was her voice echoing back
at her.

Dawn's heart was in her mouth as she hurried
outside. Usually she would be happy to avoid the
dratted man; now when she needed him, he'd
disappeared. She had a feeling of dread rolling
in her stomach. Intuitively she knew that Eleanor was in immediate need of a doctor's care.

'Mrs Fenton?'

Dawn whipped around at the sound of that familiar baritone…a voice she had heard recently

after a long, long silence from him. She stared almost without breathing as a tall male figure approached along the path. The pale sun behind his head was burnishing his fair hair with a silvery halo, making it impossible for her to read his expression. But she imagined her shock at seeing him was plain on her face.

Chapter Four

'Mr Valance?' Dawn uttered in astonishment.

'I thought it was you, Mrs Fenton. I was just about to ride off.' He gestured to a horse tethered close to the lychgate.

'What on earth are *you* doing here?' Dawn blurted out the first thing that came into her head and in her agitated state it sounded rather rude.

'I have an estate over yonder.' He jerked his head in the direction of the coast. 'Croxley Grange.' He gave her a half-smile. 'It is quite a coincidence that we appear to be neighbours. I would have mentioned it in London, but you seemed in a rush to get away that day.'

Indeed, she did regret having left him before discovering that news. But she'd no time to dwell on it now. The spontaneous surge of excitement at seeing him so unexpectedly hadn't lessened her anxiety over Eleanor.

'I came to find the vicar, but he doesn't appear to be around.' Jack thrust his hands into his pockets. 'Unfortunately, I'm in need of the fellow's services. An elderly servant has passed away. I wanted to speak to Mansfield about a funeral.'

'Oh… I'm sorry…' Although still in turmoil Dawn issued an automatic condolence. Her fear for Eleanor and her unborn child had put a throb in her temples to beat in time with the erratic thump beneath her ribs. 'I am also searching for the vicar. He is married to my stepdaughter and she is very unwell. The doctor must be brought to her without further delay. She is with child and close to her time.'

'Do you want me to fetch the doctor?' Jack offered with a concerned frown. 'Wilson is not far away; he recorded the death at the Grange just a short time ago.'

'I would be most grateful, sir, if you would find him and bring him urgently to the vicarage.'

Jack extended a hand to her. 'Would you like a ride home?'

'No…thank you… I can easily walk. Please be quick, sir, I beg of you. I am very worried about Eleanor.'

Jack dipped his head, then strode to his horse, swinging up lithely into the saddle. He wheeled the stallion about and, with a raise of his hand in farewell, spurred the magnificent beast into a furious gallop. Dawn stared after the blur of horse and rider, entranced by a maelstrom of emotions. Gladness and overwhelming relief at having his help, astonishment at seeing him again were all jumbled together, but overriding it all was still her fears for her stepdaughter. With her skirts in her fists she raced back the way she had come.

'I think you were right, Mama… I think the babe might be coming,' was the panted greeting Dawn received when she burst into the sitting room. Her stepdaughter was bent double over her aching abdomen. 'But something is not right.' Eleanor raised her frightened eyes, peering at Dawn through lank strands of fair hair that had loosened to drape her forehead.

'Hush…the doctor is on his way,' Dawn soothed, kneeling by the side of Eleanor's chair. She took her trembling hands, chafing them. 'I could not find your husband, but I was fortunate enough to bump into a gentleman I know from town. Mr Valance told me he lives close by. He has ridden straight away to fetch Dr Wilson.'

'You should have waited and asked Peter to go, Mama.' Eleanor sounded anxious.

'I should have done no such thing,' Dawn said quietly. 'The doctor's visit is long overdue.'

'I don't know the name Valance,' Eleanor gasped.

'Never mind…it doesn't matter,' Dawn soothed. 'Are you able to get upstairs, do you think? Or would you rather wait here for the doctor to examine you?'

'I must get to my bed and lie down. Peter won't like the doctor looking at me here. It is not seemly… He will be cross.'

'So am I cross.' Dawn struggled to control the volume of her voice. 'Your husband's negligence is unforgivable.' She got to her feet and with an effort gently assisted a groaning Eleanor to stand up. 'If you feel it will be too much for you to manage the stairs, then you must stay here.' She muttered to herself, 'And etiquette be damned.'

Eleanor made no more than a few steps towards the door before whimpering.

Dawn gently helped Eleanor reseat herself. It was a great pity that Mrs Grove had just left. The woman might be getting on in years, but she would have been another helpful pair of hands. 'Would you like a drink? Some lemonade?'

'No…don't leave me…' Eleanor gasped, tightening her clasp on Dawn's fingers.

'I won't… I swear…' To prove it Dawn gave her stepdaughter her other hand to hold as well. 'It will all be fine…you'll see, my dear,' she croaked out in reassurance, but turned her head to shield the anguish in her eyes.

After what seemed like a wait of an hour but was probably less than half that time, there was the sound of rapid footsteps in the hallway. Dawn sighed in utter relief. Gently easing her hands from her stepdaughter's cold grip, she hurried to open the door, hoping it was the doctor and not the vicar returning.

'Please, come in here, sir.' A tubby gentleman was heading down the hall, bag in hand. She'd guessed he was Dr Wilson a moment before the fellow barked that name, doffed his hat, then carried on into the sitting room. Jack Valance had entered the house, too, but was tactfully loitering a distance away.

'Might I be of any assistance?' He took a few steps closer to Dawn.

She knew that they might need him. The middle-aged doctor would have no better success than would she in getting her stepdaughter safely up the stairs to her bedchamber. Yet it would be more practical and less embarrassing for Eleanor if the doctor attended to her there.

'You have already been a great boon to us, sir, but if you *would* just wait a moment, there might be something else.'

'Anything. Just name it.'

Dawn gave him a grateful smile, then quickly went back to the sitting room. Having closed the door, she turned about. She needed no spoken verdict, she could read the bad news in the doctor's grim features.

'She has lost the child.' He had ushered Dawn closer to the wall to keep their conversation from his patient's hearing.

'But…surely it is just coming early?' Dawn's argument emerged in a desperate murmur.

'I fear the baby is dead, ma'am, and has been for a while. An infection has set in and made Mrs Mansfield very ill.'

Dawn felt frozen in shock, yet far back in her mind she realised she had known that a tragedy was about to happen. And so had her stepdaughter. Swiftly Dawn blinked away the tears that had started to her eyes. Eleanor's gaze was on her, watching for a sign of reassurance, and she would give it, false though it was. This was no time for bald truths that might make the poor girl hysterical. She forced her lips into a fiercely encouraging smile for Eleanor.

'It would be better if she were upstairs on her

bed so I can examine the lass properly and then do whatever is necessary.'

'I agree, sir.' Dawn gulped.

'Is her husband not yet home? Where is the man?' he hissed. 'How has it come to this? His wife must have shown signs of distress for many days. Are you a relative, madam?' The doctor rattled off his whispered questions.

'Mrs Mansfield is my stepdaughter. I arrived from London just today on a visit. As for the vicar, I've looked in vain for him at the church, hoping to bring him back,' Dawn informed him.

'If her husband's help isn't to be had, Mr Valance must assist us, if he will. Is that gentleman still waiting outside?'

Her brief nod prompted the doctor to go into the hall to speak to Jack. Dawn approached Eleanor and said lightly, 'Mr Valance will help you upstairs, my dear. It is not a task either I or the doctor can do for you, I'm afraid.'

Eleanor was past caring about etiquette; she was in too much pain to be bothered at the prospect of being manhandled by a stranger.

Jack swiftly entered the room and took Eleanor's arm, gently and efficiently easing her to her feet. He half-carried her to the foot of the stairs, then, with a murmured warning of what he had to do, lifted her up with great care and delicacy before ascending with her cradled in his arms. Dawn followed close behind, giving directions to the bedchamber.

'Would you fetch some hot water, m'm? As much as you can manage?' Dr Wilson was taking off his jacket and rolling up his sleeves.

Dawn nodded. 'Of course… I'll do it now.'

Once Jack had laid Eleanor on the bed, he withdrew. Dawn undressed Eleanor to her underclothes, then pulled the sheet up. Dr Wilson accompanied Dawn to the door to instruct quietly, 'When you go below please ask Mr Valance if he would be of assistance once more and fetch home the confounded vicar. He should be here with his wife.' He shook his head. 'I would have Mansfield's explanation for his inaction when it is quite obvious that this woman is gravely ill.'

'I've no idea why the vicar delayed fetching you.' Dawn could guess, though. The moment she'd started to disrobe Eleanor and seen the fading bruises on her stepdaughter's arms, she knew. Soon Dr Wilson would also see them.

The doctor issued a grunt that mingled his sadness and anger. 'The moment he turns up send him directly to me. I shall be here some while, I think,' he added bleakly.

Dawn managed to give her stepdaughter a reassuring smile before she exited the room and stumbled, blinded by tears, down the stairs. She knew she mustn't crumble; she had a job to do and she would do it. She found Jack Valance pacing up and down the hallway and he wheeled about, immediately striding towards her on hearing her footsteps.

'How is she? Can I do more to help? Tell me if there is any small task that might be done.'

'She is gravely ill,' Dawn murmured through lips that quivered. 'Thank you for your offer to help. The doctor asked if you would search for the vicar and make him come home. But there is something else you could do first, if you don't mind.' Dawn concentrated on practicalities to prevent herself howling. 'Would you fetch some buckets of water in from outside?' Having received his immediate nod she carried on quickly towards the kitchen, knowing he would follow. When there, she busied herself checking the heat of the range. She threw a log into the fire to stoke it up. But her shoulders had started to shake, betraying her silent sobs.

Jack drew her into his arms. 'I'll assist you with anything at all…but you mustn't give up hope, not yet.'

He also knew, then. Dawn nodded fiercely, knuckling wetness from her eyes. She broke free of his embrace though it had felt wonderfully warm and tender.

They both worked silently, he bringing the buckets and she decanting the water into pots to heat up. When he had brought her a dozen filled pails she murmured her thanks and told him that she had enough for now and he must go quickly to find the vicar.

As she'd continued to toil at the stove he had put his hands on her shoulders, moving them in a caress of encouragement before leaving. How she had longed to lean into him for his strength and comfort. But she hadn't turned around, even when she heard the back door click shut. She had remained dry-eyed and concentrated on her task. With a steaming jug in either hand she had made the trip upstairs half-a-dozen times, knocking, then leaving the water outside the closed door. Finally crushed by it all, Dawn had sunk to the floor and stuffed her fists to her lips to silence her own scream. She'd known Eleanor was fighting for her life now it was too late to save her child. Then when it had become quiet she'd sprung up, berating herself for her weakness. She'd stumbled again down the stairs to renew her efforts with kettle and pan.

The commotion at the back door as Mansfield finally burst in wasn't enough to stop her furious industry. She carried on, not trusting herself to look at him. But she said stiltedly, 'The doctor is upstairs with Eleanor. He said you should go to her immediately.'

'How dare you go against my wishes?' Peter snapped. His face was livid with indignation and he jerked on Dawn's arm to turn her about.

'Go to your wife, sir, without further delay.' Jack had entered the kitchen behind the vicar and in a single stride had soon positioned himself between Dawn and her enraged stepson-in-law.

'My thanks for bringing me here, sir, but I don't believe I invited you into my house,' Peter spat. 'The name Jack Valance means nothing to me. Now what in damnation is going on? What havoc has been wreaked in my absence, Mrs Fenton?'

Jack uttered in a voice that dripped ice, 'Not that it matters much, but I am your new neighbour. What does matter is that you should go to your wife, sir, before it is too late.'

'It is too late…if you wish to see her, or your son alive.' Dr Wilson had entered the kitchen, wiping his hands on a towel. He looked exhausted and immensely sorrowful. 'I did all I could for her…but I was summoned here far too late.'

Peter Mansfield gawped at the doctor, oblivious to Dawn sinking slowly to her haunches, covering her face with her hands, her whole body shaking with silent sobs.

'What? What are you saying?' Peter roared. 'Never tell me that I had a son at last and you've let him die, sirrah.'

'No... I have not done that. The child has been dead for some time. And your wife has perished because of carrying his corpse within her for too long. *You* have let your wife die, sir. Had I been summoned at the first sign of her fever Mrs Mansfield might have been saved.' The doctor was a-quiver with suppressed fury.

Dawn was aware of a heated conversation going on between the vicar and the doctor, but she understood none of it. Part of her wanted to spring up and dash up the stairs and see for herself that the awful news was true, but she felt enervated by grief, unable to move a muscle.

She felt a pair of gentle hands lifting her up, taking her away from the arguing men and into the living room. Jack eased her into a chair. A moment later she had risen, determined to tend to Eleanor in some small way. Jack urged her to sit, then squatted down close to her.

'I know you want to go to her. But first you must take a few sips of this to steady yourself.' He held out a brandy flask, got from his coat. When she simply stared at it, he held it to her lips. Like a child she drank, wincing as the liquor burned her throat. She allowed him to make her swallow another mouthful before she shook her head, declining to have any more. She wiped the back of an unsteady hand over her burning lips.

Jack straightened up, allowing her to rise from the chair before enclosing her in an embrace.

'I thank God that her little daughter is asleep and knows nothing of what's gone on,' Dawn finally said hoarsely, burrowing against his shoulder.

'Amen to that,' Jack murmured. 'Would you like me to stay? I'll remain just outside on the lane. It would be as well to leave the house. The vicar is distraught and better not to provoke him with my unwanted presence.'

Dawn blinked up at him with bloodshot eyes.

'I'll always be close by, Mrs Fenton, if you need me. Remember that.' Jack brought her fingers to his lips. 'Remember that,' he repeated in a velvety voice before letting her go.

Chapter Five

The bishop had come from Colchester to conduct the service, allowing the newly widowed vicar to join the mourners on the dull March day that Eleanor Mansfield, aged twenty-one, was interred in the Wivenhoe churchyard with her infant son resting in her everlasting embrace.

The funeral had been speedily arranged on the wishes of her husband, then carried out a few days after Eleanor died. Though the time elapsed was short, by then Dawn was able to contain her grief for Lily's sake. For the same reason the fury and disgust she felt for the Reverend Peter Mansfield also went undisplayed, yet simmered, unabated, within. He had taken no responsibility for the tragedy, maintaining that he had bowed to his wife's wishes in not summoning the doctor to fuss over her. When Dr Wilson had returned the following day to record the death, he had quizzed Peter over the marks on his wife's arms. Those had been explained away as injuries received at times when Eleanor had collapsed. Florid in the face, Peter had made it clear that he deeply resented the implications being made. A distraught Mrs Grove had confirmed that indeed her mistress had keeled over on occasions and she had been the one to find Mrs Mansfield on the floor.

The only person who knew the truth could no longer tell it. So Dawn had no option but to give the vicar the benefit of the doubt. The physician's face had betrayed his scepticism over what he'd heard. The only meagre comfort Dawn had was from knowing she would never again think of, or refer to, Peter Mansfield as her family. He was nobody to her. Yet she must continue to tolerate him because she couldn't bear to lose touch with her beloved granddaughter.

She glanced at Lily, playing with her toys on the parlour rug, quite oblivious to the fact her mother was gone for ever. Of course the child had asked for her, but had seemed satisfied to know that her mama was with the angels in heaven. Yet every time Dawn answered her granddaughter's sweetly innocent question she was sure Lily would be affected by her distress, though she did her utmost not to show it.

Presently the child danced the little doll on her lap, singing to the gift her grandma had brought her. Dawn smiled wistfully. It seemed such a long, long time ago that she had happily browsed the Regent Street shops for presents for Lily. Yet just a week had passed. And almost every minute of every hour of those days had been filled with heartache.

'A gentleman caller, m'm.'

Mrs Grove had quietly entered the sitting room, stirring Dawn from a sightless contemplation of the greensward beyond the window pane. The woman was still haggard from constant weeping. The cook had had to be revived with smelling salts after learning of her mistress's passing.

'A Mr Valance asks to see you, but says he understands if you would like him to go away.'

'No... I should like to see him, Mrs Grove.' Had she really felt a little thrill? For days past Dawn had been numbed by grief and sure she'd never know any other emotion.

She stood up, brushing down her creased skirts. She had no deepest mourning clothes with her, but had sewn a black armband on the sleeve of her lavender gown. She imagined she looked a wreck from weeping so used her hanky on her tear-smudged cheeks, then attempted to neaten wisps of chestnut hair, tucking them into their pins. She was still conscious of Jack Valance's appeal, she wryly realised, or wouldn't bother readying herself to receive him.

The door opened and he came in, his grey eyes immediately locking with her dark green stare, shadowed by pain.

'I will not stay long. I understand you might not want visitors. But I had to come to say…' He hesitated as though unsure how to proceed. 'I am just so sorry for your loss.'

Dawn smiled. 'I know you are, sir. Thank you, not only for your condolences, but for all the help you gave to us.'

'Would that I could have done more,' Jack said vehemently. He approached and gently took her hands in his.

She allowed him to hold them, liking the feel of his warm palms wrapped around her cold fingers. 'I was expecting you might come to the funeral.'

'I was not invited and doubted that Peter Mansfield would wish to have me just turn up.' He paused. 'I wanted to come back sooner to see you. I didn't in case I was being intrusive. I've not stopped thinking of you, though, for a single minute.'

Dawn hadn't stopped thinking of him either,

despite the horror of losing her stepdaughter. Dawn had wished Jack had come to the funeral, but understood his reasons for staying away. The vicar had made it clear he wanted a small, discreet affair when his wife was laid to rest. He'd intimated it was from respect for her, but Dawn suspected it was to shield himself from disapproving looks. News might have circulated about the circumstances of Mrs Mansfield's demise.

In all, the mourners had numbered just a dozen and most of those had comprised Peter's ecclesiastical colleagues. A few neighbours and Dr Wilson had come to the wake at the vicarage which had lasted less than an hour.

'What will you do now? Will you return to London?' Jack enquired.

'Yes... I must. I cannot stand to stay here with him. Neither, I think, does he want me to. At times I feel so angry that I cannot hold my tongue so am a constant reminder of his terrible neglect of Eleanor.' Dawn frowned, remembering the vicar's curt good morning to her when they had passed earlier in the hall. For her part she would sooner ignore him and keep her distance. When in his orbit she felt a compulsion to leap towards him and pummel him for what he'd done. 'Peter still blames me for interfering, even though the doctor severely rebuked him for failing to get his wife the help she so desperately needed.' She glanced at Lily. 'Yet... I cannot bear leaving the poor little mite behind when I return home. I wish I could take her with me and care for her.' Her voice broke and she shielded her distress behind unsteady fingers.

Jack gently drew her into his arms. 'Come... You have endured a tragedy, but are coping admirably with it and I know you will continue to do so.' He paused, brushing rogue chestnut curls away from her spiky wet lashes so he might gaze into a pair of bright green eyes. 'The most sensible thing would be for the vicar to put his daughter into your care in London, at least until he sorts out a good nursemaid to take charge of his daughter.'

'I have already suggested to him all of that, but because he knows how much that arrangement would please me, he has dismissed it out of hand.' She knuckled fresh tears from her eyes. 'The child is his responsibility, he says, and must stay with him. Yet he pays Lily no heed whatsoever. He doesn't deserve to have the dear little thing.'

'Am I right in thinking it is not just this calamity that has coloured your opinion of Peter Mansfield?'

'I've never liked him. Now I loathe him,'

Dawn admitted with unsuppressed vehemence. She clamped together her lips; she had confided too much. She hardly knew Jack Valance, yet was telling him very personal things. She had felt that immediate connection to him years ago, almost from the day they'd met. But he obviously hadn't felt the same way about her to so easily forget her and go abroad without a word. She had allowed him liberties then…and was doing so now, standing quietly within his embrace as though it were her natural place to be. But it wasn't; if what she'd heard was true he had a fiancée. Though she knew he was simply comforting her, she stepped away from him. Just in time, as it transpired.

'Ah… Valance. How are you, my good fellow? My servant said you had arrived.' Peter Mansfield strode into the room and extended his hand. His attitude was completely different to that on the day he had first met Jack. Then he had treated him as an interloper instead of a guest.

'My condolences on your loss, sir.' Jack shook hands.

Peter huffed a sigh. 'Thank you. I wanted a son more than anything.' A silence followed, but the bereaved husband made no mention of missing anybody else as he plunged his hands on his hips. 'I have heard talk in the village that you have taken up residence at Croxley Grange, Mr Valance.'

'It is a temporary stay. My preference is to reside most of the year in London.'

'We had heard that a viscount had taken over the whole estate.' Peter clucked his tongue. 'The gossips concoct such fantastical tales.'

'On this occasion they are correct.'

Peter's grin appeared to freeze on his face. '*You* are Lord Sterling?' he eventually burbled.

'I am.' Jack gave a slow nod.

'Well…what splendid news. While you are in the vicinity you are very welcome to visit the vicarage whenever you wish, my lord.' Peter gave an obsequious bow.

Dawn darted a glance from beneath her lashes at Jack. He was watching for her reaction to the news he was an aristocrat. She was surprised to hear of his elevation, but then there had been no reason or opportunity for him to discuss his business with her. Years ago, when she'd believed them to be growing closer, he'd told her a little bit about his family. He was the younger son of a baron with a meagre allowance and few prospects, he'd said. She'd known things were different for him now. Emma's husband had described his friend's change in circumstances as

Valance having found his feet and his fortune. And in rather a magnificent way, it seemed.

'While you are in Essex, my lord, you must meet some of the local dignitaries,' Peter declared, strutting to and fro across the rug. 'I would most happily attend any social function you hold at the Grange and bring the bishop along with me to introduce you...'

'As you are in mourning, sir, I doubt you would wish to socialise for some while,' Jack smoothly said. 'In any case, I have no plans to entertain during my brief stay, so you will miss nothing at Croxley Grange.'

Dawn had listened to the vicar's blatant social climbing with mounting disgust. Not a single word or look to mark his guilt or sorrow on losing his wife. Yet, before the wreath on his front door had withered he was shamelessly wheedling for an invitation to dine with the new owner of the big house.

'I deeply regret that I did not have a chance to become better acquainted with your wife.' Jack knew he had the fellow squirming and he wasn't about to let him off the hook. What he *was* determined to do was get Dawn what she wanted, and what the child needed. And what *he* needed. In London she would be close to him.

'My stepdaughter would have liked an opportunity to know you better, too, sir,' Dawn blurted out when it seemed Peter was intending to remain tight-lipped about his dead wife. Moreover he now appeared sullen. Well, let him sulk! She would not allow Eleanor to be forgotten so easily, or to be kept from a conversation to protect *his* ego!

Jack crouched down to stroke a finger on Lily's soft cheek and be rewarded with a shy smile. 'Mrs Mansfield's daughter is her image; a lasting tribute to her mother. You must be very proud of your little girl, sir.'

Peter made a non-committal noise, fiddling with his neckcloth and his perambulation of the room became speedier.

'Yes, indeed, she is like her mama.' Dawn again broke the silence and she gave Jack a grateful smile. Although no word of a plan of action had passed between them she sensed he'd decided to be her ally against Lily's father.

'Have you arranged tea for Lord Sterling?' Peter barked. He resented being put in his place. He barely glanced at Lily even though a pointed reference had been made to her. In turn the little girl seemed oblivious to the fact her father was close by.

'I want no tea, thank you,' Jack said, straightening up.

'Please take some port, then, my lord.' Peter didn't want to lose his illustrious guest before he'd inveigled himself into the fellow's good books. He was also inquisitive about what was to become of the largest estate for miles around. He strode to the sideboard and poured two glasses of ruby wine without offering Dawn a drink. 'Do take a seat, my lord; you must tell me all about your plans for Croxley Grange.' He gave Dawn a sharp nod so she would sit down, allowing the gentlemen to do likewise.

Dawn returned to her chair, not for the vicar's sake, but for her own. She also wanted to keep Jack Valance's company. For as long as possible. After days of being battered by anguish, his presence today had actually lifted her spirits, made her feel more alive than could even Lily's sweet company. Constantly fretting over her granddaughter's bleak future living with a parent who seemed careless of her existence was guaranteed to depress Dawn.

'We heard the house was run-down and had been returned to the Crown on the death of the previous owner. Viscount Welham had no heir. He was an odd fellow—kept very much to himself and sadly contributed little to the community.' Peter took a swig from his glass. 'It was most disappointing that the man was no proper benefactor to good causes as one in his position should be.'

'The Grange will be restored to a sound condition—other than that I have no plans for any major changes.' Jack politely sipped at the port that had been forced into his hand, then placed the glass on a table.

'Oh…a great pity, sir; the presence of gentlemen of your standing is sorely needed in the area.'

'I will give to local charities, whether or not in residence in Essex,' Jack said with a hint of a sardonic smile.

Dawn glanced at him, biting her lip on her own faint amusement. So Mr Valance, or Lord Sterling, as she supposed she ought to think of him, was aware that the vicar was brazen with his begging bowl for church funds.

'If I may ask, sir, what plans have you for your daughter's care following your wife's sad passing?' Jack sat back in his chair and turned a relentless gaze on the vicar. 'Your work obviously keeps you occupied late into the evening at times. When I came upon you on the evening of the tragedy you were still on duty.' Jack knew very well that on the night he had fetched the vicar back to his dying wife's bedside, the man had been miles away in a bawdy house. Mansfield had made a blustered explanation of his presence upstairs. It was his calling to preach against sin, and as though to prove it, he'd produced a bible from his pocket.

'Indeed, I am busy,' Peter said pompously, barely blushing at what his guest had alluded to. 'A wedding here and a funeral there and all manner of sick and needy folk taking up my time. Of course I will always be available to you, my lord.' Peter had been pleased to receive a prompt payment from Sterling for the servant's funeral.

'Will you hire a nurse locally to care for your daughter or engage a woman from an agency in London?' Jack wasn't to be put off pursuing his goal.

Peter gave a heavy sigh, wondering what ailed the man to be constantly bothering with domestic issues that were none of his concern. 'I suppose something of the sort will eventually be done. But I have a servant here during the day and the child is docile enough to need little attention.' He turned to Dawn. 'Surely it is time for her nap.' He flapped a hand to let Dawn know he wanted Lily removed from the room.

'She has only recently woken up,' Dawn said truthfully and with a hint of stubbornness. 'And Mrs Grove is to retire from your service, as you know, sir, so will not be here at any time to care for Lily.' The cook had just that morning told Dawn she'd informed the vicar of her intention to quit. 'Lily must never be left alone, she is far too young—'

'I believe I know my duty to her,' Peter interrupted. 'A new woman will soon be engaged in Mrs Grove's stead.'

Dawn wasn't about to be put off by his stony stare or clipped words. 'Lily needs to be properly nurtured. She is a lively child at times and very bright. She should be occupied and educated with toys and books and cared for by somebody who cherishes her. She is my granddaughter and I have offered to take her with me to London so you may attend to your duties here. And I will do that at no cost to you at all, sir.' Having rattled that off, Dawn paused for a breath.

'Why, that sounds like an excellent idea, Mrs Fenton,' Jack declared heartily, ignoring the furious floridity that was rising above Mansfield's collar. 'If the vicar is agreeable to that sensible solution I know our mutual friends will be delighted to have Lily as a playmate for Viscount Booth.'

'Viscount Booth?' Peter echoed stiffly.

'The Earl of Houndsmere's firstborn. Lance Harley is a good friend of mine. He mentioned to me only the other day at dinner that in his opinion children need friends from an early age if they are to thrive. Your daughter, I would say, is about the same age as their son and would make an ideal companion.'

'I believe that friends are important, too,' Dawn spoke up with a private smile for Jack to thank him. 'And so does the Countess of Houndsmere believe in children socialising. Emma would gladly welcome Lily into her home as readily as she does me. Young Bernard is a delightful little boy and would adore having Lily to play with.'

The Reverend Peter Mansfield was aware that Dawn had lofty friends, but he'd paid the connection scant heed before, as he'd never seen a way to benefit from it. Now he suspected he might. He also suspected something else. 'You are *previously* acquainted?' He swung a glance between the couple.

'Indeed, we have known one another for many years,' Jack confirmed. 'Mrs Fenton and I have close mutual friends in the Earl and Countess of Houndsmere. It is a very odd coincidence that we met by chance in Essex. Would that a happy rather than sad event had occasioned it.'

Dawn was discreetly watching for Peter's reaction and a burgeoning optimism started to make her heart race. Though she displayed not a jot of *her* feelings she was sure the vicar was considering the likely benefits to be had from his daughter getting to know an earl's heir.

Jack had been observing Mansfield, too, and knew it would be as well to act immediately. He got up and walked to the window, looking out with a heavy sigh. 'It is hard to believe that the recent fine spring weather has so quickly disappeared. I shall need to return to London without delay. I cannot be snowbound when I have important meetings in London to attend. Those clouds blowing in look threatening. A heavy fall followed by a thaw will flood the roads for weeks.' He turned back and crossed his arms over his chest. 'If you wish to travel home with me today, Mrs Fenton, I have a good coach and a fast team of horses. We can outrun the worst of it with ease.'

'I *would* like that, sir, thank you.' Was this really happening? Dawn thought wildly. Was she really going home—*so soon, please, God*—with her beloved granddaughter at her side?

'Will it take you long to pack, ma'am?'

Dawn forced herself to sound calm when replying, 'Not at all, sir.' And that was the truth. With all the commotion that had met her arrival Dawn had only removed a few necessary items from her trunk. All that was required was those to be replaced and the lid to be dropped down again.

'And your daughter, sir? Is she sensibly to come with us while you attend to planning her future and engaging the necessary staff?' Jack's tone of voice made it clear he would think the vicar a fool if he refused.

'Yes...you may take the dear child to London then, I suppose.' Peter gave a gracious nod. 'In her absence I will endeavour to sort out a suitable nurse until a governess can take over the task.'

'I expect it will take many months to find the right candidate,' Jack said. 'In the meantime you will be content knowing your daughter is perfectly well cared for and is making fine new friends in London.'

'I'll pack Lily's things with mine,' Dawn blurted, standing up, wanting to make ready for the journey straight away. She felt an urge to dash to Jack and hug him for what he'd done for her, but knew she must not act in any way that might pique the vicar's resentful nature. She managed to manoeuvre into position to send Jack a look that she hoped he would understand. She wanted him to wait and take them with him now. Once he was gone, even if only briefly before returning to collect them, Peter might brood and retract what he'd just agreed to.

Jack walked away from the window where he'd been studying storm clouds and picked up his drink. 'If I might impose on you, Mrs Fenton, would you hurry, please? I shall wait for you to ready yourself. It would be expedient to set on the road without delay.' He paused. 'In the meantime I will speak to the vicar and hear of his plans for the upkeep of the church. I have noticed, sir, that the perimeter wall of the grave-yard appears unstable.' Jack took a sip of his port. 'Is the roof in good repair?'

As though to add her weight to the decision to flee this house Lily sprang up and started whizzing about the room, whirling her dolly in a hand.

'Oh, do take her away with you,' Peter snapped impatiently.

'I will be ready to set off when you are, Mrs Fenton. I have nothing of note to collect from the Grange other than my valet. And he will follow when he is ready. We should be back in London by nightfall.'

'Thank you.' Dawn waited for his eyes to skim past the vicar and tangle with hers, as she knew they would. But though he displayed no more than polite friendliness in his smile Dawn knew what was in his mind. Her triumph and pleasure were equally hidden. The Reverend Peter Mansfield must never understand how overjoyed she was to have her beloved granddaughter going home with her.

Chapter Six

'I will always be in your debt, my lord. I don't know how I can ever repay you for the wonderful help you gave to me and to Lily.'

No flirting, Jack told himself sternly as a rogue thought of how he'd like this desirable woman to please him infiltrated his mind. He gazed into a pair of glowing green eyes, then leaned forward on the coach seat to take the slender fingers she held out to him. She squeezed his hands strongly in gratitude and he caressed the soft skin beneath his thumbs. It was innocent, he told himself, letting her go and gazing out into the gathering gloom. There was nothing seductive in a kind touch.

'There is one thing you can do for me that will be ample reward,' he said with a half-smile. 'No more "my lord", please. I remember you called me Jack years ago, at my insistence, it's true. And I believe you permitted me to use your name, when we were alone.'

'I would like that, sir...' Dawn gestured a bashful apology as he raised a wry eyebrow. 'It is a habit that I will soon break now I feel we are becoming friends.'

'I hope we are already friends, Dawn,' he said quietly, but held back on hinting he intended they'd eventually be more than that. Since their reunion in London he'd spent just a few hours in her company, yet she'd already crept back beneath his skin. It wasn't so long ago he'd sworn he'd never again let Dawn Sanders mean too much to him. Yet within a week of being home in England his sensible intention of avoiding her had been overtaken by a restless need to be wherever she was. He had arranged to dine with their mutual friends, guessing that the Houndsmeres would invite her along, too. He'd also guessed she might stay away to avoid him and she had. But it had done nothing to lessen his need to see her. He'd rather be spurned than know she was indifferent to his presence. Spotting her on Regent Street had been a stroke of luck. Once he'd spoken to her, he'd known she was no more immune to him than he was to her.

After that meeting all logic had been over-taken by memories of how much he'd once wanted her. He had a mistress who was sensual and amiable enough to satisfy his need for female company, yet he'd taken Pauline home from Regent Street that day and hadn't visited her since. She had twice called on him, though, uninvited and much to his annoyance, to try to rekindle their relationship.

Jack hadn't had a pressing reason to travel to Essex. Once he'd discovered that Dawn was heading in that direction he'd decided to visit his estate in the hope of seeing her again. Now he thanked the Lord he had set out on the road, even if for mile upon mile he'd mocked himself for acting like a moonstruck fool obsessed with his first maid. But that was forgotten now, overtaken by genuine relief that he'd been in the right place at the right time to be of service. He felt immensely glad to be removing Dawn and her granddaughter from Mansfield's clutches and the depressing atmosphere at the vicarage.

Despite all of that, he regretted that the timing couldn't have been more inappropriate to hint at how they had once felt about one another. He still wanted her and hoped she still had similar feelings for him. But holding her, soothing her with kisses and caresses, as a lover would, had to wait. For now kind words and condolences must suffice. Jack knew for decency's sake he must be very patient. Dawn needed to deal with the consuming heartache that was preventing her turning her thoughts to anything other than her granddaughter's welfare.

Jack looked at the little girl stretched out beside her youthful grandma with her head on Dawn's lap. 'She quickly dropped off to sleep after her upset.'

'I'm sorry Lily made such a dreadful racket. She can be mischievous at times, but is usually easily distracted from it.' Dawn placed a loving hand on the child's fair hair. 'The poor little mite must be so confused. I have told her that her mama is in heaven and she seemed to accept it. But in her own way, she knows something is wrong and is now missing her mama dreadfully.'

Almost from the moment they had started on their journey Lily had howled for her mother. The commotion had gone on for at least two miles before eventually petering out. Rocking her, singing to her, playing dolls with her… Dawn had tried it all, but none of it had worked. Jack had not batted an eyelash despite the fact that his temples must have been throbbing equally badly. She guessed he was unused to being around fractious children; nevertheless, he had coped admirably. He had eventually quietened Lily by showing her some sleight-of-hand tricks with a coin, producing the sovereign from behind one of the little girl's ears. Lily's sobs had transformed to giggles. Grabbing at the gold Jack had sent spinning on the edge on the seat, she had refused to hand the coin back for any more magic to be performed. She had curled up and fallen asleep with it clutched in her hand. Now Dawn eased the sovereign from her slumbering granddaughter's fingers and returned it to its rightful owner. 'I know it is hard to believe after her tantrum, but lately Lily has been unusually subdued. She is only three, but I imagine children can be very sensitive little souls.'

'She doesn't take after her father, then,' Jack commented drily, slipping the sovereign into a pocket.

'Indeed, she does not!' Dawn responded with muted force. 'She is the image of her mama in looks and temperament and I thank the Lord for it.'

'Was it an arranged marriage?'

Dawn knew he was circuitously asking why her stepdaughter would have tied herself to such a repulsive individual. Dawn wasn't sure why the marriage had come about either and wished fervently now that it never had.

'The Reverend Peter Mansfield was an acquaintance of my late husband's from the days before I married him. When Eleanor was seventeen the vicar approached Thomas to ask for his daughter's hand and his suit was accepted.'

'And your stepdaughter had no objection?'

'She was exceedingly close to her papa. He advised her to accept Peter and she did. Eleanor implicitly trusted her father to have her best interests at heart.'

'And what did you think about it all?'

Dawn contemplated for a while before answering. 'I think my husband loved his daughter very much. She resembled her mother and was a reminder of his first wife.' Dawn knew he was remaining quiet in the hope she'd explain that comment. 'I felt no jealousy for my predecessor. It was not a love affair between us, but a convenient arrangement that suited us both.' She didn't want to sound disloyal to her husband, yet there was no doubt in her mind now that her stepdaughter's marriage had been a dreadful mistake. 'I thought that at seventeen Eleanor had time to wait a while and get to know the vicar better before committing to a betrothal,' Dawn said carefully. 'I didn't like him from the start, although he did put more effort into being genial back then.' She paused, wondering whether to confess that she'd almost argued with Thomas over Eleanor's future.

Just a few hours in Jack Valance's company after years apart and yet she felt she could bare her soul to him…tell him anything. And she had never felt that way with Thomas in several years of marriage. 'I aired my concerns and Thomas tried to allay my uneasiness about the match. He believed Mansfield was just trying too hard to impress his prospective bride and in-laws.' She hesitated, then added, 'My late husband wanted to see Eleanor quickly settled. He'd had some business setbacks, you see, and his debts were mounting.'

'A father would want to know his daughter was provided for in those circumstances,' Jack said fairly.

Dawn nodded agreement. 'Thomas wanted her dowry safely transferred to a husband in case creditors seized it and ruined Eleanor's marriage prospects.'

'An understandable action,' Jack said.

Dawn began to nod, then a frown furrowed her brow and she shook her head instead. 'But even with my husband's reassurance I was still not convinced it was the right thing for Eleanor to do at so tender an age. She wasn't very mature at seventeen and Mansfield was already over thirty when they were married. I believed a younger man might have suited her better, but allowed myself to be swayed from making a fuss. I had been part of the family just a short while and was conscious that Eleanor was not my daughter. Things would have been very different had she been my flesh and blood.' Dawn gazed at Jack, explaining, 'A second wife has a tricky path to tread when joining a ready-made family. I got on well with Eleanor from the start, but she was very much her father's child and I didn't want to come between them.' A wave of sadness made her bite her lip to disguise its trembling. 'Perhaps with hindsight I should have said and done far more.' She choked a bitter sound in her throat. 'How useless is wisdom when it comes too late.'

'We're all guilty of knowing the right thing to do after the event,' Jack said gently.

She gave him a grateful smile, then looked fondly at Lily. 'I will be more vigilant with her... and speak up at every opportunity if I think I should to protect her. I hope that Peter will always allow me to see her. It is hard to know his moods sometimes or what he will do.'

'He will do what he believes will benefit him. At present he hopes that your connections might serve his purpose of getting to know an earl and his heir.'

'You have understood him rather well after so short an acquaintance,' Dawn said ruefully. 'It took me longer to fully appreciate how unpleasant and devious he is.'

'There is nothing unique about the Reverend Peter Mansfield. Such fellows are ten a penny,' Jack said contemptuously. 'Whereas women with your qualities are rare indeed.'

Dawn felt a little flustered by his praise. He hadn't smiled when complimenting her and looked quite severely serious. 'Thank you, but I think any grandma would do the same.' She chuckled to lighten things between them. 'Anyway…please don't have me too virtuous or I will surely let myself down.'

He did smile then in a way that brought heat to her cheeks. 'Oh… I don't want you virtuous, Dawn. Heaven forfend…'

Jack saw a glimmer of comprehension in her eyes before she looked away and began soothing her fidgeting granddaughter with a gentle touch. She understood what he wanted. But he'd been right in thinking that her devotion to the little girl was all that mattered to her right then. It seemed odd to think of Dawn being a grandmother when she was clearly younger than Lily's father.

'You had no children of your own?' he asked.

Dawn shot a look at him. Did he know of her own lost baby? She doubted that her best friend would have mentioned anything so personal.

'I'm sorry. That was impertinent of me.'

'I don't mind speaking of it. I nearly became a mother, but miscarried. My husband had had his accident just two weeks previously and the doctor blamed the shock of it on causing me to lose the child.' The lump in her throat had made the explanation sound very husky.

Jack thrust his fingers through his fair hair in a show of regret. 'I'm sorry... I had no idea. I shouldn't have asked and made you dwell on yet more heartache you've endured.'

'I think of it often without any need for a reminder, and anyway I like to talk to you.' Dawn was gazing at the darkness beyond the coach window. 'I always enjoyed our conversations.' She felt his eyes lingering on her profile and slowly met them. It had been the first proper reference to their romance years ago and she deduced from his reaction that he hadn't forgotten about any of it either. She avoided his steady stare by concentrating on Lily and stroking the child's hair. 'So...tell me all about your adventure abroad, if you will,' she said lightly. 'I imagine you saw many lands and peoples. It must have been an exciting time for you.'

'Indeed...and not all of it pleasant.'

'Oh? You found your adventure a disappointment?' If he had, she thought acidly, it had taken him a long time to return from it.

'In part,' he answered and lifted the leather blind at the window, peering out into a wintry scene. 'I'm afraid that the bad weather has caught up with us.'

Glancing past him, Dawn saw a swirl of white flakes spattering against the glass. She had noticed that the carriage had lost pace and seemed to be moving in a more laboured way.

'It might be as well to put up somewhere rather than risk the roads further along. The winds have changed. We are driving into the snow as we head south.' He rested his elbows on his knees, leaning towards her to ask, 'Would you mind if we broke our journey at a tavern and spent the night there?'

'I'd sooner reach London safely. I know how treacherous icy roads can be.'

A frown and a gesture were Jack's way of apologising for prompting her to think of her husband's coaching accident. 'I can only marvel at how you have coped with everything that has happened to you.' His eyes gleamed with warmth before he straightened up and sat back against the squabs, his expression again concealed by shadows.

'Thank you,' Dawn murmured. 'But all families endure tragedies and I mustn't think fate has been particularly unkind to me or I will feel depressed.'

'I don't want that. I want life to improve for you. And it can. Shall we put up at the inn and see what tomorrow brings? At sunrise there might be little more than March frost in the air.' Jack hadn't been prompted by lust to suggest they overnight together. His honest intention was that they all arrive safely in London. And once there... What then? He'd gone away years ago wanting to marry her, but what could he now offer to the woman he'd once hoped to be his wife other than an informal arrangement? They were both older, wiser, battered by life. Why would she object to having everything he could bestow but his name? Doing without her in his life would be impossible. The years apart hadn't cooled his feelings for her as he'd hoped they might for life to be uncomplicated. Being close to her didn't simply elicit a residue of longing that left him nostalgic for youthful days. He wanted to kiss her...finish what he'd started back then when more innocent and less knowing of life's cruelties.

She'd wanted him, too, years ago and just the memory of her ardent response to his kisses and caresses had the power to stir his loins. But she was parrying his attempts to flirt...guarding herself from him. She might have poured out her heart and confided her worries about her grandchild's future, but she'd not let him know her personal emotions, especially towards him.

'If we are slowed down to a snail's pace by blocked roads, Lily will get hungry and mischievous.' Dawn was aware he'd been brooding on something. Believing he might be waiting for her to properly confirm she had no objection to putting up at a tavern, she said lightly, 'We should stop for the night. I'm afraid my nerves certainly can't stand another tantrum.'

Jack gave a wry smile. 'Nor mine...' He rapped on the roof for the driver to pull up.

The vehicle slowly skidded to a halt on the ice and Dawn realised that the sooner they were safely in the warm and dry the better she'd like it.

A gust of cold air blew in as Jack got out to speak to the driver, making Lily stir. Dawn tucked the blanket more closely around her granddaughter and continued to lull the child. Her free hand twitched the blind aside so she could see where they were, but thick white flakes were obscuring her vision.

After a few minutes Jack climbed in, bringing a frosty scent with him. He reseated himself, idly brushing ice crystals from his glistening hair. 'The Bell Inn is about a mile up ahead; we can pull in there.'

* * *

'Would your husband also like a cup of hot chocolate brought up to your room, my lady?'

'My husband? Oh, no… You misunderstand… Lord Sterling is my travelling companion and will require a separate room. I'm sure he would like a hot drink, though. And some warm milk for the child, please.' Dawn's colour had risen, but she realised it was as much her fault that a misconception had occurred.

The proprietor of the Bell public house had been rushing to marshal incoming vehicles when they had turned in on to his slush-covered courtyard. Having noticed a crest adorning the coachwork, the fellow had tramped over, demanding the driver give the identity of his aristocratic passenger. Jack had sprung down and introduced himself, then set about arranging for the stabling of his horses. The solicitous landlord had helped Dawn and Lily alight, quickly ushering them towards the tavern to shelter from the quietly falling snow. He had summoned a serving maid to attend to them before disappearing to see to others abandoning their journeys.

Dawn had been concentrating on keeping Lily protected from the crush of travellers and had not thought much about it when the landlord addressed her as 'm'lady'. Quite naturally the fellow had assumed Lord Sterling was with his wife.

'I wasn't told you needed two rooms, m'm.' The serving girl looked flustered. 'I've just let the farmer and his family have the only other one. We're bursting at the seams now the weather's brought folk to a halt. Strangers are topping and tailing in what beds we've got.'

'Is everything to your satisfaction, m'lady?' The landlord had hurried back inside, knocking snow from his shoulders. 'Never fear, His Lordship is on his way now he's attended to his fine team of horses. My daughter will fetch you a hot toddy while you wait for your husband in the back parlour.' He jerked his balding pate at his daughter to get her to quickly fetch it.

'She's not his wife.' The girl looked as though she might wink at her father.

He gawped, then quickly subdued his surprise beneath a bland expression. Quality conducting a discreet tryst in his country tavern was a common enough occurrence. A couple turning up with a bastard in tow was more unusual, though, and he wished they'd picked a better time for it. He had a multitude of cold, hungry folk cramming every nook and cranny. 'A nice hot drink to warm you up, m'm?' he repeated his suggestion, then nodded at Lily, sucking her thumb.

'The child might like some cake or crumpets and a milky drink. My girl will fetch it all for you if you'd like to sit down in there.' He gestured to a door further along the hallway.

Lily had understood something nice was on offer. She tugged on her grandma's skirts, nodding her small head, then held out her hands to be picked up.

'Is there a problem?' Jack had picked a path through the throng in the shadowy corridor, lit by guttering candle flame. 'Here, let me hold her.' He courteously took Lily as Dawn shifted the toddler in her weary arms.

'All is being attended to, my lord.' The landlord bowed. 'I'm just about to take your companion's order. We have beef roasting in the oven if you've an appetite for a hearty dinner.'

'The lady wants a separate room,' his daughter chirped up. 'But the farmer took the last one for his family.' She jerked her chin at a couple huddled together in a recess. Between them stood two young children hiding from people barging to and fro.

'Well…yon farmer must try an inn further along.' Her father hissed from the corner of his mouth, then turned a smile on his eminent guest. 'Do sit in the back parlour, my lord. There is a good fire and comfy chairs. You will have it to yourself till midnight if you wish. Thereafter a party of tinkers is bedding down in there. It's the only space left.' He attempted to guide Dawn towards the room, but she hung back.

'Please don't make that family travel on in this weather. We will manage with what we have.' Dawn sent Jack a bashfully enquiring glance, hoping he wouldn't be embarrassed into agreeing if he didn't want to. But she couldn't in all conscience send people back on the road again on such a night simply to preserve her modesty. Jack was a thorough gentleman, she was sure, and she was a widow, not a swooning maid, unused to the sight of a man without his shirt on. They *would* manage somehow.

'Of course, we will manage very well,' Jack endorsed with a subtle smile. 'Would you like a dinner?' he asked Dawn. 'I think I could do justice to a plate of roast beef.'

'Thank you…yes…' Dawn had noticed a wonderful savoury aroma wafting in the atmosphere and it had made her stomach grumble.

The landlord snapped his fingers at his daughter to make her hurry to fetch the meals. Before she headed off the girl slid Jack a lascivious look from under her lashes. In Dawn's opinion any woman would be mad not to jump at a chance to share the bed of a tall blond gentlemen as handsome as Jack.

Chapter Seven

⁂

Once the steaming plates of roast beef and vegetables had arrived Lily had set her sights on that rather than her buttered crumpets. She had abandoned her low stool, situated a cosy distance from the fire, and attempted to climb on to her grandma's chair at the dining table.

Dawn had settled the child on her lap, feeding her a small helping in between taking her own mouthfuls of succulent roast meat. Jack had devoured his meal with the speed that only men seemed able to achieve, then had lifted Lily away from the table, allowing Dawn to finish her dinner in peace. He had taken the child to sit by the fire with him and had played spin the coin to keep her amused.

Having eaten her fill, Dawn placed down her cutlery and dabbed her lips with a napkin, feeling more relaxed than she had in many days.

Now that Lily had turned her attention to her doll, Jack was lounging back in his wingchair, one hand draped over the arm with a tumbler of cognac oscillating between thumb and forefinger. Dawn watched him with a wry smile as he patiently returned to Lily the doll she lobbed on to his lap. The toy was immediately plonked back on his knee and this time he allowed it to stay there until the toddler held out her hands for it.

He had been a boon from the moment they had met at Wivenhoe church, and he had volunteered to fetch the doctor. But Dawn knew she mustn't think of Eleanor now or tears would flow. Once back in her own home in London there would be time enough to grieve for her stepdaughter. She transferred her gaze to Lily; the child had settled down quietly between Jack's spaced feet. She seemed perfectly at ease with him despite having known him such a short while. He would make a good father…a good husband, too, Dawn realised. He was tolerant and kind with children and not too lofty to lend a hand and give his wife a rest… She pulled herself up short. She'd painted a picture in her mind of them as a family and they were far from that. Once back in town they had separate homes and lives to go to. At present all was quiet and harmonious for her, but the reality might be very different in a month's time. Would Peter Mansfield allow her to keep custody of the daughter he seemed to view as a nuisance? He could come and take Lily away, as was his right, and Dawn feared that if that day arrived, her heart might break. She blocked the bad thoughts; concentrating on the here and now was what she must do or she would drive herself mad with worry.

Her eyes returned to Jack's fire-daubed profile as he gazed into the leaping flames in the grate. He was brooding on something and Dawn suspected she knew what it might be. They hadn't spoken again of their sleeping arrangements, but neither of them had forgotten that shortly they would go upstairs together. A moment later she was proved right in believing he had bedtime on his mind.

'I'll overnight in the stables…'

'What?' Dawn was aghast at the idea of him attempting to rest in such a draughty, freezing cold place.

He turned his head her way to smile and said, 'Believe me, I've slept in far worse places. It isn't a problem for me, honestly.'

'You will not sleep outside!' Dawn spluttered. 'There's no need. The landlord's daughter told me all manner of strangers are sharing bedrooms and I'm not too precious to do the same when needs must.'

'Are we strangers, Dawn?'

'Perhaps not,' she said. 'Which makes the idea of you suffering frostbite on my account even more ridiculous.'

A thought occurred to her. She had forgotten about Miss Sarah Snow rather too quickly. Putting up at a hostelry with a woman might be something he would sooner avoid having to explain to his intended. Perhaps he wasn't being gallant but pragmatic when offering to allow her the room to herself. Awkward though it was to refer to gossip about his betrothal, Dawn realised she had a valid reason to do so. She got up from the dining table and settled in the other fireside chair so they sat face to face.

'I completely understand that you might wish to keep it quiet that you shared a tavern chamber with me,' she said carefully. 'When we get to London I promise not to mention a word of this episode to anybody. Even Emma will never know of it.'

He placed down on the hearth the glass of cognac that had moments ago hovered at his mouth. 'You've heard rumours about a betrothal?'

'Yes, I have… Are they true?' she blurted. Why deny it? she thought. Better to cut to the

chase than coyly probe for information as though
jealous. Even though she feared she might be.

'What have you heard?' Jack picked up the
cognac and shot it back in one swallow.

'Miss Snow is a pretty redhead and Jack
Valance has fallen in love and returned from
overseas to announce their engagement.' She
watched for his reaction to that concise statement, but could discern no emotion in his hard
profile. 'That is more or less the gist of what I
overheard while I was choosing a book at the circulating library,' she prompted him for a reply.

'I hope you came away from the place with a
better fiction than that,' he muttered drily and
refilled his glass to the top with cognac.

'It's not true?' Her heart had quickened in the
hope of hearing him confirm the gossips had
overstepped the mark. 'I'm not prying... Well,
maybe a little,' she added when he seemed reluctant to answer. 'I suppose I'm no different
to most ladies in having a rather vulgar interest in knowing which eligible bachelor has got
caught and by whom.' She managed a rueful
smile, though wasn't nearly as insouciant as
she made out. Her heart was drumming as she
waited for his reply.

No answer other than a sarcastic noise escaped his throat and it flustered her. *Did* he

think she was being vulgarly inquisitive? 'You don't need to tell me, of course,' she said quickly. 'Your business is your own affair and I'm sorry I brought it up. I just wanted you to know that I understand our enforced stop here could be embarrassing for you. I'll keep it all a secret, if you wish. It's the least I can do after all you have done for me.'

'I don't care who knows about it. Do you know what I do wish?' He took another hefty swig of cognac.

'No…' Dawn said rather hesitantly.

'I wish I'd been an eligible bachelor about six years ago.'

Her gratitude to him was clear in her limpid green gaze, as was her bewilderment as to why his mood had changed when all she'd done was sweetly offer a solution to a possible problem. He hung his head, watching his fingers rock the empty glass to and fro. He was disgusted with himself. Inwardly he'd vowed to keep things casual between them until she was settled back in her own home and had had time to mourn her stepdaughter. What did he think he was doing, acting like a sulky youth after what she'd recently been through? But he knew why he was frustrated: wanting her was six years old and being this close to her now was tormenting the life out of him. They should have kept on the road… The ice would've cooled him down, he mockingly told himself. But he knew he'd never have journeyed on, risking those roads just in case he couldn't control himself. He glanced at Dawn, frowning into firelight. The tenderness tightening his chest was still there, but overlaid with something earthier…darker. If she'd just waited another six months before marrying it wouldn't have come to this. Perhaps she hadn't loved him as much as she'd said. Perhaps he'd been a fool to have risked everything, including his life and sanity, to have her.

Abruptly he stood up and went to the window, gazing out into the dark night. 'It's stopped snowing. The sky is quite clear,' he informed, regarding the vast starry heavens. 'We should be able to set off early in the morning.'

'I hope you're right. It will be good to be home.'

'I'll sleep here in the parlour…the chair's comfortable enough.'

'As you wish,' she said stiffly. 'Wherever you sleep you can trust me to say nothing about this. Not that there is anything to hide; the whole thing is quite innocent.'

Jack smiled sardonically at the large, milky moon. 'Is it?' he muttered.

'Why do you say it like that?' Dawn took

the plunge and started a conversation she knew might lead to sparks flying. 'I'm a widow, not a debutante. I don't care what people might try to make of it. I will ignore propriety when I want to and if I believe the situation merits it. Not that I think a mention of this will ever leak out. Besides, only the Houndsmeres ever knew that once upon a time we spoke of being more than friends. And now it is in the past. Things turned out differently for both of us.'

'You make that time we spent together sound like a fairy tale.'

'I suppose it was. A girlish fantasy. When young one is allowed to dream.'

'You weren't a girl, you were twenty-three,' he said, turning from the window to look at her.

'Thank you for reminding me,' she returned tartly.

His slate-grey eyes roved her beautifully in-dignant features as he slowly approached. 'Apart from recalling your age, I seem to remember you saying you wanted to marry me.'

'Only after *you* delivered half a proposal and said you wanted to marry *me* when in a position to do so,' Dawn protested, though her cheeks had turned rosy. Indeed, she *had* made it clear she wanted him, clinging to him and kissing him as though he was everything to her on that long-ago day in Hyde Park. 'Are you hinting that you believe I should have waited...pining for you... for years in the hope that you might come back and propose properly?' She sounded disbelieving...almost angry.

'No...'

'Not a word...not a single line written in a letter of where you were or what you were doing,' she breathed. 'I didn't marry until long afterwards.'

'I know...' he said hoarsely and thrust his fists into his pockets. 'At first I wasn't in a position to be able to write to you.'

'An inability to do things seems to have dogged you,' she said waspishly.

'Indeed, it has...and still it seems to,' he returned. 'So I take it you're not bothered by the idea of me being somebody else's husband?'

'No more than I imagine you are to know I was somebody else's wife.' She'd answered brusquely and could sense the tension between them building higher, starting to crackle as intensely as the burning logs.

'I was jealous when I found out about him.' He halted just in front of her, his eyes as dark as the uncovered window behind. 'So do you still want to share your innocent bed with me?'

Dawn's small teeth sank into her lower lip as

she turned her head to avoid his heavy, knowing stare. No matter how deeply she once had felt about him, she'd never flirt with a man who was getting married. And she knew he was, even if she had no idea *why* he was. He certainly didn't act or talk as though he were in love with Miss Snow.

'It is getting late,' Dawn said. 'And Lily is tired.' The little girl was rubbing her eyes and starting to whimper.

'It's been a long day for you, too. You should get some rest.' Jack paused. 'And thank you for your concern about gossip, but I've no need to explain my behaviour or beg anybody's pardon.'

'I see… All is well then…' She managed a tight smile. She didn't want friction between them over old hurts. He had been too good to her for that.

'No, you don't see,' he growled. 'There is much I want to say to you. But now isn't the right time. When we're back in London I'd like to visit you, if I may.'

'Of course… I would like to stay friends.' Dawn smiled as the child begged to be picked up, holding out her hands to Jack rather than her grandma. 'I believe that Lily would like to be your friend, too.' Dawn hoisted the child into her arms. 'I'll bid you goodnight. But…please don't go outside to the stable. The landlord's daughter assured me our chamber is spacious. If you change your mind about sharing accommodation with the tinkers, I'm sure we can manage adequately without getting in each other's way.'

He took Lily from her as the child wriggled, leaning in his direction and stretching out her small fingers. Balancing Lily on a muscular forearm, he slid his free hand over Dawn's cheek with tantalising softness. 'Life has dealt us both harsh blows, Dawn.'

She knew of her own heartaches, but had little idea of what he'd suffered to make him say such a thing. Her eyes questioned him even as she instinctively angled her face into his warm palm. When his lips replaced his fingers at her cheek she turned towards him as though it were the most natural thing to do. His eyes were on her mouth a mere second before his lips parted them with a possessive hunger that whipped her back through years to a secret, thrilling tryst behind an oak tree in Hyde Park. Her hand raised, grasping his jacket as she returned the kiss. Through the pounding of blood in her ears she heard her granddaughter squeaking a protest. Lily was snugly embraced between them. Dawn regretted her behaviour; moments ago she'd believed herself above flirting with men who were spoken for. She quickly tried to put some distance between them, but Jack stopped her, gripping her wrist.

'I'm sorry… I shouldn't have done that.'

'Indeed, you should not…if you are engaged. Are you?' she whispered, holding her breath while waiting for his answer although she already knew what it would be. She felt guilty and ashamed. He hadn't forced that kiss on her…she had invited it.

'I believe I am.' He threw back his head and a curse was ejected from beneath his breath.

Dawn busied herself picking up Lily's doll from the rug, not wanting him to see the distress that final admission had caused her. She wouldn't pry further into that or the blows that life had dealt him. He was a man on the threshold of married life with another woman. If he was waiting for his proposal to be accepted…so be it. Or perhaps it was just something as venal as a marriage contract being pored over that was causing uncertainty and delay. Yet she knew Jack Valance no longer had need to fortune hunt for a bride. He had found his feet and his fortune, so she'd been told.

'I'll bid you goodnight now, sir.' She reached out to take her granddaughter.

'I never forgot you, you know,' he said hoarsely.

'With all the horror of it I never could put you from my mind.'

'What horror?' she whispered, her eyes raking his tense features and her hands dropping to her sides as the child snuggled into him.

'Nothing...forget I said it.' He swooped on the bottle of cognac standing on the hearth, then, with Lily safe in his arms, led the way upstairs.

Jack wasn't asleep, she was sure of it. Only her granddaughter was enjoying sweet slumber, her light, sighing snores audible in the room. Dawn guessed that he knew she was awake, too, although she was lying silently, fully clothed but for her shoes, with Lily by her side.

Before climbing on to the lumpy mattress, Dawn had placed the flickering candle stub and a folded blanket by the side of the chair he'd said he would use. He'd courteously disappeared to allow her to perform her ablutions and settle herself and Lily beneath the covers. Quietly he'd entered the chamber a while later, taking his makeshift bed in the corner.

She was feeling unbearably restless, but quelled a compulsion to rise and approach him to demand he told her about the horrors he'd mentioned. Her intention to be less inquisitive had melted as soon as she saw the raw pain in his eyes. He had soothed her distress and she was human enough to want to comfort him if she could, no matter their differences. But she knew he'd let the comment about his past slip out in an unguarded moment. He'd looked regretful afterwards for having done so. She was keen to have every detail of what had kept him away for so long. But what was the point in becoming too familiar? It was for his future wife to demand what he'd been up to, not her.

Though tempted to leap from the bed to make the spinning thoughts in her head go away, she remained quiet and still. If she moved, he would, too... They would come together again and participate in more than a conversation...she knew it. She could feel the magnetism between them even now, in the cold, silent room.

Dawn squeezed her eyes shut, feeling ashamed that she wanted him to just come over and kiss her again. She'd no liking for women who went after men when fully aware they weren't free. She'd had her spouse and her family life. Jack Valance was entitled to have those things, too, without her feeling jealous of it. Feeling chilly, she eased the sheets up to her chin and watched moonbeams pattern the walls. How many lonely nights had she stared at her ceiling beneath her father's roof, wishing that one day she and Jack

Valance would share a bedchamber? Now they were, but it was too late for them to do anything but wish sleep to claim them. She frowned at her sentimental indulgence. They weren't the first ill-starred couple whose love went awry. Those yearnings belonged in the past and she must be grown up about things now and accept he was somebody else's future husband.

She touched a forefinger to the bow of her lips where it still tingled from the pressure of his mouth. Though quick and unfinished, his kiss had stirred deep within her an excitement that her husband had never aroused. Thomas had always been gentle and considerate when he came to her room at night. She'd never refused him and had done her best to respond to him. Though a virgin bride, she had known what she was getting into when agreeing to marry Thomas Fenton and had stayed true to the vows she'd spoken in church. It hadn't just been wifely duty; she had longed to become a mother, yet it wasn't to be. She imagined that her husband had also been disappointed with the physical side of their marriage, comparing her to his lost love. But they'd never spoken of their lack of closeness and compatibility. It had just been there... between them...keeping their relationship respectful rather than loving.

She gazed at the silvery disc glimpsed between the chink in the curtains, then closed her eyes, willing herself to empty her mind and fall sleep. Still the tormenting thoughts kept coming. Her late husband hadn't been the only one who'd loved and lost. She thumbed tears from her lashes. Why be upset now? she inwardly scolded herself. She'd known for weeks about the rumours concerning Jack's betrothal and hadn't cried for what might have been after their reunion in the drapery.

She was muddling up gratitude with affection; she still felt emotional after her stepdaughter's death…that's all it was. Jack Valance had acted as a knight in shining armour during a ghastly time for her.

Tomorrow she would be different with him… cooler. After that kiss he might believe she'd signalled an interest in a dalliance. His attitude to his betrothal indicated it was no love match, whatever the gossips said. But Dawn knew she was no man's mistress. She *believed* in marriage and in fidelity. Vows spoken in church weren't just words, they were truths, in her mind, and her conscience wouldn't allow her to sully them. Not even for Jack Valance.

A release of pent-up breath flowed from her as the muddle in her mind continued to deny her any rest. As though he'd heard it and it had prompted him to take a drink she heard the sound of cognac being swigged from the bottle. Raising quietly on an elbow on the bed, she took a peek at him. The candle stub had guttered low, but she could see his broad torso silhouetted by the dying embers in the grate. He was lounging back in the armchair in the corner of the room, head tilted as though he gazed at a spot close to the ceiling. She watched him raise the bottle from the floor to his mouth. Before he drank, he spoke to her.

'Go to sleep...'

She immediately sank her head into the pillow. He hadn't sounded drunk, but harsh, and she hadn't wanted him to see her watching him. In fact she didn't know how he had as he'd not turned her way. 'I want to drop off...but can't,' she whispered. Indeed, that was the truth! Her eyes felt hot and gritty with weariness and she craved sweet oblivion.

'Are you cold?'

'A little bit...'

He'd approached her in a lithe noiseless way that only became apparent when his thighs appeared at the side of the bed. He settled over her and Lily the blanket she'd left for his use.

'You should keep it,' she murmured. 'You'll freeze.'

He lifted the bottle held in a fist close to his hip. 'This'll keep me warm enough,' he muttered. He placed the backs of warm fingers to her cool cheek so she could tell his temperature.

'You are cold,' he said. 'Do you want a nip of brandy?'

Dawn raised on an elbow to shake her head. Well, she had wanted to talk to him. She caught his hand as he stepped back as though to go, but he immediately freed himself.

'I'm sorry... I just thought you might want to talk as neither of us can sleep.'

'That's not what I want, Dawn, and you know it.' His voice was guttural and his dark figure moved away again, merging into shadows in the room.

Dawn settled down beneath the weight of the extra blanket and closed her eyes. She put her arm around Lily, lightly, to warm but not disturb her.

'Goodnight, Jack...' she whispered into the pillow before finally falling into a dreamless slumber.

Chapter Eight

A pale light woke Dawn as it filtered between the velvet curtains and striped warmth across her eyes. She turned her head on the pillow to blink at Lily. The child was stirring as well and would be fully awake soon, wanting her breakfast.

As her befuddlement cleared and memories of last night resurfaced Dawn knuckled her sleepy eyes, sitting upright. The chair was empty and a quick look about the room confirmed Jack had gone from it. Dawn got carefully out of bed, trying not to disturb Lily, and tucked the covers around the drowsing child.

On the washstand was a basin and jug. She broke the veneer of ice on the water's surface, then poured, washing quickly. She gasped as her skin stung with cold, but she was glad of immediately feeling invigorated in body and mind.

Having brushed down her crumpled clothes,

she neatened her hair, combing her fingers through chestnut tangles before deftly repinning a sleek chignon at her nape.

She knew he had laid down with them after all. She hadn't dreamt the sensation of the mattress dipping beneath another's weight settling upon it. Neither had she imagined the feel of a hard masculine arm curving about her body. And it hadn't been her husband she'd dreamed of; no phantom lover had comforted her, but real flesh and blood. She remembered turning towards him, nestling blissfully into a warm body without once breaking her sleep.

Dawn used the spotted mirror suspended on the wall above the washstand to secure the wisps of hair that had escaped her attention. She gazed into a pair of dark green eyes and wistfully shook her head at her reflection. *Leave him be...and he will let you alone, too*, whispered in her mind. *He has too much pride to bother with an unwilling woman. If you do not, you will regret it, not he. Once married...once he has his children...he might grow to love his wife and forget about you...mistress, friend, whatever it is he has in mind for you. You will end up alone... the fool who dreamt of happy endings. There are none to be had where he is concerned. You have another better cause to fight for.* Dawn turned about and gazed at her granddaughter, wriggling to the edge of the bed to jump down from the high mattress. Keeping Lily was the dream to chase.

She helped the child to her feet. 'I expect you would like some breakfast, wouldn't you?'

'Want Jack.' Lily pursed her rosebud lips.

'You should call him Mr Valance,' Dawn said, crouching down beside her granddaughter and taking her small hands to squeeze and kiss. 'And I expect Mr Valance is making sure his fine horses are ready to pull his black coach. Soon we will be at my home in London. You will like that, won't you?'

'Will Mama come?'

'I'm sure she would like to…' Dawn said huskily. She smoothed a hand over the child's knotted fair hair. 'Your mama loves you so much, Lily…and so do I.' Briskly she stood up before her granddaughter noticed tears in her eyes. 'Now, we had better give you a wash and tidy you up, young lady, then go below and find you something nice to eat.'

'Good morning. Is Mr Valance…that is, Lord Sterling…taking breakfast with us?'

Dawn had found the landlord's daughter in the

back parlour, setting the table with crockery and cutlery. Of Jack there was no sign.

If the room had been commandeered as a makeshift lodging then Dawn would not have guessed it. It was spick and span and everything looked as cosy and inviting as it had yesterday evening when they had settled down to dine. The only difference was that sunbeams rather than moonlight streamed in through the small mullioned windows.

'Good morning to you, m'm. His Lordship ate earlier and so did his coachman. They're outside readying the horses to journey on.' The girl gave Lily a smile. 'Now what can I get for you? There's eggs and bacon, or cold ham and beef if you prefer. Bread baked fresh this morning and butter and jam, or honey if you like.'

Indeed, the smell of frying bacon was evident. But it was the wonderful aroma of fresh bread wafting about the tavern giving Dawn an appetite.

'Scrambled eggs and milk for the child, please, and bread and honey with some tea will suffice for me, thank you.' She approached the window and looked out into bright light glinting on a thin covering of white. 'Thank goodness it stopped before too much snow settled.'

'It's thawing nicely now, m'm. Some folks have already left.'

'What time is it?' Dawn hoped she'd not slept too long and delayed them getting an early start.

'Just after nine, m'm,' the girl replied and with a bob disappeared to get the food.

Dawn realised she *had* overslept. At home she would rise far earlier. Little wonder she had woken so groggily, but she had felt warm and snug in bed despite being half-aware that Jack had removed the cocoon of his arm some time earlier. She led Lily to the fire to warm herself by its glow, showing her how to hold out her palms, then rub them together.

'Good morning.' Jack entered the room, crisp winter air clinging to his coat.

'You should have woken me sooner,' Dawn said. She avoided lengthy eye contact by settling Lily on a chair at the table. She felt bashful with him which was silly, she told herself. They'd done no more than what was sensible by sharing a bed and keeping each other and Lily warm on a bitter night. Yet she knew because of it there was an increased tension throbbing between them.

'There was no need to disturb your sleep. You looked comfortable.' He picked up a log from the basket, lobbing it into the embers, then forcing it further in with the toe of his boot until flames leapt up.

'Did you manage to sleep well?' she asked politely, still attending to her granddaughter. She'd not mention that she knew he'd come to bed with them.

'I rarely sleep well.' He sounded remote and approached the window to plant a large hand either side of the wonky black-timbered casement. 'The sky to the south is clear...we should manage the rest of the journey home with no further trouble.'

The landlord's daughter backed into the room with a loaded tray and started setting out their breakfast on the table.

The amount of food on display was far too much for her and Lily to eat. After the servant withdrew she said, 'If you're still hungry, I can offer you...' Her voice tailed off as she became aware of his ironic expression.

'I've eaten, thank you,' he said with studied politeness.

'Well, take some tea, sir, at least,' she said, rather flustered.

'So we are back to formality, are we?' He turned back to the sunny vista.

Dawn didn't answer. What did he expect from her? she thought exasperatedly as she spooned scrambled eggs on to a plate for Lily and buttered her some bread. Why act familiar when they were on a path to grow apart? Or was she right in suspecting he'd deem his marriage no barrier to being close to other women? She'd offered to talk to him last night as neither of them could sleep, to help while away some long dark hours. But he hadn't wanted that, he'd said. And she knew very well what he had wanted. But she wouldn't fool herself that she alone roused his lust. She recalled the blonde woman he'd been squiring about town. Perhaps he intended to discreetly keep seeing his *chères amies* after the wedding. It wasn't an uncommon arrangement among people of wealth and pedigree. A refined wife to produce legitimate heirs and a lover to satisfy a gentleman's earthier needs. And if that was the sort of man he was, then she should thank her lucky stars that she *hadn't* waited any longer for him to return and marry her. She might by now have been a lonely, bitter woman, trying to ignore whispers about her husband's latest lady friend.

Dawn took a bite of bread and honey, swallowed, then kept her voice level when saying, 'We shan't be long eating this, then we can set out on the road.'

Jack pushed himself away from the window and came to the table.

'There's no rush and no need to bolt your food. The horses are rested and refreshed. We'll make good time and be back by noon.'

Lily held out her spoon, offering him some scrambled eggs.

He ruffled her fair hair. 'I'll go and pay the shot. We'll all soon be home,' he said before quitting the parlour.

No doubt it would be a blessed relief for him to get back to normality with his friends and family, Dawn thought. He had been hijacked by an odd, tragic episode and who could blame him for wanting to put it behind him? Whatever store he put on marriage was his own affair, but there was no getting away from the fact that he *did* have a wedding and all that entailed in front of him to concentrate on. And she had her granddaughter's well-being as her priority. She'd wanted a child of her own to love, to fill a lonely place in her heart, and although Lily wasn't her flesh and blood, she adored her. And that was enough.

'Oh, my dear, I can't believe what has happened. I'm so very sorry to hear the news. I was desperate to come and comfort you. What can I do to help?'

'Please tell me not to blub so much, Em,' Dawn said wryly. 'I fear I am turning into a veritable waterworks.'

'I'm not surprised to hear it and you should cry as much as you need to,' Emma said gently, dabbing at her own eyes with her hanky.

Moments after she had received Dawn's letter, and before properly digesting the awful news, the Countess of Houndsmere had hastened to ready herself to visit her best friend. A brief message had informed her that Dawn had returned early to London following the tragic death of her stepdaughter in Essex. Emma *had* been primed for bad news. Just hours earlier she had got the gist of the calamity from her husband. The Earl had bumped into Jack at his club where he'd learned that his friend had escorted Dawn home from Essex following very sad circumstances. Under intense interrogation from his wife the Earl had explained that he didn't know all the ins and outs as his friend had believed it best that Dawn broke the news about her family. But now, having sat with Dawn for an hour, listening to the story unfold, the Countess of Houndsmere was struggling to combat her shock.

'I must buck myself up or Lily will sense

something is wrong,' Dawn croaked. Her friend's tears had prompted more of her own.

She had been home for almost a week and had believed herself coping well with her grief. But sometimes a certain way Lily smiled like Eleanor would stab another ache beneath her ribs and make her retreat to a corner where she might weep unseen.

'Yes…we mustn't upset her, she's a real darling,' Emma agreed, straightening her shoulders with a livening sniff.

The two young women had been deep in conversation while Lily played with her toys on the rug by the fire. Several times the child had looked over at them as though wondering what kept them huddling quietly together, hankies in hands. Dawn had so far managed to avoid receiving visitors, or answering any awkward questions, other than Polly's. The first day they'd arrived home Dawn had had to send her maid to find her bed to calm down. Polly had started howling on learning why her mistress had brought her granddaughter home with her and Dawn had feared her distress would frighten Lily.

Emma, of course, was different. Dawn relied on her as a confidant and greatly valued her advice. After some days spent settling Lily into her new home, she had written to her friend. She'd known that the letter would prompt an immediate visit. It was good to be able to share the burden of her fears for Lily's future with her best friend. While the child's father still loomed in the background Dawn always had a worry on her mind.

'Mansfield sounds as though he is either a buffoon, or a monster.' Emma commented quietly from behind her teacup, then took a sip. 'Thank goodness you managed to make him see sense and could bring Lily to London.'

'It seemed he would continue to object until Mr Valance stepped in. Or Lord Sterling I suppose I should call him now.'

'If I'd known about that I would have told you the last time I saw you. I had no idea of Jack's title until he came to dine with us that evening.' Emma paused, looking reflective. 'He seems different to how I remembered him and not just in looks. That exotic foreign air suits him, but I'm not sure I like how cynical he has become. It was lovely to see him, of course, for he is such good company and made me laugh a lot. But he hardly mentioned becoming a nobleman or owning a vast estate in Essex. Lance told me later that Jack had been rewarded for combatting piracy and recovering plundered cargoes for the Crown. It all sounds very thrilling.'

'It does!' Dawn could only agree and made no attempt to disguise her awe at hearing about it. Every time something new was revealed about Lord Sterling she realised how little she knew of Jack Valance.

'It would be easier, though, to extract blood from a stone than get Jack to talk about himself, or his future plans.' Emma rolled her eyes.

'Indeed, he can be reticent when he wants to be, which is most of the time,' Dawn said a touch acidly.

'You mean his betrothal?' Emma put down her cup, gazing into her friend's eyes. 'Those whispers you overheard at the circulating library proved to have some foundation. Did he tell you about it?'

Dawn shrugged. 'He seemed to want to avoid the subject and I decided not to pry. With all that had gone on it seemed inappropriate to be nosy.' She gave a smile. 'Don't look so mournful, Em. Our very brief romance is long past. Why should Jack not get married and have his family life?'

'He is not in love, that's why,' Emma said bluntly. 'It is an arrangement and I am surprised that he has entered into it when he has the means now to settle down with a soulmate. The girl is an orphan and he is her guardian. Perhaps he feels duty bound for some reason.'

'She is an orphan and he is her guardian?' Dawn echoed in astonishment. That she also had *not* known, although she'd guessed his heart wasn't involved. No man in love would sound so cavalier about overnighting at a tavern with another woman in case he hurt his fiancée's feelings.

'Lance knows no more than that about Sarah. He says although he and Jack are old friends, from mutual respect they never delve too deeply into matters not willingly shared.'

'We all have our secrets.' Dawn knew that included her. Though she and Emma were also old friends she wouldn't speak about bedding down with Jack at a tavern on an icy night. Some things were too precious to share. She knew that Jack wouldn't mention it to a soul either. Looking back on it, Dawn realised it had been a rather sweet episode that she would cherish. Just for one night they had been bound together as a couple...a family...even if it had been a make believe that had dissolved as quickly as the snow in morning sunlight.

After an amicable quiet, Emma asked in concern, 'Tell me true...are you really coping with it all? You know I will do anything in my power to help with Lily. It is such a great change in both your lives.'

'Yes… I am coping, I promise.' Dawn gave a smile. 'And every day that passes I learn a little more about how to handle a little girl with a mind of her own.'

Emma chuckled. 'Thank heavens Jack was in Essex and could help you quickly come home.'

'I like Jack. He does magic…' Lily piped up.

'We all like him,' Emma said. 'And *I* like *you*, young lady. And I know somebody else who would love to get to know you.' She got up from the sofa and went to Lily, sitting in front of the fire. 'I have a little son called Bernard and I know he would like a friend.'

'Has he got a doll?'

'He's got some bats and balls and a rocking horse and tin soldiers, but I'm not sure that he has a doll. Would you share yours with him?'

'If he shares his things,' Lily said pragmatically, hugging her doll to her chest.

'Of course…that's only fair.'

Dawn got up from the sofa to see if there was any tea left in the pot. She felt she had talked enough about her woes now and it was time to find out how her friend had been.

'You look well, Em. Are you feeling better now?'

Emma strolled to join her and helped herself

to a treacle biscuit from the plate. 'Now the horrid nausea has passed I'm feeling fit as a fiddle.' In between nibbles of biscuit she added, 'Which is just as well as there are months yet to go.' She patted her small bump. 'Will you see Jack again, do you think?'

'I expect he might call when he has a moment. He promised Lily he would spin the coin with her again. She liked him, especially playing with his sovereigns…and keeping them,' Dawn added wryly.

'Clever girl.' Emma chuckled.

'The teapot's empty. Shall I ring for Polly to make more?'

'I'd love to stay longer, but I ought to be going.' Emma sighed. 'I promised Bernie I would be back in time to have tea with him before his bedtime. Then my sister-in-law has invited us to dine this evening.' She paused. 'Are you observing mourning and not socialising or will you come over soon and bring Lily so the children can play together?'

'Eleanor wouldn't want me to keep her beloved Lily cooped up instead of making a new friend. And I shall be quietly going about my business as usual. So we'd love to come over so Lily can meet Bernie.'

'I'll send the carriage one day next week then.'

Emma said a fond goodbye to Lily, placing a kiss upon her fingertips, then patting those on the little girl's rosy cheek.

Dawn accompanied her friend into the hallway, holding Lily by the hand so she might also wave goodbye to Emma. Polly was in the process of brushing down the stairs and as Dawn closed the door the maid said, 'It has turned quite fine this afternoon, m'm. Shall I take Miss Lily into the garden and give her a push on the swing? It will be time for her tea soon.'

'Thank you, Polly. She would benefit from some fresh air.' Dawn had noted her granddaughter yawning while sitting warm and comfortable in front of the fire. She didn't want Lily napping or she wouldn't sleep at her bedtime.

Polly took the excited child's hand. Lily had heard the magic words 'garden swing' and was keen to get to it.

Dawn watched them from the dining-room window, smiling contentedly as a laughing Lily swayed to and fro beneath a bough of the apple tree. Her husband had told her that Eleanor had loved playing on the garden swing as a child. Thomas would have adored to see his little granddaughter enjoying it, too, Dawn realised with a lump in her throat.

She turned away and returned to the parlour,

aiming to tidy the tea things on to the tray. Instead she seated herself at the table, resting her sharp little chin in her hands and dwelling on what Emma had recounted about Jack's adventures overseas. She understood what her friend meant about him seeming to be a different man to the one they'd known. He *was* harder in character and quite wickedly good looking. She wondered what had occurred to rob him of his carefree spirit. He'd obviously endured dangers; no buccaneer gave up his booty lightly. Perhaps Jack Valance had suffered greatly for his transformation into Lord Sterling.

And why was Sarah Snow his ward as well as his fiancée? How had he met her? On his travels, Dawn guessed. It was quite an intrigue… but one that she must not allow herself to get too involved in. His life, his future, his wife…they were not her concern.

The journey home from the Bell Inn had been as speedy as Jack had promised. It had been quiet, too. As the horses had thundered on through countryside, bringing them ever closer to London, Dawn had been increasingly aware of a subdued atmosphere. She had retreated into pondering on the practicalities that awaited her at home: buying Lily clothes and a few more toys were top of her list. She had rushed to get away from the vicarage and had grabbed only a handful of her granddaughter's things. Jack, too, had seemed to prefer to brood than talk, although she had felt his stormy gaze on her profile on many occasions. Even Lily had been quiet, behaving herself for the duration and only indulging in a minor tantrum when it was time to say goodbye to Jack. He had helped them alight, then had assisted the driver in carrying in Dawn's trunk, stowing it in her bedchamber. He had loitered while Dawn briefly introduced her maid to Lily, then asked Polly to take the child off to the kitchens for some refreshment. She had wanted to say a private, uninterrupted goodbye to Jack and to renew her heartfelt thanks for all his help. Though courteous, he hadn't seemed to want to tarry. A featherlight kiss to the fingertips he'd raised to his lips, then he had repeated his commiserations on her loss and secured her permission to call again.

But...so far she'd seen nothing of him. She was eager to see him, she realised, far too eager, and that wouldn't do. All her good intentions to keep their friendship platonic could so easily unravel. Yet she hadn't changed her mind about being an attachment to his life once he was a married man. If he was unfaithful, that was a matter for his conscience. She couldn't allow him to seduce her into abetting him in adultery. She would end up hating herself...then him...

Abruptly Dawn got to her feet, knowing she needed to keep herself busy to keep the yearning to see him at bay. She stacked the used crockery on to the tray, willing herself to stop thinking of him. She would take Lily out to the swing again after her tea, she decided, and properly tire her out before reading her a bedtime story. Then tomorrow they would sally forth to the shops.

She couldn't cocoon Lily or shut herself away from probing questions about her granddaughter. She would bump into neighbours and acquaintances who would be curious to know who the pretty little girl was and how long she would be staying with her. Eventually, when Lily was older, she would ask questions herself about half-recalled memories of her mother. And her granddaughter deserved to be told the truth about her baby brother, too.

At first Dawn had not felt comfortable leaving Lily's side for a minute. But Polly had fallen into the role of nursemaid exceptionally well and Lily liked her. Probably because the maid spoilt her dreadfully.

Dawn approached the window to gaze along the street. The peaceful neighbourhood looked as it had just a short while ago...before her life had changed so dramatically. She spotted people she knew going about their business. The lime trees were unfurling their leaves again now the cold snap had passed. She let the curtain drop into place, then a second later again whipped up an edge as her mind registered having glimpsed a face she longed to see.

She held her breath, peeping at the tall handsome gentleman with very fair hair, mere yards away. She knew he was heading towards her front door.

Chapter Nine

A rat-a-tat made her hastily smooth her skirts, then begin tucking loose chestnut curls behind an ear. She whisked into the hallway, then hesitated to take a deep breath with her hand hovering in mid-air. What did she want to say to him? What would he say to her? He had looked rather stern and purposeful as though this wasn't simply a courtesy call. Had he news from Essex about Peter Mansfield? She recalled that Jack had said his valet would follow him home at a later date. The servant might have turned up and told his master something of note…

Whatever reason had brought him she was simply glad to see him. Quickly she opened up in case he went away, believing nobody home.

'My apologies; I should have sent word of my visit… Is it a bad time?' He glanced past her, wondering why she'd attended her own door when he knew she had a maid. 'May I come in?'

'Yes...of course, sir.'

Jack stepped into the hallway and she immediately gave him a welcoming smile.

'Have you forgotten we agreed not to be so formal, Dawn?' he reminded her.

'It is a shame you didn't come just a little earlier. Emma was here with me.' She avoided responding to his ironic remark. 'It was wonderful to see her, too.' Dawn had brought a quirk to his lips by making it quite obvious that she was delighted he'd called. 'Please come and sit down, if you will.'

'How have you been? And Lily?' he asked, accompanying her towards the parlour.

'We are very well, thank you. Lily has settled in nicely...better than I dared hope. My maid has taken her into the garden for some air. Soon it will be her teatime.' Once inside the cosy room, Dawn said, 'Oh, please do have a seat.' She indicated a fireside chair, then took the one opposite. The embers in the grate crackled quietly, the only sound in the room as they settled to sit face to face, much in the way they had at the inn.

'I must bring up something,' Dawn said, feeling flustered beneath his steady, thoughtful regard. 'I omitted to reimburse you for settling our bill at the Bell and that was very remiss.'

'You've no need to pay anything,' Jack said. 'You and your granddaughter were my guests, travelling with me at my request. It was a pleasure having your company.'

'Are you sure about that? Have you recovered from sharing your coach with Lily?' Dawn asked.

'Just about,' Jack replied, sounding equally rueful. 'Anyway, she was very good on the last leg home.' He rested his elbows on his knees, frowning at his interlinked fingers. Having remained so for some moments he suddenly looked up. 'What I haven't recovered from, Dawn, is you. Being with you, lying beside you…wanting you…'

Dawn rose abruptly. She had been congratulating herself for managing to keep things simple and friendly between them despite her heart having flipped at the sight of him. 'I've not offered you refreshment,' she blurted out. 'Will you have some tea?'

Jack was also on his feet and reached her in one stride, gripping the tops of her slender arms and holding her still as she would have slipped away. 'Please don't try to avoid this. You know very well how I feel about you.'

'I'm afraid you are wrong about that, sir,' Dawn retorted, attempting to wrest herself free of him. 'My recollection is that our romantic attachment ended long ago. You went abroad and when you did not return I got married. And you are now betrothed to Miss Snow and I wish you both well for the future.'

He abruptly released her and turned his back to her. His coarse laugh preceded, 'Do you think I'd be here if I really believed that to be true? You don't wish me well. You wish I'd come back when I said I would.'

'Perhaps. But that is all over with now.' So she hadn't fooled him with her martyred speech, neither had she really wanted to. She was glad he understood he'd let her down. And in case he didn't, well she'd add something else to make sure of it. 'You did not write, as you said you would, or come back, as you said you would.' Her accusation made him swing to face her, but she put distance between them this time. Mentioning his betrayal had brought back bitter memories that were making her feel tempted to lash out and hurt him as he'd hurt her.

Thomas Fenton had never known she'd married him on the rebound and pining for a lost love. There were things they never spoke of; she imagined he wouldn't have been interested in knowing about it anyway. After all, he, too, had been pining for *his* lost love though he rarely mentioned her. Eleanor had been the one to tell Dawn about her mother.

Thomas had deserved her respect and loyalty as he had given those things to her. It was the least they could do for one another to make up for the lack of real emotion in their marriage. She had wanted to be a perfect wife…but she hadn't been, any more than Thomas had been a perfect husband. Locked in her heart had been the image of this man. And now she was feeling guilty and a fool; she wasn't sure that Jack Valance had ever been worthy of such blind devotion. She wasn't sure whether she had really ever known him at all.

'Oh, I did come back…but I was too late.' Jack kept his tone level; there was nothing to be gained from blame or regrets. Yet…had she waited just a little longer…kept faith in him…

'What?' Dawn gasped.

He turned to face her, an abrupt gesture displaying his frustration. 'I was far too late. Lance wrote and told me that you were to be married. By the time I got the letter in Tangier about a year had elapsed. I knew it was a fool's errand, but I came back anyway. I saw you with him. You looked happy together.'

Dawn closed her eyes, momentarily speechless with shock and anguish. But how could she have guessed at any of it? 'Don't make me out to be the culprit in this. If you were delayed, why did you not write and explain?' she cried. 'A single sentence asking me to wait would have sufficed. I heard nothing from you before or after I was married.' The sting in her tone came not only from sorrow, but from vexation now she knew how tantalising close she had been to having the man she'd really wanted.

'Little point in writing once you became Mrs Fenton, was there?' He sounded sarcastic. 'Once I knew it was hopeless I went back to Tangier and took up where I'd left off.'

Dawn moistened her lips with a flick of her tongue, aware of his stormy grey eyes immediately drawn to the movement. 'Tangier? What were you doing there?' she demanded.

'Trying to make money enough to approach your father for your hand in marriage without him laughing at me.'

'My father would never have done that!' Dawn sounded indignant on her father's behalf. But her affluent stepmother would have had something to say about the match. Julia had refused to provide a dowry for her stepdaughter. Thomas Fenton had proposed knowing his bride could provide nothing but her services as a substitute mother to Eleanor.

'Your father would have guffawed at my impertinence.' Jack gave a cynical smile. 'And I wouldn't have blamed him. When I went away I had nothing other than a stack of unpaid debts and a reputation for being a wastrel.'

'I didn't think that of you,' Dawn said earnestly. 'I liked you very much.'

'I know and I felt the same way about you.' He raised a hand to cup her flushed cheek. 'You were worth changing for, Dawn. And that's what I did. I went abroad and I changed…acquired wealth and a title so I could come back and you'd be proud of me. And it was for nothing. I wish I'd stayed here and taken a chance on you agreeing to elope with me.'

Dawn was so overwhelmed by what he'd revealed that for a long moment she simply stared at him, their gazes inextricable. Finally she said quietly, honestly, 'I wouldn't have eloped and smeared my family with scandal.'

'I guessed as much…that's why I never suggested it.' His hand dropped from her face to be plunged into his pocket.

'But I was of an age to marry openly without my father's consent.'

His frown hardened in dawning comprehension. 'You would have gone against your father's wishes and suffered scrimping and scraping, to be with me?'

'I'd have done what I could to help us improve our lot,' she replied flatly. 'Surely that is what being married is all about: pulling together towards a good future as a couple?'

'You would have moved from your father's comfortable house to live in a poky room with me as my wife?' He sounded unconvinced and his narrowed eyes never left her face though he prowled to and fro.

'I expect so...' Dawn abruptly turned away. His arrant disbelief was making her question her own answers. *Had* she spoken the truth? Would she have suffered deprivation for the man she loved? 'What does it matter now?' she cried in exasperation. 'Why are we even talking about this when it is all too late?' She marched away from him, feeling close to tears, wishing he'd not come and so thoroughly upset her equilibrium. Yet...she'd longed to see him and didn't want him to leave so soon. But if he stayed, would he tell her what she yearned to hear? That he still loved her and wanted *her* to be his wife? If he were honest and decent, as she hoped he was, surely he couldn't live a lie with Miss Snow knowing his heart wasn't in it? Or had Jack

Valance's transformation to Lord Sterling changed him thoroughly? Was he arrogant enough to believe he could have his cake and eat it?

If they both calmed down they might have a chance to talk in an adult way about what might be done to put things right for everybody. A man of honour surely wouldn't want his fiancée to know he didn't love her and never would because he'd already given his heart. Or was she being woefully unsophisticated to still think that love and marriage went hand in hand? Well, if she was, it was too bad! Dawn knew she couldn't change the person she was. And if he was different now…more callous and selfish…it would be as well to find out sooner rather than later. If he only truly cared about himself, it would help her to get over him to know about it.

'Will you have some tea, sir? Lily will be back indoors in a moment and I know she would like to say hello.'

'I don't want any tea, thank you. And I didn't come to play with your granddaughter…sweet though she is. I want a grown-up conversation with you.'

'On that we are in complete accord,' Dawn said quietly.

'Good. I intend to start by saying what has

needed to be said for many a long year. And
I'll begin with this. I'm glad I didn't ask you to
live like a pauper for my sake.' He sounded controlled, if bitter. 'It was worth fighting for something decent to give to you, even if the doing
of it wasn't as easy or as pleasant as I'd fool-
ishly expected. I lost the race against time, and
Thomas Fenton, but I kept my pride. I hope I
still have your good opinion, too.' He frowned.
'Had I not gone away and we'd started married
life in straitened circumstances, the struggle
would have driven a wedge between us eventually. You would have ended up despising me
and that would have been impossible to bear.'

Dawn's heart plummeted. So it seemed that
even long ago when she'd fallen in love with
him his ego had been his first love. And she
hadn't even realised it. 'What you've just said
proves how little you really understood me and
how wrong it would have been for us to become
husband and wife before we knew one another
better. I would have waited longer for you had
you asked me to. But you did not and we took
different paths in life. And while we are having a *grown-up* conversation, sir, perhaps you
would like to make a mention of the most important thing that you acquired while away on

your travels. As well as your title and riches I believe you also gained a fiancée.'

He tipped back his head and cursed soundlessly at the ceiling. 'Yes… I did.'

An ache gripped her ribs, making it hard for her to breathe. She had vainly hoped it might be a mistake…that the young woman who was his ward was just hoping to be his future wife and nothing had been properly agreed. But he had admitted it now. She clung to the chair back for support, feeling enervated. Fate had indeed been unkind to play such cruel games with them.

'I believe you are also Miss Snow's guardian as she is an orphan.' She tried to keep her voice steady, but it seemed shrill to her own ears.

'All of that is correct,' he said distantly.

'I see…'

'No, you don't see.' He swung to face her. 'You think me self-centred. You believe I have come here with little thought to the consequences for all involved. I have not. I have done my damnedest since we got back from Essex to put you from my mind. But I can't.' He gave a gruff laugh. 'A hellhole of an Ottoman prison couldn't bring me low. But you can, Dawn, it seems.'

'You were in *prison*?' she breathed.

'I was captured and unable to do anything at

all other than survive as best I could for many months.'

'Is that why you couldn't write to let me know where you were and when you might return?'

'An enslaved man isn't afforded such luxuries as pen and paper out there.' He paused, then added with searing honesty, 'I would have bartered my soul for a chance to contact you and beg you not to lose faith in me.'

Dawn's face had whitened in shock and her green eyes glowed with spontaneous tears. 'I'm so very sorry. I had no idea of what you'd been through,' she whispered. She imagined he had suffered dreadfully.

'I know and I wish I had kept it that way.' He swiped a hand across his mouth in regret. 'I shouldn't have told you about it and upset you. I'm not after sympathy. And I don't blame you for giving up on waiting for me. I'm glad Fenton made you happy.' He slowly approached her. 'But I'm here now and you're free—'

'But you're not,' Dawn interrupted quietly. 'Are you?'

'My heart is. It's always been yours.' He raised a hand, brushed the back of a finger against her cheek. 'It's you I want.'

Dawn turned from him. 'I'm not as sophisticated as you, sir. You will need to explain further what you mean by that.' Was he really saying that he still felt the same way about *her*, but nevertheless intended to marry somebody else? His fiancée was buying her trousseau, yet her future husband was attempting to woo an old flame. The poor girl! An idea circled in Dawn's mind that made tears sting her eyes. She might have been that poor girl. If she had become Mrs Valance, how long would the happiness have lasted before she discovered her husband was visiting past loves? She would have trusted him...adored him, just as no doubt Sarah Snow would when she became Lady Sterling. Yet he wasn't worthy.

'My marriage will not affect how I feel about you. I wish things were different, but they are not.' Jack approached her again, blocked her path as she would have escaped him. 'We are both adults and can give and receive love and comfort, if not wedding vows...'

'I think I must stop you there, sir, before you say something to offend me.' Dawn's voice was clipped and cold. 'I have the gist of your proposition and it is unwelcome. Thank you for calling, but I think you should leave now.'

He growled a laugh deep in his throat. 'Did I imagine that you kissed me back...or that you cuddled up to me in bed, after inviting me to use it? Have you been so long widowed that you've forgotten what follows when a woman reacts like that to a man?'

'I did not... I was asleep when you laid down,' she protested, her face furiously red.

'But you knew I was there, didn't you? You were conscious of that.' He took her hands, tightening his grip when she would have pulled away. 'I want you and I know you want me. As my mistress you will be as close to me as my wife... closer...'

Dawn snatched herself free and whipped a hand across his face. She turned away, feeling ashamed of what she'd done. The blow had left a white imprint of her fingers on his lean bronzed cheek.

He didn't seem angry, or hurt—in fact, he smiled.

'I did offer to leave you alone and sleep in the stables. As I recall, you insisted that I did not.'

Dawn flushed scarlet. 'I... I believe I said there was room enough for us to share a chamber without getting in each other's way,' she spluttered. 'More fool me for having been worried for your health sleeping outside.'

'I don't mind the cold. I prefer it to the heat. A rat-infested cell in Tangier in high summer—' He broke off and threw back his head to contemplate the ceiling as though deciding what to say and do next. Abruptly he strode towards the door. 'My apologies. I shouldn't have come. Please forgive me and forget about what happened here this afternoon.' He snapped a bow and was in the hallway close to the exit when Dawn caught up with him. She couldn't bear the thought of them parting so coldly.

'I'm sorry you suffered while abroad. Truly I am.' She raised a hand as though to touch his arm in comfort, but curled those fingers into a fist. 'And whatever you may think, I do sincerely give you and Miss Snow my best wishes. You deserve some peace and happiness after what you have endured.' She was aware he wanted to leave…and she was detaining him. He kept his face averted and his hand remained on the handle, ready to pull open the door. But she didn't want them to be bad friends after all he'd done for her. Without him she wouldn't have her granddaughter safe by her side. 'Please don't allow this to come between us…' Her small teeth nipped her lower lip as he curtailed her attempt at reconciliation with a brutal laugh.

'It's too late for that as well, Dawn.' He put a hand to her face, turning it up firmly so she couldn't avoid the searing look he was giving her. 'But you're right, let's be adult about it. If we meet at the Houndsmeres' or elsewhere, I'll play my part of genial fellow.'

'Will you play your part of faithful husband?' She couldn't believe she'd let that slip out. Especially as she already knew the answer to her question. She might have turned him down, but others wouldn't. He was a rich, handsome aristocrat on the prowl for a mistress and could take his pick of women.

'What do you care?' he asked. 'You do care... that's the problem. And it's mine, too,' he added self-mockingly.

'You've no idea how callous you sound, have you?' She curled her fingers over his to remove their warmth from her face. 'Emma said she believed you a changed man to the one she knew. And indeed you are different.'

'And so are you,' he returned silkily. 'You're not a virgin of twenty-three now. You're a widow with a granddaughter, for God's sake.'

'You think that the fact that I'm older and have had a husband has somehow stripped me of morals?' she demanded indignantly.

'No... I thought those damnable years apart might have shown you as it has me that happiness is not won lightly and, if found in among the dross, should be snatched at.'

'You are soon to vow to love and cherish a

young woman who might actually believe you
mean what you tell her in church, sir.' Dawn
sounded aghast at his duplicity. 'You may cheat
her if you will…it's a matter for your own conscience. But I will not be the one to abet you
in it. I know how I would feel if my husband
cheated on me.'

'Was he faithful?'

Dawn shook her head in censure. 'The fact
you even ask me that is proof you are deplor-
ably cynical, sir.'

He laughed, quite amused. 'I prefer to call it
realism. Marriage, as you know, is no romantic
dream no matter how much you wish it to be.'

Had she known that Jack would taunt her
with the practical arrangement she'd had with
Thomas, she wouldn't have disclosed it. As husband and wife they had shared affection…and a
bed. Their life together had never been an ordeal.
Yet Jack had sowed a seed of doubt. If Thomas
had been richer, would he have kept a mistress?
'Yes, I do know that marriage isn't all sweet-
ness. For some of us there is more to it than passion: respect and honour and duty are equally
important.'

'Yes, they are…' Jack agreed sourly. 'There
is no need to tell me that, I assure you.'

His hand was tightening on the door handle.

Dawn could tell he wanted to leave, but equally was torn in two, as she was, because not all had yet been said. Once he'd gone their differences would hold them apart and thus the rest might never be aired if they didn't speak of it now. And there was something niggling at her.

'Why on earth would you wish to get married with your attitude? Surely not for her dowry when you now have enough riches of your own.'

'Money?' He barked a laugh. 'Would that it were that simple,' he muttered. 'I'm marrying for respect and honour and duty and every other damnable scruple that you believe me incapable of possessing. And I wish you were right and I was without conscience. But it seems I am not; it is constantly with me so I must put you from my head instead.'

He yanked open the door and was out on the top step when Lily appeared.

'Jack!' The child hurtled along the hallway and launched herself at his legs, making him disentangle himself, then step down a step before crouching to speak to her.

'Stop that, Lily.' Dawn spoke sharply and the child looked at her wide eyed.

'Sorry, m'm, I didn't know you had company.' Polly had also picked up on her mistress's tone.

She hurried forward to take Lily by the hand and draw her back into the hallway.

'Say goodbye to Mr Valance, Lily. He is very busy and must leave now.'

Dawn noticed the sardonic glint in his eyes as he slowly rose to his full height. As the child murmured her polite goodbye, he turned and descended the steps, springing aboard his curricle pulled by the pale-flanked horse she'd admired before. On that occasion on Regent Street he'd had a flamboyant blonde on his arm.

Dawn closed the door before the carriage had pulled away. She watched her granddaughter being led towards the kitchen for her tea. But her mind was still with Jack. She was glad she'd stopped herself from sounding jealous by taunting him with an undeniable fact: he seemed in no need of a mistress as he already had one.

Chapter Ten

'You must be nice and let Lily have a turn on the rocking horse, Bernie.'

The boy looked mutinous, but did as his mother bade him and got off the ride to allow the little girl to use it. He sank down to the rug to play with his tin soldiers, but not before having delivered a tug to Lily's fair curls on passing.

Lily pursed her lips, pinching him in retaliation before climbing on board and swaying serenely to and fro.

'Well… I think they like one another,' Dawn said ironically, making Emma chuckle. At the back of her mind she realised it was probably true. Although the children competed with one another for everything—even the last biscuit on the plate had been broken in half to appease them—they followed one another around and had done so almost from the moment they'd been put in the same room together.

'Perhaps a run around in the garden is in order,' Emma suggested.

Dawn knew her granddaughter was happy today despite her skirmishes with Bernie. That had come as a relief to Dawn. Over the last few days the little girl had started to tearfully ask about her mother again and this time her grandma's explanation about Eleanor being with the angels in heaven hadn't pacified Lily. Neither had allowing her to play on the swing brightened her for long. But the promise of a trip to meet the boy with the rocking horse had finally distracted her. When the Earl's coach had arrived earlier to convey them to Grosvenor Square Lily had kneeled close to the window to peer out at passing scenery, impatient to arrive at their destination.

Dawn realised it would take a while for her granddaughter to get used to her new surroundings. In a way it was a comfort to know Lily had loved her mama and missed her so much. Not once had the child asked about her other parent.

The door of the nursery was opened and the newcomer immediately received a boisterous greeting from his young son.

'Well, this all looks very civilised,' Lance

remarked with a smile, ruffling the boy's dark locks.

'Bernie just pulled Lily's hair.' His wife arched an eyebrow at him.

'Lily pinched him back,' Dawn gamely admitted.

'Sounds fair…' the Earl pragmatically judged. 'Will you come downstairs and say hello to Jack? He's accompanied me home from White's.'

Dawn felt her stomach somersault, but she gave Emma an easy smile. Her friend was gauging her reaction to the news. Not long after they'd settled down with the children in the nursery Emma had asked if she'd recently seen Jack. Dawn had admitted that he'd visited in the week and that they'd parted rather frostily. She hadn't disclosed much of what they'd spoken about. Jack might not have told the Houndsmeres about his harrowing time in a foreign gaol and she wouldn't betray his confidence on that score. Neither did she want to admit that he'd propositioned her in case Emma branded him a selfish philanderer. Dawn had to admit, though, that he certainly fell into that category and she wasn't sure why she felt compelled to protect him from criticism. Her casual explanation that their contretemps had arisen from a simple misunderstanding about his long silence had been readily accepted by Emma. Dawn wished it had been the trifle she'd made it out to be, then she wouldn't feel flustered at the prospect of being brought face to face with him.

'Of course, we'll come and say hello to Jack.' Emma stood up from the sofa.

Dawn rose, too, beckoning her granddaughter. 'Lily will like to see him, I'm sure,' was all she said.

Jack was stationed by the window in the drawing room, gazing out over the gardens. When he turned about, Dawn fleetingly allowed her eyes to skim on his, giving an equally mannerly greeting to the one she'd received. She managed to keep an ironic edge from *her* voice, though, when replying that she'd been very well, thank you. Something it seemed he'd been unable, or unwilling, to do.

Lily had immediately trotted towards Jack to tell him about the rocking horse she'd played upon. Dawn felt a poignancy stealing over her as she watched them together. From the first moment he'd met her granddaughter he had been kind to her…far kinder than Dawn had ever witnessed the child's father act towards Lily.

'Shall I ring for tea?' Emma suggested brightly. 'Or will you gentlemen take these two scamps into the garden to play chase and give our nerves a rest?' She chuckled. 'We will join you in a little while once we are sufficiently recovered.'

The children appreciated that idea and started their game by racing towards the door.

Knowing Emma as she did, Dawn guessed there was a reason for her friend buying them some time on their own. Once the youngsters' excited whoops had faded away she turned on Emma an old-fashioned look. 'So…what have you to tell me, my dear?' she asked.

'Well, let me first say that I haven't arranged Jack's visit in an attempt to matchmake. I *would* adore to see you together, if it were at all possible, but I fear it isn't.' Emma sighed and squeezed Dawn's fingers. 'Other than that I have wanted to ask you something all afternoon, but dared not speak in front of Lily. She is such a knowing child.' Emma frowned. 'You've had more than a tiff with Jack, haven't you? I hate to see you upset, Dawn, and I know you are. Please don't be brave and say you're not.' She sighed. 'I probably shouldn't ask…but we *are* best friends. So…has he reluctantly offered to call off his engagement for your sake and made you feel horribly guilty for wishing that indeed he would?'

'He's offered nothing of the sort,' Dawn replied ruefully, hugging Emma in gratitude for her concern. 'Jack has made it clear he intends to wed Miss Snow.'

'What has he in mind for you, then?'

Dawn gave a shrug, but she felt her cheeks growing warm and knew her friend wasn't fooled.

'Ah, I see...' Emma linked arms with Dawn to draw her to the sofa. 'I suspected as much. And you have said no, haven't you?'

There was no point in prevaricating. Emma was too astute. 'Did you also imagine I might say yes, Em?' Dawn sank on to the cushions.

Emma vigorously shook her head. 'Not for a moment did I think it. I know you were tempted, though, just as I was tempted when Lance asked me to be his mistress.' Emma perched beside her friend, turning to face Dawn. 'That's how I can recognise the signs of people in love, beset by obstacles to their happiness.'

Dawn frowned. 'I hope I have not made my weakness too obvious. I wouldn't want Jack to ever know I gave a second thought to his proposition.'

'You behave very properly with him. But I know you still love him,' Emma said softly. 'And it's clear he's not over you. Though you did your best to avoid looking at him, he couldn't take his eyes from you when you entered the room. I cannot understand what he thinks he is doing persevering with this betrothal to Miss Snow.'

'He has his reasons,' Dawn quietly championed him. 'He spoke of duty and honour being at stake. I shan't pry into it. If he wants to tell me, he will.'

'Apparently the girl is pretty, but has no dowry. One would be forgiven for thinking he must be head over heels in love with Sarah Snow to have proposed.' Emma sat back and crossed her arms over her middle.

'It isn't a love match, he admitted that.' Dawn nibbled her lower lip. 'Who am I to decry a practical arrangement with a spouse? It suited me well enough.'

'So you didn't argue with him because you found out Sarah is ensconced at his Essex retreat?'

Dawn whipped a glance at her friend. 'Is she?'

'I was astonished when I found out, but apparently it is all quite proper. She has a plethora of maids and a chaperon and he is here in London. I imagine he will follow the same routine after the nuptials, leaving his bride out in the sticks while living his own life in town.'

'They might grow closer, in time.' Though her heart ached to know the truth in it, Dawn sincerely hoped Jack Valance *would* discover that happiness among the dross that he'd spoken about. His inner demons might in time be quietened by the contentment his wife and children brought to him.

'I'm not sure *I* would feel so charitable about it,' Emma said. 'He virtually proposed to you before he went away. Then returned with a fiancée.'

'I got married, Em, while he was away. And he knew it.'

'And why should you not? He'd had plenty of time to nip in first,' Emma stated bluntly. 'Did he expect you to sit on the shelf, twiddling your thumbs?'

'No…' Dawn clucked her tongue. 'He told me he was pleased that Thomas married me.'

'Well, I don't believe that and I doubt he does either,' Emma trumpeted.

Dawn walked to the window and gazed out at the mellow scene of two gentlemen laughing together, then intermittently joining in the children's game of dashing hither and thither on the verdant, sunlit lawns. 'Perhaps it was my fault.' Dawn spoke almost to herself. 'Perhaps if I'd *really* loved him then I *would* have waited longer before getting married.' She gave a sigh. 'But nobody had heard from Jack…not even

Lance. So I listened to my stepmother when she impressed upon me that Thomas Fenton's proposal was probably the only one likely to come my way. I had no dowry and I imagined Julia was right. I couldn't countenance the prospect of more years in my childhood home with a stepmother I didn't like, but must give way to...' Dawn tailed off into silence as the unpleasant scenario played out in her head. For a moment longer she stared, blurry eyed, unaware that Jack had turned towards the house and caught her watching him.

It was too late to duck out of sight so she brazened it out and raised a hand, and got an ironic bow for her trouble.

'Nobody would have turned down a rescue plan in those circumstances,' Emma said stoutly. 'Your husband was a nice man. I liked him and so did Lance.'

'I liked him, too,' Dawn said quietly, returning to Dawn's side. 'And how I wish it had eventually come to more than that between us...then I wouldn't mind one bit about what Jack Valance got up to.' She made an apologetic gesture. 'Enough of this maudlin poring over what might have been,' she said. 'Let's go and join the others in the sunshine. Then if you don't mind lending me a carriage again I should take Lily home. She'll need an early bedtime after all this excitement.'

Dawn realised *she* was full of excitement, too, and acting like a silly girl infatuated with a secret swain she knew was a rascal. She was impatient to go outside to be near him, torture herself with the bittersweet pain of wanting what she mustn't have.

She should have made an excuse to leave, she realised, and avoided him altogether. But taking the coward's route would have denied Lily her chance to spend time with Jack. And that wasn't fair. The child had few kith and kin and another friend for her should be welcomed.

As the ladies promenaded along the corridor towards the garden door Dawn forced her mind from Jack and to a sobering matter she had to attend to when back home. That morning she had received a letter from Lily's father. She intended to quickly answer it. She knew that what really interested the Reverend Peter Mansfield wasn't enquiring about Lily's well-being. He'd barely touched on that. The gist of the missive had been to discover how well acquainted Dawn was with Lord Sterling and whether she had received an invitation to his forthcoming wedding. That news of Jack's betrothal had spread didn't surprise Dawn. But the idea that Peter Mansfield might start inveigling for an invitation to the wedding…or worse, to conduct the service… made Dawn fervently hope that the ceremony would take place in town and be a quiet affair.

What had additionally worried her in his letter was a heavy hint that if His Lordship intended to remain at his London mansion for a while then Peter would pay a visit to town to speak to him. It was time, he wrote, to renew his acquaintance with Lord Sterling and also to accompany the child when she went to visit the Houndsmeres' son and heir. When Dawn returned home she would set pen to paper and inform Peter that the Viscount was shortly planning a trip to Essex to socialise with his country neighbours. She hoped that might keep the odious vicar right where he was.

Having joined in the game of blind man's buff and been caught by Bernie, Dawn retreated to relax beneath the magnificent plane tree. Jack, also out of the game, having allowed himself to be caught by Lily, strolled to stand beside her.

'It is hard to believe the weather has improved so rapidly since the snows.' Believing she had found a neutral topic of conversation Dawn burst out with it…then soon regretted it.

He grunted a laugh, glancing at her blushing complexion. 'Yes…best we don't revisit that episode, isn't it,' he said. 'Let's talk about something else. Have you heard from Mansfield yet?'

'I have. Just this morning,' Dawn was glad to change the subject. 'I shall write later and tell him that Lily is completely fine.' She gazed at the child, pink-cheeked and laughing as she played with the puppies. How happy she seemed! And seeing her so filled Dawn's heart with joy, too. But the spectre of her father was never far away and Dawn's smile soon faded. 'The vicar is angling for a reason to visit so he might again make your acquaintance and get to know the Houndsmeres.'

'I can't promise him a welcome if he turns up at my door,' Jack muttered drily, gazing off into the distance.

'I shall inform him that you are about to return to Essex in the hope it will keep him there.'

Jack laughed soundlessly. 'Would you like me to now say that's my intention to give some truth to the lie?'

'I didn't think it was a lie,' Dawn retorted. 'As Miss Snow is at your house in Wivenhoe I thought you might soon go back there.'

'Why would I do that?' he asked levelly.

'To see how she is in the manner of a fond fiancé?' Dawn tartly suggested.

'Miss Snow is just fine without me. In fact, I

also had a letter today. My fiancée informs me of how happy she is.'

'Obviously she has no idea of your true character then or what is in store for her as your wife.'

'She knows me as well as she needs to and is content that being married to me won't change her life in any way.'

Dawn wasn't sure what to say to that. It certainly *was* a business arrangement then, if the prospective bride and groom had no hankering to see one another and intended to carry on as though they were single.

'No comment to make?' He turned to her. 'No accusation about my callousness in leaving her all alone?'

'Why on earth don't you set the poor girl free and let her find somebody who might cherish her and actually make her a loving husband?' Dawn rattled off in a suffocated tone.

'God in Heaven,' he ground out. 'Don't you realise that's what I want above all else? Unfortunately, it's not that easy. I wasn't the only one at the mercy of brutes. She was, too. I swore to her dying father that thereafter she'd always be safe with me.' He sighed, shook his head in regret…a wordless declaration that he'd said too much. Abruptly he turned on his heel, informing quietly, 'I'm leaving now. I'll just say goodbye to your granddaughter and the others.'

Dawn wasn't letting him walk away after that astonishing revelation. She grabbed at his wrist double-handed and held on to it. 'You can't just go without explaining some more. I don't understand.'

'I know you don't understand,' he said. 'And there's no point in explaining, is there? It won't change anything.' He turned his head, expelling a heavy sigh. 'I'm sorry, I should learn to keep my mouth shut. That's the second time now that I've spoken thoughtlessly. And I'm sorry to have come here and spoiled your day with your friend.' He faced her, twisting his hand in her grip so he could entwine their fingers. 'I swear I didn't know you were here... I didn't come to ambush you. Lance kept quiet about having visitors this afternoon. We were supposed to talk business in his study. But it can wait until another day.'

She'd harboured a secret hope that he *had* come here to bump into her. But it seemed that was a conceit. 'There's no reason for you to go, sir, or to delay your meeting. I've already told Emma that it's time to take Lily home or she will get overexcited.' Dawn extricated her fingers from his warm clasp.

'I'll give you a lift as we're setting off at the same time.'

'My ride back is already arranged, thank you.'

'Lily will prefer to travel with me,' he coaxed with a quirk of a smile.

'I know...and thank you for kindly taking notice of her. But our spending time together isn't a good idea.'

'I like the idea of it...' The words sounded mild, but his eyes held sultry amusement.

Oh, he knew how he affected her, she realised. Was he confident that if he got her alone she'd be amenable to a seduction this time? Would she? Was she able to withstand him? Years ago when he'd secretly kissed and caressed her she'd felt dizzy with emotion. At the inn he'd aroused the same sort of thrill in her. Even now the memory of that kiss made her flesh fizz as though champagne bubbles showered her skin in places where his mouth and fingers had been.

The fact that he made her feel young and innocent again confused her. She wasn't either of those things now...as he'd bluntly pointed out to her. She was a mature woman in every sense. Even if that experience of carnality with Thomas had been plain and basic, it had taken her from girl to woman and stranded her there. But in one respect she was unchanged: girl or woman, she believed that adultery was sordid and shameful. And thus she knew there could be no future for them.

Dawn shook herself from her introspection and started to move past him, about to call to Lily that it was time to go home.

'You're right...you deserve an explanation.' Jack caught her hand, drawing her backwards before she'd taken more than two steps. His expression had grown serious...bleak, even. Yet he frowned as though unsure of his decision to open up to her. 'If you let me take you home, I'll relate it all. I've said too much now not to carry on. You should know how this damnable tangle started. But it's not a pleasant tale.'

Dawn could see the conflict darkening the backs of his eyes. Would she be gracious and tell him he had no need to unearth painful memories for her sake? She couldn't; she was greedy to understand what had kept them apart and destroyed her youthful dream of growing old with this man. So in tacit acceptance of their pact she said, 'Thank you for offering us a ride, sir. I am ready to leave now.'

Chapter Eleven

Polly peeped at her mistress's distinguished guest. She had gulped when the child had addressed him as Jack. Nervously she'd whispered to Lily to call him Lord Sterling, but the little girl seemed adamant that wasn't his name. Polly had only clapped eyes on the fellow last week, yet she'd served Mrs Fenton since her marriage. It was obvious, though, that her widowed mistress and the handsome Viscount were close enough to be on first-name terms and Lily had picked up on it.

'Your granddaughter is all ready for bed, m'm,' Polly announced. She clung determinedly to her charge's tiny wriggling fingers to prevent Lily scampering into the room.

Dawn had risen from her armchair to welcome in the blonde angel clad in her nightclothes. 'Come here, my dear.' She held out her arms and

Polly allowed Lily to trot into her grandmother's embrace for a goodnight kiss. 'Sweet dreams…' Dawn murmured against the child's fair brow. 'Now be a good girl and go quietly to bed.'

Jack was also on his feet and his expression didn't alter when Lily said solemnly, 'Night night, Jack.'

'Goodnight, Lily, sleep well,' he answered.

Once Polly had ushered the child from the room Dawn gave him an apologetic look. 'I have asked her not to be so familiar with you, but Lily doesn't understand about etiquette.'

Jack chuckled, gesturing he believed the matter trifling.

'I know you don't mind, but it isn't appropriate.'

'You trust your maid to be discreet, don't you?'

'Of course—Polly seemed quite shocked, though.'

'There are worse things that can happen to make a maid seek her smelling salts.'

Dawn decided not to probe further into that enigmatic remark. A scandal might indeed be just a breath away if she were not exceedingly careful to avert it. With that in mind she politely offered him some refreshment. 'Would you like a cup of tea? Or there is some port. I shall fetch it as Polly is busy.'

'I need nothing, thank you.'

So far they had talked of incidentals, anticipating an interruption when Lily was brought to bid them goodnight. The uncommonly humid day had given way to an overcast sky and Dawn had remarked that a storm was brewing while gazing out of the window. In addition they had discussed how well the children had taken to one another on their first meeting. The promise of more outings had satisfied both youngsters on parting and Master Bernard had waved from the doorstep as his new friend was driven away.

Now there was no further need to delay with polite chit-chat, Dawn realised. Once her maid had settled Lily for the night Polly would retire to a cosy spot below stairs. A silence had already settled on the house and the premature dusk brought on by the sombre heavens had fostered an atmosphere of intimacy in the room. The glow from embers smouldering in the grate had traced their standing silhouettes on the wall. Another log was needed, as was a lighted lamp, but Dawn was loath to speak of mundanities and spoil this poignantly romantic moment. It would soon be ended and he would go. She had no right to detain him for long and would sit alone in the twilight, spellbound in that bedevilling fantasy of what might have been had fate not turned against them.

Dawn snapped herself from her trance and turned to the window again to avoid a pair of eyes that seemed as turbulent as the distant horizon. He knew of her inner yearning, she was sure.

A couple who lived at the other end of the street were hurrying past, no doubt keen to get home before the black nimbus rolled closer. They had slowed down to look at the sleek vehicle and fine horse stationed outside her house. Dawn knew she was risking gossip. Her neighbours were used to seeing the Houndsmeres' carriage by her door, aware of her friendship with the Countess. But a gentleman's racing curricle being too often in evidence would raise eyebrows. She didn't want people speculating on why Lord Sterling, soon to be married, was paying Mrs Fenton frequent visits.

A sudden flash of lightning scored a jagged line through the sky, focusing her attention. The first fat raindrops fell slothfully to dribble like tears on the window glass.

'The storm has started and your tiger will get soaked, poor lad.' Dreamy nonsense done with, Dawn concentrated on practicalities.

'He knows to move the vehicle under cover.'

He did, too. The boy was just changing position to put the carriage into motion. Dawn watched him skilfully employing the reins—nevertheless, she knew the moment that Jack approached and stood close behind her.

'Do you want me to go, Dawn?'

She glanced over a shoulder at him. 'Of course not. I want you to stick to our bargain and tell me your troubles. It is only fair as you know all of mine.' She hoped that her light teasing might clear a path to the start of this difficult conversation.

'Indeed, you have had some bad luck and sad times, haven't you?' He stroked her face with tender fingers, turning her about to face him.

'And so it seems have you, my lord.' She instinctively welcomed his caress by pressing her cheek against his palm.

'Don't call me that, even in jest. I'm still Jack to you...not a stranger.' He paused. 'The stranger is the fellow who gave his word to wed a girl he hardly knows.'

'You hardly know me.' Dawn attempted to move past him. She knew she must learn to accept him mentioning his marriage without getting snappy. But a sharp pain was tightening her chest.

'That's not true; it seems I've known you all my life.' He used both hands to cup her face, keeping her close to him. 'That's how it was for me from the first moment we met.'

Dawn knew what he meant. Never had she, before or since, been so immediately in tune with another person. She lifted her eyes to meld with his and receive a ghost of a smile.

'Are you sure you want to hear details of my foul past?'

'I do,' she said quietly.

His thumbs brushed against her jaw, then abruptly he walked away. Coming to a halt by the fireplace, he immediately commenced his account of those missing years. 'I left these shores having sought employment as a mercenary in service to the King. The work was perilous, we were told, but there were riches to be made. There was a group of us: other men of all ranks who had served in the army and navy were recruited to the same mission to bring a halt to piracy off the coast of Tangier. Cargoes were being plundered from English ships and those of our colonies and the threat to shipping lines and the Crown's coffers was of grave concern.'

'I believed most of the pirates had given up or been captured.' Dawn was quickly absorbed in the tale and moved closer to read his expression. So far he had sounded quite remote as he reeled off facts.

'After Napoleon's defeat some rogue brigands saw an opportunity to resume their activities. The King wanted them quashed before they wreaked havoc on Gibraltar. One of my colleagues was Sarah's father. Robert Snow had retired to Tangier after serving as a naval officer. He was a widower and his only child was living in Tangier with him. Like me, he needed money so volunteered to join the group and, like me, he came to bitterly regret his decision.'

Dawn perched on an armchair and indicated that he should sit, too. He declined with a vague headshake, staying where he was, his face dappled by shadows.

'We had some success in skirmishes with the pirates, but unfortunately several of our men were killed and our numbers depleted. Our foe got more vicious as they fought to retain their toehold in the Mediterranean. We were boarded just off Tangier and, as I was the highest-ranking officer, I was taken to their hideaway to be questioned.'

Dawn sprang up and went to him. She had heard the hoarseness in his tone and needed no description of what had happened to him next. The horrors he'd spoken of had been encountered when he was a prisoner under interrogation. She slid her arms about his waist, cuddling him in comfort. 'You need not speak of your treatment at the hands of those barbarians. Tell me of your escape and how you managed to get home at last.'

'I didn't escape… I was rescued by Sarah's father. He hadn't come for me…but for his daughter. Sarah had been abducted and was also being held and used as a bargaining tool, as was I. Those brutes wanted to ransom us both… that's the only reason we kept our lives. But for Sarah…just sixteen…her ordeal was so much worse than what I suffered. Yet she is an intrepid little thing and vowed she wouldn't let those savages destroy her.'

Dawn felt tears squeeze through her lashes as she listened. She moved her arms from Jack's waist to slide them about his neck and hold him tightly. Still he kept talking, the words muffled by her shoulder.

'Her father was wounded in the rescue mission and, though it seemed he would pull through, he succumbed to his wounds less than a year later. Before he died he reminded me that I owed him my life. Undoubtedly I did. He made me promise to marry his ruined daughter and to protect her with my name. He bade me do anything in my power to make Sarah happy. Eventually I agreed to it. I gave him my solemn word.'

Dawn moved back from him to gaze into his dark, tortured eyes. 'You came back to England and saw me with my husband before you gave that promise, didn't you?'

'Yes. I believed you lost to me and returned to Tangier filled with regret and bitterness.' A bleak laugh preceded, 'I nurtured those feelings…they helped me take revenge on those who'd captured Sarah and I. Together with the other men left in our group I pursued them until they were all either killed or incarcerated. Sarah's father passed away shortly afterwards. I knew Robert wouldn't allow himself to rest in peace until we'd finished the job he'd helped us start.' Jack paused, staring into the flames in the grate. 'Sarah had got used to me visiting her father in the hospital and, though her ordeal had left her angry and wary of men, she grew to trust me. She agreed to the marriage, as I did, to pacify her father, not out of any affection we had for one another.' He frowned. 'But she seems settled now. In her letters she tells me she likes being close to the sea again at Wivenhoe. She seems content and nobody is happier to know it than I am.'

'The poor child.' Dawn hadn't realised she was crying until she tasted salt on her lips. She used the palms of her hands to clear the tears from her face. 'I'm so sorry, Jack. So very sorry for what has happened to you and to Sarah.'

'The worst of it is that I want to break my vow to a dying man. I want you.'

'You will not do that!' Dawn enclosed his chin in a small hand, forcing it up so their eyes met. 'You will never forgive yourself. You told me you feared me despising you for having nothing to give me. Now I know what has caused all of this I'm fearful, too. I don't want *you* to hate *me*. If you go back on your word for my sake, you will surely never rest easy and neither will I. It is not just your conscience at stake now, but mine as well.'

'I know…and that's why I didn't want to tell you and burden you with it. Yet…' he groaned '…yet, if I can't be with you, the longing will drive me insane. You feel the same way about me… If you didn't…if you'd given yourself body and soul to somebody else…it would be easier to bear than this. Knowing you are now free but I am not is the worst kind of torture.'

In a single stride he suddenly brought himself too close for her to avoid him and his lips swooped to slant silkily over hers. Dawn made a token resistance, tried to free her mouth from one that was hot and desperately hungry. She knew she should reason with him, but her desire was being stoked by his skilful hands and lips, enfeebling that corner of her mind that warned her to be sensible. She'd had many long, barren years of being sensible. As he nimbly flipped her bodice buttons from their hooks she arched her back, pressing into him, impatient to have his famished fingers on her naked skin.

Jack's growl of passion rasped deep in his throat and he lifted her off her feet, then walked them both to the sofa, lowering her into the cushions. In an instant he had followed her down, wedged a knee between her thighs while his mouth, alternately rough then delicate at her lips and breasts, made her squirm in delight. Years-old need had been unleashed, stiffening his loins like iron, and Dawn felt the thrust of his manhood scorching her through her cotton gown. He freed her mouth to plunge his lips against her throat and through panting sobs Dawn cried softly. 'Oh…we must not. This isn't right. You must go, Jack.' Yet even as she said it her spine left the cushions. She closed the gap between them so she could abrade her taut nipples on the rock-hard sinews of his chest.

'I can't go! Don't make me… I swear I'll stop if you say…' Jack growled out in frustration.

Dawn sighed, unable to gainsay him, ceding

gratefully to his dominance as she was pressed back into the sofa and quietened with another potent kiss. She felt the tension leave her bones and undulated sensually beneath him as he lavished slow kisses and caresses on her exposed pearly flesh.

His mouth relinquished her pulsing lips, slid a moist trail to her breasts. Dawn was lost in excitement… Her body had craved this man's touch for far too long to be denied. She whimpered, panted her ecstasy into the shadowy atmosphere as his tongue leisurely flicked, circled, relentlessly teased her. Her fingers were tangled in his silvery hair and, wriggling her calves free of her hampering skirts, she snaked those slender limbs around the brawny strength of him, rocking her pelvis against his in an age-old rhythm.

Jack gave a ragged groan and pinned her hips against the cushions. 'You will agree to become my mistress? Please, say you will…'

A crash of thunder swallowed her answer and it seemed he wasn't about to repeat what he'd said. An oath exploded beneath his breath, but barely penetrated Dawn's sensual torpor. A second later he had lithely gained his feet. Jack reached the door a fraction before it opened and managed to block a view into the room with the breadth of his body. Dawn struggled to a seated position, fumbling with her clothes, her heart pounding in shock and embarrassment. What on earth had she been thinking of, behaving in such a way? In her own home…downstairs on a parlour sofa! And Polly must have seen them!

'I'm sorry, my lord, a visitor has arrived to speak to Mrs Fenton,' the maid whispered, keeping her eyes lowered. But the deep blush on her cheeks wasn't so easily hidden. She'd tapped on the door before entering and hadn't seen much at all of what had been going on in the dark parlour. The Viscount had been quickly on his feet, protecting his lover. But the maid could guess what she'd interrupted and why no lamp had been lit. Polly was just thankful she had reacted swiftly and had managed to barge the visitor back into the hallway. She didn't like him, whoever he claimed to be.

Dawn knew that a few of her buttons were still open, but she'd sooner leave those than draw attention to herself by fiddling with them. She crossed an arm over her gaping bodice and used the other quivering hand in neatening her tangled locks.

'The Reverend Peter Mansfield is here to see you, m'm,' Polly hissed.

Dawn would have preferred the devil himself

to have called, but she said clearly, in a strong voice she barely recognised as her own, 'Please ask him to wait in the hall. I will just be a moment.'

'I will not wait, madam. I have travelled a distance and am wet through from the rain and in need of a hot drink.' Peter yanked the maid out of the way and stomped over the threshold. It was obvious he had not known that Dawn had company. Polly had mouthed her warning quietly enough for him not to have heard what was said.

He swung a glance from one to the other of the occupants of the dim parlour and his fleshy lips took on a hint of a sneer. 'Well…how nice to see you again, my lord.' He jerked a bow. 'I was not expecting to bump into you here. I trust I'm not disturbing anything.'

'You are. Mrs Fenton and I have important matters to discuss,' Jack bit out coldly. 'Perhaps you would do as the lady asks and wait in the hall until she is ready to receive you.'

'But…she appears ready to receive you…' Peter remarked too innocently. 'So may I take a warm by the fire? I promise not to interfere in your…business.' The vicar looked past Lord Sterling's athletic physique, his eyes alight with lasciviousness as they settled on Dawn's slender figure. 'It seems I have come to check on the child's welfare not a moment too soon. I would see her at once.' He turned to the maid, demanding, 'Bring her, if you please.'

Dawn stepped forward, but not too far in case the vicar saw her dishevelment. But she had surfaced from the drugging sensuality that had mired her senses and she had conquered her embarrassment, too. There would be time enough later to rue being caught out acting like a disgraceful wanton.

'Your daughter is in bed asleep, sir,' she stated firmly. 'And it would have been better had you arrived at a more fitting time.' She put up her chin. 'I have only just received your letter informing me of your intention to visit and was not expecting you without prior warning.'

'So I gather, madam,' the vicar purred with heavy insinuation. 'I set out early, having seen the signs of bad weather.' A flash of lightning seemed to vindicate his decision to beat the storm to London. 'I broke my journey to take refreshment at the Bell. The landlord related that some weeks ago Lord Sterling's party were not so lucky in avoiding the spring snows and were forced to overnight at his establishment. How unfortunate for you both...'

Dawn knew exactly why he'd brought that up. He wanted her to know that he believed her

Jack's paramour. After what he'd just interrupted, she couldn't blame him for jumping to that conclusion. But for a few more minutes she would have succumbed to that sensual web Jack had spun. They would have been, in every sense of the word, lovers caught in the act.

'Step outside, sir, I wish to speak to you,' Jack growled with such authority in his tone that the vicar appeared to shrink into his shoes. Jack didn't wait for Mansfield's response. Taking the interloper's elbow, he propelled him into the hallway, shutting the door after him.

'Here…let me do that, m'm.' Polly nipped over, her fingers swiftly fastening buttons, then smoothing down Dawn's dress. Having neatened her mistress's clothes, she circled Dawn, securing silky chestnut curls back in their pins with swift, capable hands. The maid stood back and gave her mistress a satisfied nod. 'There, much better. Are you ready for a lamp to be lit now, m'm?'

'Thank you Polly,' Dawn replied, though her heart was still hammering, making her feel faint. She took a deep breath. There was no point in putting this off. She had to deal with Mansfield, hopefully to send him away to return tomorrow. She didn't care what he said; she wasn't going to wake up her granddaughter to see a father who cared so little for her that he hadn't once called Lily by her name.

Then in the meantime she must devise a way to persuade him to return to Essex…without her beloved Lily. She imagined that might be no easy task. Had the vicar turned up to say he had employed a nurse for his daughter and was taking charge of her? The thought of losing Lily made Dawn swallow a spontaneous sob. Swiftly she went into the hall to start to buy herself some time…and found it empty.

Chapter Twelve

The speeding curricle was abruptly brought to a halt outside the Stag and Hounds. Immediately Jack threw the reins to his tiger, then jumped down. 'Get out.' He beckoned curtly to his passenger.

'But… I don't understand…' Bewildered, Peter Mansfield swung a glance between the Viscount and the tavern doorway. Some rough-looking sorts were congregated there. But they remained idle, as though gentlemen of means pulling up in this seedy district were not an uncommon sight.

'I promised to find you a bed for the night,' Jack drawled. 'You'll find one in there that should suit. It's a bawdy house. Have you brought your bible?' he tacked on sarcastically. He'd come round to dislodge his unwanted passenger with a rough tug, but managed to refrain from hurrying Mansfield towards the entrance with a shove.

'I will receive you tomorrow morning at ten o'clock to discuss various matters. Vale House, Bruton Square. In the meantime you will stay away from Mrs Fenton.'

'What's the meaning of this?' Peter fumed indignantly, steadying himself after his rough handling. 'I'll visit her if I wish. You cannot prevent me seeing the child.'

'We will talk of that tomorrow.' Jack jerked a nod at the tavern in dismissal.

Peter puffed out his chest and stood his ground. When the Viscount had escorted him from Dawn's house, promising him a bed for the night, he'd believed the man was offering hospitality in his Mayfair mansion and had readily gone with him. But the curricle had headed fast in the opposite direction, towards the eastern outskirts of town. En route the Viscount had ignored every one of his questions. In fact, it was only on reaching his destination that Lord Sterling had bestowed on him a look, or a word.

Peter guessed that Dawn was the man's strumpet, but that mattered as little to him as did the child's welfare. He'd come to London to foster his own interests and had been handed on a plate a most wonderful way to do so.

Dawn had never liked him and had opposed his marriage to Eleanor, whereas Thomas Fenton had been easily exploited. Now it seemed his widow might be, too. Dawn would be mortified if salacious gossip started about her. Lord Sterling wouldn't relish it being known either that he'd been discovered in flagrante when about to take a bride. Of course his ego and reputation would survive any amount of tattle, but Dawn—respectable madam that she was—was a different matter entirely. His Lordship seemed protective of her, so Peter knew he had a useful advantage. The master of Croxley Grange was now the most influential landowner in the area. And Peter needed such a friend to protect his interests along the Essex coast.

'See he is well looked after.' Jack tossed some coins to the pimps lounging by the door. He grunted in sour amusement as the vicar licked his lips having spotted a comely harlot. She'd emerged from the portal at the sound of gold hitting the cobbles.

'Say goodnight to Mrs Fenton for me, won't you?' Peter called slyly as the Viscount sprang aboard the curricle and set it in motion.

Jack didn't answer; he knew he was being goaded. He swore beneath his breath instead. Would his damnable bad luck never turn? The vicar had assumed he'd go back to see Dawn now and God knew he wanted to. If he returned there, she would let him in...but the closeness they'd shared as a couple...the fusing of their bodies and lives that Jack so desperately wanted...he knew that was now as far out of reach as it had ever been. He had seen in her face her regret and shame and he understood how she felt. They shouldn't need to resort to grubby snatched trysts, or to hiding their feelings for one another. They were soulmates...people who fitted together perfectly. But nothing in life was right for them...or even tolerable.

On reaching the centre of town he drove towards her street and halted the vehicle at the corner, deliberating on whether to knock on the door. The house was in darkness. The hour was late and she would have retired for the night. He shouldn't disturb her. Yet he was desperate to see her. He wanted to hold her...to soothe her anxiety over what would happen now with her granddaughter.

Jack knew that was Dawn's greatest fear: losing Lily to Mansfield's callous custody. And his own fear was having to live his life without Dawn in it. Yet he understood why she felt cheated. Her rightful place was at his side, as his wife. He'd braved cruelty with her face imprinted on his mind, her soulful green eyes promising him a future that would be worth the pain and suffering. He'd thought that life lost to him when Dawn married and had allowed obligation to take him headlong into another sort of prison. He couldn't renegotiate a marriage contract with a dead man. Yet he knew if he seduced Dawn into a role she didn't want she would lose respect for him and for herself. Love and trust would wither beneath resentfulness whether or not they wanted it to. But he'd tasted her now and she'd been every bit as sweet as he'd remembered. She wanted him as much as he wanted her, and the devil at the back of his mind was urging him to damn his morals to hell and finish what he'd started.

Dawn had been listening for a sound of an approaching vehicle and had observed the curricle stopping in the distance. She had wondered if he might return to speak to her. But…much as she was desperate to know what had happened, she wasn't sure she was strong enough to see Jack again just yet. It seemed he felt the same way about her. From behind an edge of her bedchamber's curtain she glimpsed the glow of a struck match and knew he was sitting smoking, thinking about whether to come closer and knock on her door. If he decided to do so, what would she do? Send him away? Let him get close enough for another seduction? She closed her eyes, unequal to the test, willing him to go away. As though he knew her that well, he flicked the reins and the vehicle was expertly backed up and disappeared from view. She wiped her wet eyes, wondering what tomorrow would bring. She guessed it would bring Peter Mansfield back again and she must be ready to receive him this time. She let the curtain drift back into place and sat down at the dressing table, staring at her shadowy reflection, illuminated by a single candle flame. Her eyes looked huge and soulful in the pale oval of her face, glittering and dark. She unpinned her thick chestnut tresses and pulled a brush through them, wondering what Jack had said to get rid of the vicar. Wherever Peter was she knew it wouldn't be long before she saw him again. As exhausted as she felt, she mustn't rest yet; she must scour her mind for sensible arguments to offer up to persuade him to let her keep Lily.

'A letter arrived while you were out, my lord.'

Jack heard his butler speak as he strode past, but was so lost in dark contemplation that he didn't absorb what the fellow had said.

Crawley hurried after his master, nipping in front of him so the Viscount couldn't avoid the silver salver being whipped up and thrust towards his elegant waistcoat. 'A letter, my lord. It was delivered post haste from Wivenhoe.'

Jack muttered his thanks and took the parchment, proceeding towards his study. He tossed the letter to the desk, immediately pouring from the decanter and despatching the cognac in a single swallow. He refilled the glass before throwing back his head and growling his frustration at the ceiling. He was already regretting leaving the blasted vicar to his own devices. The fellow might take his fill of pleasure, then hail a hackney to return him to the centre of town. Mansfield wouldn't be as bothered as he was about disturbing Dawn, or her neighbours, at this time of the night. He had his faux concern about his daughter to bandy about as an excuse for acting uncouth.

Gulping at brandy again, Jack prowled to and fro, wondering whether to return to the Stag and Hounds and satisfy himself that Mansfield was still there. He was hoping the vicar liked a drink as much as he liked a harlot and would sink too far into his cups to think of venturing out again.

Jack knew he wouldn't sleep after what had gone on. But he must wait until morning, then go back and see Dawn... What he'd say though, he'd yet to decide. Nothing had improved for them; it had got worse. He still had an unwanted duty to fulfil to Sarah and Dawn still had her granddaughter as her priority.

Thinking of his fiancée had reminded him of Wivenhoe. He grabbed the parchment and sat down in the chair behind the desk, breaking the seal and frowning in anticipation of reading about a problem at Croxley Grange. He was hoping that another old retainer hadn't popped his clogs in his absence...

Jack's frown deepened as some of the paragraphs he'd just scanned, but not digested, started to penetrate his preoccupation.

He stood up, rereading the letter and a thin white line circled his mouth as his back teeth ground together. Indeed, there was a problem... and it couldn't be worse. A second later he was again in the hallway and sprinting for the vestibule, calling for the racing curricle to be brought round without delay. Even with this awful news about Sarah's life being in danger he couldn't put Dawn from his mind. He returned to his study, grabbing pen and paper to dash off a note to her explaining that he'd been called out of town on business that couldn't wait, but that he would be back by her side as soon as he was able. He sealed it and shoved away the inkstand just as he recalled that the Reverend Peter Mansfield was due to visit on the morrow. A note was swiftly penned to him, too. Jack hoped that his demand for an urgent meeting at Croxley Grange instead of Bruton Square would take the confounded vicar immediately back to Wivenhoe so Dawn and her granddaughter would be left in peace.

Jack gave the letters and his instructions for their despatch to Crawley, then took the stairs two at a time, intending to get a few essentials for his trip to Essex.

Sarah was missing from home and her chaperon was beside herself with worry. A Revenue man had been abducted by smugglers operating in the area, the woman had written, and the fear was that Sarah might have been snatched for ransom, too.

'My name is the Reverend Peter Mansfield and I have an appointment with your master.'

Having snapped out his business, Peter whipped off his black hat, secured it under an arm, then peered along his nose at the butler. Servants at an address such as this would be more used to welcoming gentlemen in expensive tailoring than in clerical garb. Though not at this ungodly hour in the morning, of course. Only lesser mortals attended to their affairs so unfashionably early. Though no mention had been made of it Peter had bristled, believing the butler might have expected him to use the servants' entrance.

Crawley raised an eyebrow at the man's abrasive tone. He had been expecting the vicar, if not his superiority complex, so allowed him over the threshold to inform him the appointment had been cancelled.

A blush stained Peter's cheeks. If the Viscount thought to play a game with him by summoning him, then refusing to receive him, he'd not suffer such an insult lightly.

Crawley could see the man looked ready to explode so added mildly, 'Lord Sterling wishes me to convey his apologies for postponing your meeting. He has been called urgently and unexpectedly to Wivenhoe, but has left you a note.' The butler turned to the magnificent gilt console table on which reposed two parchments and selected one. He held it out, then proceeded towards the great doors in readiness to let the unpleasant fellow out.

'One moment…' Peter was immediately alert to the fact that Lord Sterling had left a note for somebody else before quitting town and he could easily guess who the other recipient might be.

He sidled closer to identify the name written in black ink, subduing his excitement on having his hunch proved right. 'I should like a little refreshment, if you please. Your master invited me to partake of breakfast with him,' Peter fluently lied. 'I would not have forgone my meal had I known I was to come here on a fool's errand.'

Crawley raised a fastidious eyebrow. 'Indeed, sir,' he intoned. 'How very unfortunate you are.' He paused, hoping the fool would just take himself off now the door had been opened for him to use. But he waited in vain to see the back of him. 'And of what would you like to partake?' Crawley eventually asked.

'A glass of something to drink will suffice. Port, if you have it,' Peter snapped.

A stiff bow was Crawley's acceptance of the order. A few moments ago the servant's attitude would have irked Peter, but far more was now at stake than the man's insolence. He must find the audacity to steal that letter the second the butler's attention was occupied.

As the manservant marched off to speak to a footman stationed in an alcove Peter shot out a hand, palmed the parchment and slipped it into his pocket.

Left alone, he felt his confidence returning. He glanced about at the hallway. It was quite lavishly appointed and Peter guessed the drawing room was a fine sight to behold. His chest swelled in satisfaction. He could soon have this rich aristocrat at his beck and call.

When the port arrived he haughtily grabbed the goblet from the tray the footman proffered and hastily downed it before turning to leave. The butler had obviously thought himself too high and mighty to bring it himself. That had suited Peter; the footman hadn't glanced once at the bare top of the console table. The butler would have been more vigilant. Peter descended the sweeping steps to the pavement and hurried away, smirking.

'Shall I tell him you are indisposed, m'm?' Polly enquired. Her mistress hadn't been able to disguise her disappointment on hearing the visitor's name. The maid sympathised; she had been sorely tempted to shut the door in the beetle-like fellow's face when answering his loud rat-a-tat.

Dawn frowned, wondering what to do. She had expected Jack to first put in an appearance to discuss yesterday's excruciating episode. But she'd seen nothing of him so would have to do without hearing his opinion on how to tackle the problems Mansfield could present. Polly had done her best to keep the vicar from witnessing her mistress's misbehaviour. But Mansfield wasn't a fool…he knew what he'd disturbed with his untimely appearance. Thankfully he'd no proof that Lord Sterling and Mrs Fenton *were* any more than friends. So she would endure any amount of his snide looks and comments if he would just go away and leave Lily with her.

'You'd better show him in, please, Polly.' Dawn sighed. 'I'd as soon get this meeting over with.' Before the maid quit the room Dawn asked, 'Is my granddaughter up and dressed? Her father might ask to see her.'

'She is, m'm. Lily's just finished her breakfast.'

A few moments later Polly showed the unwanted caller into the parlour and Dawn turned about to greet him with a serene expression. She didn't need to study his face to know he was feeling smug. Every precise step that brought him closer to bow exaggeratedly seemed designed to mock her.

'Good morning, Mrs Fenton. I trust I find you well?'

'You do, sir,' Dawn replied, but had no intention of enquiring how he was. 'Take a seat if you will.' She indicated a chair.

He fluttered some indolent fingers, declining the offer. 'I have come to collect the child. I have an invitation from Lord Sterling to go immediately to Croxley Grange so will be heading home shortly.'

Dawn felt as though she'd received two physical blows. So he was claiming Lily and he wanted to taunt her with Jack's absence. She curled her fingers about the chair back to steady herself. She wouldn't let him see how he had affected her and paused to control her voice before replying. 'Lord Sterling is going to Essex?'

'Oh…did you not know?' Peter feigned surprise. 'I imagined he might have told you. You seem such…*close* friends,' he purred. 'His Lordship penned me a note so I'm aware he is even now at Wivenhoe. He set off last night, eager to get there as soon as may be. Obviously there is nothing of importance to keep him in London and he wants to be with his future wife.'

Dawn avoided Peter's horribly spiteful smile by rearranging a candlestick on the mantel. Yesterday Jack had taken charge, removing the vicar from her house to protect her from humiliation. But he wasn't here to perform that office now. He had returned to Sarah without even telling her of it. She instinctively knew Mansfield hadn't made up the story to rile her, though he was undoubtedly capable of such nastiness. Now she understood Jack's reticence to call on her late last night. He had come back to see her to tell her he intended to quit town but, in the event, hadn't found the courage to do so. He'd obviously concluded that a clean break would be best and had headed straight to Wivenhoe.

Putting distance between them in case Mansfield caused mischief was sensible. A week ago Dawn would have been the one to suggest they took such a course of action to avert a scandal. But not now. She couldn't forget the bittersweet passion they'd shared and she was greedy to have more of it…but on what terms? She wanted Jack, despite knowing it was wrong and despite knowing she must always come second. He'd made his difficult choice and she loved and respected him the more for it. Yet, if all he could ever give her were crumbs of his time and affection, would she be tempted to snatch at them?

She mustn't! Dawn clenched her hands at her sides and took a deep breath, trying to stiffen legs that felt like jelly and a backbone that seemed pitifully weak. She must be strong and follow Jack's lead; she must let him go as he had cut her adrift. All she had left was her pride and her granddaughter. She would fight like a tigress to keep both.

Do not condemn him too soon…before you know for sure that his conscience proved after all to be stronger than yours. The post might bring a letter of explanation, she comforted herself. *He might not have so brutally severed ties.*

Peter had shifted to a position that enabled him to observe the raw emotions that were flitting over Dawn's features. He could see that she was hurt and bewildered...and indignant by what she believed to be the Viscount's defection. It pleased Peter to think he might have so easily started to drive a wedge between the lovers. From beneath his brows he ran a lustful eye over her lush figure. Oh, he could understand what the Viscount saw in her. She might not be in the first flush of youth, but she had the firm flesh of a woman who had never swollen with child. Her pert bosom and curving hips were separated by a sweetly slender waist that seemed to beg a man's hands to girdle it. Her face, though not strictly pretty, had a classical, almost handsome set to the features. Well-defined dark brows soared above large eyes of the most glorious green and her full pink mouth was enough to lure his eyes and start him thinking of kisses and more...

Peter had always thought Dawn an attractive and desirable woman. From the moment they'd been introduced he'd known that he'd sooner bed Thomas Fenton's wife than his daughter. She didn't feel anything similar for him, but Peter wasn't put off by the idea of breaking a woman to his will. He'd punished his late wife…as the wanton had deserved. And he always chose the whores who tried to hide from him.

Dawn's attraction for him also lay in the fact that she'd beguiled a powerful man. Once he'd read the letter that Sterling had sent to her Peter had been in no doubt that the man was smitten with Mrs Fenton. *She* was the Viscount's weakness.

And Dawn's weakness was her granddaughter. Peter was banking on her agreeing to do anything to keep the child. So, he should strike now while she was feeling vulnerable, believing her lover had abandoned her and her granddaughter would soon be lost to her. Never would he more easily persuade her that what she needed was an ally.

'Please arrange for my daughter to be readied for the journey.' Peter perched on the edge of a chair. 'Perhaps some tea while I wait…' He took out a snuff box and used a pinch, looking very much at his ease.

'Lily is settled here,' Dawn blurted, striving to hide her panic. 'Why do you want to take her with you? She has made friends with the Houndsmeres' son,' she added in desperation.

'I must thank you for introducing the child to

such worthy people. When next we are in town I
shall accompany my daughter on a visit to your
noble friends. I do regret that I haven't the time
on this occasion. Lord Sterling has summoned
me and that fellow wields influence in my neck
of the woods. I won't let him down.' Peter added
smoothly, 'Perhaps we could all visit the Earl
and Countess on another occasion…as a family.' He got to his feet and took out his pocket
watch, consulting it with a sigh. 'I need no tea…
the hours are flying by.'

'You must allow me time to explain to Lily.
She is young, but bright and sensitive, too. Another disruption in her life will greatly upset her.
She has not seen you for so long she may be confused as to who you are.' Dawn had moved to
the door as though to bar him going to get his
daughter. Even when Lily had lived beneath her
father's roof the two of them might have been
strangers for all the notice they took of one another. 'I beg you will allow me a few days to talk
to her. If you return at the end of the week, it
will give me time to prepare her for the journey.'

'I understand your concern and it does you
credit. You are fond of the child.' Peter saun-
tered to Dawn to take one of her hands in his.
He patted at it, but when his fingers started to
stroke her skin she immediately pulled free of

him. 'It is indeed commendable that you feel so deeply for her, being as you are no *real* kin,' he reminded Dawn of her place in the same mild tone. 'The child needs a woman like you to mother her.'

'Indeed, she does…' Dawn started to relax, even managing to return him a tight smile. Was this a sign of negotiation? Would he back down? She believed she knew the Reverend Peter Mansfield well enough to guess that, if he did, he'd angle for something in return.

She imagined he hadn't yet engaged a nurse and neither did he want to, due to the expense involved. 'You wish to take Lily to Essex, but who there will care for her, sir?'

'Well…you may continue to do so, my dear, if you agree to accompany me back to Wivenhoe. I know you have friends in town, but you have a friend in Essex, too…in the Viscount. Perhaps it might suit you to again be close to him.'

Dawn felt heat flood her complexion at that bold insinuation. So he knew very well who she yearned to be with. And it wasn't just her granddaughter.

So what would she do? Return to Essex with him to stay close to the two people she cared most about? 'You must allow me some time to think about this. I am not prepared to make a snap decision.'

'Very well, my dear.' Peter sounded the soul of consideration. 'I shall allow you your way and return tomorrow. But I cannot wait longer. I go home tomorrow to attend to business and, with or without you, will take the child with me.'

Chapter Thirteen

'Why… Mrs Broome…what a lovely surprise to find *you* here.' Dawn's voice held mingling astonishment and delight at seeing a friendly face.

'La…it is good to see you, too, Mrs Fenton. I had no idea you'd be coming back with the master. He told me you had returned to London and taken his daughter with you for a holiday after that sad business with her mother.' Mrs Broome clucked her tongue and glanced at the little girl. 'What a terrible shock that must have been for you all.'

'Yes…it was.' Dawn's last recollection of Eleanor, frightened and in pain, would always haunt her mind, especially here. The fine vicarage should have made a cosy home; instead an oppressive atmosphere always made her heart sink on stepping over the threshold. She thanked the lord that Lily, too young to be aware of what had happened, wouldn't be tormented by bad memories of her mother as she grew.

'I've been looking forward to meeting the little lass.' Mrs Broome injected some jollity into her tone. 'The master said he'd bring her home so I've prepared her room. What a pretty little thing she is.'

So, it had been no spur-of-the-moment decision that Mansfield had made to reclaim Lily, Dawn realised. 'Indeed, we shall stay in Essex… for a short while,' she replied carefully. 'You've brought kittens with you.' She changed the subject, a smile in her voice. Her granddaughter had crouched down to look at two squirming bundles of black and white fur in a basket in the corner of the kitchen.

'The master wasn't keen on letting me keep them, but I told him they'll turn into good mousers. I'm used to having a cat guarding the larders.'

'Lily has taken to them.' Dawn wondered why she'd not thought of getting a pet for her granddaughter.

'Well, let me make you a nice cup of tea after your journey. I've baked a currant cake. I bet you'd like a slice, wouldn't you?' Mrs Broome chucked the child under the chin. 'The poor little mite looks done in. I expect she needs to get early to her bed.' The woman set the kettle to boil on the hob.

Dawn, fatigued from lack of sleep and constant worry, settled herself and Lily at the kitchen table.

During the journey to Essex in the creaky hired rig, little conversation had passed between them. But the vicar had briefly answered one of Dawn's questions before crossing his arms over his chest and starting to doze. He had employed a new housekeeper and the woman seemed competent. Dawn had been glad to hear it. She'd not relished the idea of taking on that chore. Lily had been well behaved from the moment they'd set out, playing with her doll or napping. But she had asked her grandma about her friend Bernard. The little girl had been pleased to hear she would see him again soon. And so had the vicar seemed contented by that answer. A beam of satisfaction had tipped up his fleshy lips, although he hadn't opened his eyes.

Much as Dawn would have liked to snooze away the miles she had been fretting too much to do so. The previous night had seen her rampant thoughts denying her any rest during hours that seemed endless. When the sky was at its blackest she had abandoned her bed to stare out of her window. Wishing on a star wouldn't help, she'd scolded herself. Spurring herself into action, she'd dragged her carpet bag from the top of her clothes press. For a frantic ten minutes she had packed her things; the idea of fleeing with her granddaughter to somewhere that Mansfield wouldn't find them had seemed a sensible solution at three o'clock in the morning. With first light came the return of her reason.

Such mad behaviour would gain her nothing but a charge of abduction. A court would side with the child's father and she could be banned from ever again seeing her granddaughter. As a blush on the horizon had brightened her bedchamber she had continued making ready to travel…to Essex. With heavy heart she knew she had only two choices: let her granddaughter go, or move to the vicarage to care for her. But she would never stop trying to persuade Peter Mansfield that his daughter's prospects…and also his own…would be better served if Lily were raised in town, socialising with the Earl of Houndsmere's son. Intuitively Dawn understood that if Lily were to thrive she needed to be kept at a distance from her father.

Dawn knew she would work tirelessly to bring about their return to London. Jack might have put distance between them, but she was certain he wouldn't turn his back on her. If things got unbearable for her and Lily at the vicarage, she would swallow her pride and ask for his help. Mansfield believed he had her pinned beneath his thumb, but he had a weakness, too. The fellow still seemed in thrall to the benefits to be had from being classed as Lord Sterling's friend. Dawn was well aware that Jack despised the vicar as much as she did, but was confident he would play along with it, promising Mansfield all manner of pomp and circumstance while throwing his weight behind reasons why Mrs Fenton and her granddaughter should return to town.

And, in the meanwhile, the unexpected, wonderful discovery that she had a friend at the vicarage had given Dawn a boost. She was curious to know how Mrs Broome's employment had come about.

'Well, do you remember my daughter taking a fancy to that lad at the Bell?' the woman commenced answering Dawn's question. 'She found out there was a vacancy going and took a fancy to having that, too. Now Betty's a tavern maid and the couple are sweethearts, hoping to wed next spring.' Mrs Broome set the cups while carrying on her tale. 'Once she up and left I couldn't afford the rent on my cottage so needed full-time work, or another husband.' She guffawed.

'I decided to stay fancy free and looked for a position as a cook. I heard that the vicar at Wivenhoe had lost his wife and was advertising for a housekeeper so applied for the job. I remembered you saying he was kin of yours and took that as a good sign.' She poured tea, frowning. 'Anyway, he offered me the position and I took it.'

'And do you regret it?' Dawn felt rather guilty that her connection to Peter Mansfield had been taken as a recommendation about his character.

'Not yet...' Mrs Broome replied diplomatically. 'If ever I do regret it, then I'll leave. Now my daughter's marrying Sam Crocker I might head towards London and better opportunities if things don't turn out right for me here. The girl's got to stand on her own two feet, like I had to. Betty will be sixteen when she weds; that's the age I was when I got married. Then the following year my daughter was born and the year after that I lost my husband to the influenza. It's always been just me and her, but I can cope with life on my own.'

'Indeed, I believe you can,' Dawn said admiringly. This was no Mrs Grove, scared of her own shadow and believing in hobgoblins haunting the area. Dawn felt blessed to have the unexpected boon of Mrs Broome's company during her stay.

'And so are you one of life's capable sorts, so I reckon,' Mrs Broome returned the compliment.

Dawn smiled and drank her tea, wondering if the vicar understood how strong a character his new employee was. It was hard to believe that the woman was barely older than she was herself. The housekeeper looked closer to forty than thirty. But Dawn could tell she was energetic just by observing her going briskly about her business in the kitchen.

'I like to go into town and run errands so if you've something needs fetching, just you tell me.' Mrs Broome gave a smile. ''Course I don't venture out much at night and neither should you, m'm. But I expect you already know about all of that from when you were here before.'

'What do you mean?' Dawn hoped she wasn't wrong in thinking the new housekeeper was more down to earth than her predecessor.

'The smugglers.' Mrs Broome bluntly explained. 'We all know about them, of course. But everybody holds their tongues. See no evil, hear no evil.' She dropped a wink.

'Smugglers?' Dawn's chuckle faded away as she saw the woman was deadly serious. Dawn had heard about the illicit trade, of course; it was common knowledge that contraband reached London. But she had no proper idea of what went on along the coast and how smuggled goods were brought ashore from France.

'Some folk says free traders are a good thing,' Mrs Broome whispered, tapping her nose. 'How else would the likes of commoners afford tea and lace like rich people do?'

'Ah... I see you have met Mrs Broome.' The vicar had entered the kitchen, unseen and unheard by the conversing women until the moment he chose to make his presence known.

Dawn felt a familiar chill cloak her, recalling how months ago he'd crept up on her in the kitchen when she'd been speaking to Mrs Grove. They'd been discussing how poorly Eleanor seemed and how the vicar appeared careless of his wife's deterioration and suffering.

'I've made tea for Mrs Fenton, sir. Would you like a cup before dinner?' Mrs Broome appeared indifferent to discover he'd been listening to her gossiping.

Peter inclined his head. 'I shall have a tray in my study, Mrs Broome.' He turned to Dawn. 'Perhaps you and the child should take your refreshment upstairs. The parlour would be a more appropriate place for a lady.'

'I'm content here, thank you.' Dawn was aware of the emphasis he'd put on 'lady'. He wasn't about to let her forget that he knew about her indiscretion with Lord Sterling. And she wasn't about to let him dictate to her how she behaved. 'Lily likes watching the kittens while I talk to Mrs Broome.' She intended to frequently seek the woman's company so he might as well get used to seeing them together.

'As you wish, Mrs Fenton. We can talk about things at dinnertime in any case.'

Dawn knew the only way she could tolerate being under his roof was to spend as little time as possible in his company. She wasn't going to dine with him but with her granddaughter, then she would retire early. Peter went out again and she turned back to her cake, taking a bite. It was delicious and she told Mrs Broome so. She asked for another slice and received a beam of pleasure along with a thicker wedge of crumbly currant cake. Dawn was determined not to allow Mansfield to deflate her good mood. Yet at the back of her mind she was wondering whether she should, after all, have taken her chances absconding from London with Lily.

The following morning Mrs Broome was in the process of clearing away the breakfast crockery when she announced, 'I shall be off to town later this afternoon. Cupboards need filling. Can I fetch you back anything, m'm?'

'Thank you, no. Actually…if you don't mind, we shall accompany you,' Dawn said brightly, helping Lily down from the dining table. 'I intend to take my granddaughter out most days as the weather is fine. She shouldn't be cooped up.'

Mrs Broome looked delighted at the prospect of having their company. 'It's a bit of a walk for her little legs though, m'm,' she pointed out.

'Oh, the vicar has a dog cart we can use. I'm quite able to drive it.'

'So am I,' Mrs Broome said flatly. 'But he told me not to when I suggested fetching the groceries in it.'

'Well, he hasn't told me not to use it,' Dawn said. 'If he's out in the gig, and the pony and cart are sitting idle, then I don't see how he can object to his daughter being given a ride to town. Besides, it is sensible for us to bring back what the cupboards lack rather than waiting for the boy to deliver later in the week.'

Mrs Broome gave an emphatic nod. 'Quite right, too, m'm,' she said.

An hour later they were out on the rutted road with a balmy breeze at their backs. The two women had settled into an amicable quiet, with Lily seated between them on the bench. It had been a long time since Dawn had driven a vehicle, but she'd not felt nervous at the idea of harnessing the pony, or of taking the reins. Excitement and relief at having escaped the vicarage were lifting her spirits making her more than usually appreciative of the countryside. The clear azure sky and verges sprinkled with scarlet poppies were a glorious sight. The hedgerows rustled with wildlife and intermittently rabbits broke free of bramble to dart away over the fields. The pony was elderly and well behaved, maintaining a steady if slow trot that allowed Dawn to loosen her grip on the reins, then settle back to enjoy the ride.

As they passed the brow of a hill they had a clear view of Croxley Grange rising up in all its turreted glory away to the west. Dawn had no need to have that reminder of Jack Valance. He was never far from her thoughts. Days had passed since he'd held her, kissed her, yet the vivid memory of their fiery passion was enough to revive a phantom pressure on her skin as though he still tantalised her with his touch. She mentally shook herself, concentrating on the road ahead. She must do without him and cope alone with her problems if she could. Jack had quit town without contacting her and in doing so had conveyed a message more honestly than could a letter containing his regrets.

She noticed a pothole ahead and slowed the mare to steer her around it. The breeze had patted colour into all their complexions and Dawn smiled as her animated granddaughter pointed to a hare that seemed to be challenging them to a race. The creature was bounding in front of the cart, then suddenly it veered off towards the meadow through a gap in the hawthorn.

'The rich fellow who owns that big house is a handsome rogue by all accounts.' Mrs Broome had noticed the direction of Mrs Fenton's gaze a moment ago. 'He's soon getting wed, though, so lots of hearts will be broken.'

'Have you seen anything of Lord Sterling's fiancée?' It had slipped out before Dawn could curb her tongue.

'Only the once…in the distance…and hemmed in by a throng of people dancing attendance on her.' Mrs Broome tickled Lily's cheek as the child fidgeted on the seat. 'Refined young ladies have to be kept under lock and key, away from the likes of lusty lads, don't they?' She chuckled. 'I'd have a job keeping my girl indoors now she's courting. If you've a comely daughter, you've got a worry until she's safely wed, no matter your station in life.'

It seemed that news of the Viscount's return to the area hadn't yet spread. But it would. Dawn guessed the wedding announcement wouldn't be far off either. She urged the pony to increase pace as she glimpsed the signpost up ahead. They were approaching town and a few minutes later she was heading along the dusty main road to stop the cart in a lane behind the green.

'There's my friend over there,' Mrs Broome returned a wave to a woman who appeared to be loitering in the hope of a chat.

'Please go and speak to her, if you want to, and run your errands,' Dawn urged when Mrs Broome politely stayed by her side. 'I'd like to have a look in the drapery. Lily needs new vests. We can meet back here by the cart in an hour or so.'

The drapery was busy so Dawn walked on past the shop with the intention of returning later to make her purchases. Up ahead she'd spotted somebody she knew. Mrs Grove had served Eleanor well and Dawn didn't want to miss an opportunity to say hello to the old housekeeper and ask how she fared. The woman was leaning on a stick as though aches and pains had crept up on her since she'd retired.

'Jack!' Lily tugged on her grandma's hand to gain her attention.

Dawn had almost jumped from her skin on hearing Lily squeak out loud the name that constantly circled her head. She crouched down to shush the child, then glanced in the direction of Lily's pointing finger.

And indeed it was him. He was some distance away on the opposite side of the road. It seemed to Dawn that her heart ceased beating for the time it took her to straighten up. He looked impeccably distinguished, sporting a snugly fitting grey tailcoat with his strong legs encased in buff breeches and polished Hessian boots. His silvery hair was being whipped on to his brow by the breeze and the hand he'd splayed on the curricle was lifted to push the stray locks from his eyes.

She wasn't the only woman who was watching the lord of the manor. A couple of young ladies hurried past, whispering excitedly behind their gloved fingers about Lord Sterling being in town this afternoon. He appeared about to help his companion to board the curricle. But he didn't... he remained where he was, his head turned in Dawn's direction, having just spotted her.

She was too far away to read his expression, but as their eyes remained locked she imagined his feelings were as ambiguous as her own. She tossed up whether to raise a hand in acknowledgement or simply turn away to carry on about her business. Perhaps he was annoyed, thinking she'd followed him. Well, she hadn't. She'd far,

far sooner still be in London. She would have done anything rather than meet him again like this…out in public…when he had his fiancée by his side. And she knew that the petite Titian-haired young lady who was standing by the Arabian, rubbing its nose, was Sarah Snow.

Perhaps he was embarrassed at the idea of introducing them. Well she'd no qualms about meeting his future wife. In fact, Dawn realised she would sooner get the introduction over with. She put up her chin and set off determinedly in his direction, clutching tightly at Lily's hand as the child tried to slip free and fly ahead to greet him.

Chapter Fourteen

'This is a nice surprise, Mrs Fenton. Most unexpected, too.'

'Indeed, it is unexpected,' Dawn answered crisply, aware of his ruefulness. 'I'm sorry for intruding. Lily spotted you and wanted to come and say hello.'

Jack's mouth took on a sardonic slant as he detected an undercurrent of *froideur* in her tone. 'There's no need for an apology. I'm always pleased to see you and your granddaughter. I believe you know that.' His dark fingers ruffled Lily's fair curls, but his attention soon returned to Dawn. She understood the blunt question blazing from his grey eyes, then he turned to his companion and made introductions.

'I have heard about you, you know,' Sarah Snow said, taking the hands Dawn had extended to her in welcome. 'I know about you, too, Miss

Lily.' Sarah crouched down to speak to the little girl. 'I know that you like to spin sovereigns. So do I. Major Jack taught me the trick of it.' She tutted. 'I must remember to call him Lord Sterling now, mustn't I?' she whispered to Lily. 'May I take her to have a look in the toyshop window?' she asked Dawn. 'It's just there.' She pointed to a premises close by.

'I'm sure Lily would like that,' Dawn answered with a smile. She had been wondering how to engineer a brief, private moment with Jack before they parted. He ought to know what had brought her to Essex. For the foreseeable future they would be neighbours and needed to be prepared to bump into one another. It was a tormenting situation, knowing they must appear to be just acquaintances. From the satirical set to his features, Dawn guessed that Jack was also brooding on the farce involved.

Sarah led Lily away and Jack casually took Dawn's arm, tightening his fingers when she would have slipped free. A mulberry tree close by beckoned as shelter and he steered her beneath its branches. Dawn's mind slipped back through the years to a day when he had manoeuvred her in just such a way in Hyde Park and had kissed her quite determinedly. From that moment she had fallen in love with this man and forlornly realised she had never stopped. Yet the passing years and her changing life had done nothing to bring to fruition a love that seemed doomed.

'Did you come to Essex to find me? Has something happened in London that needed my help?' Jack demanded the moment they were in shadows cast by whispering leaves.

'I did not come to find you and I don't need your help,' Dawn returned succinctly. Oh, she did need his help, but realised that she must learn to do without him. She had seen them together now... Jack and his fiancée. Sarah Snow was no longer a faceless young woman, but real flesh and blood. She was sweet and friendly and innocent...and deserved to be happy after what she had been through in Tangier. While watching them together, unobserved, Dawn had seen Jack smile fondly at his future wife. He might not love Sarah, but he wasn't indifferent to her either. And neither was Dawn. Sarah had done nothing to harm her; the young woman believed that Mrs Fenton was exactly who she purported to be...an acquaintance of her future husband. Dawn couldn't act the hypocrite or the liar to promote that fallacy while wanting to have Jack to herself. So she must leave them both alone... deal with her problems alone...

'You're quiet…what's the matter? Is it Mansfield bothering you?' Jack asked.

Dawn shrugged, keeping an eye on her granddaughter. Lily was eagerly browsing the toys in the shop window, pointing this way and that as something caught her eye. 'I hoped never again to set foot in Wivenhoe, that's all.'

'It sounds as though Mansfield *has* interfered.' Jack frowned. 'Why did you not wait for me? I would have dealt with that weasel. He won't go against me and risk losing the funds I've promised him for the church. Didn't you believe that I'd fulfil my promise to return by the end of the week?'

Dawn shot a look of confusion at him. 'When did you promise any such thing? I've not seen or spoken to you since you left my house without even saying goodbye.'

'Apologies for that, but I thought you'd want me to eject Mansfield with all due haste after his untimely arrival,' Jack drily excused himself. 'And I did come back to say goodnight… and more besides…' His eyes studied her face, dropped lower to move in a caress over her figure. His voice became husky as he added, 'Your house was in darkness. I imagined you were in bed…' He gave a hollow laugh. 'So indeed it took some noble self-restraint to stop myself banging on your door.'

Dawn felt her cheeks fizzing with heat as a silver glint in his eyes burned her skin.

'I didn't think you'd appreciate me disturbing the neighbours,' he roughly explained. 'So I did the decent thing and went straight home...to a message that I was needed urgently at Croxley Grange.' He planted a hand on the tree trunk. 'Did you not believe that I would return in a few days as stated in my letter?'

'Your letter?' Dawn echoed. 'I've not received a letter from you.'

Jack took a step towards her, frowning. 'Before I left town I wrote you a note. I gave instructions to my butler that it was to be delivered before noon the following morning.'

Dawn shook her head in dismay. 'I didn't receive it.' Knowing he hadn't just gone away without a word caused a surge of relief to ripple through her. She felt bereft, though, not to have received that small token of his regard. A message from him would have comforted her and emboldened her against Mansfield's threats to take Lily. She might have stood her ground with her granddaughter in London, knowing Jack was on his way to be her ally. But she had allowed Mansfield's spite to sow seeds of doubt in her mind. She had agreed to come to Essex, believing herself abandoned by Jack and on the point of losing Lily.

In a way she realised she was glad she *had* panicked and come to Wivenhoe. Meeting Sarah had given her a fresh and vital perspective on the reality of all their situations. She must stop relying on Jack and stop hoping his betrothal would flounder. Slowly but surely she must withdraw from his life, even as a friend, because the temptation to want more would never leave her. And, if he chose to cheat on his wife, Dawn could at least comfort herself with the knowledge that the betrayal wouldn't be tormenting her conscience.

Jack limited his frustration at knowing the letter had gone astray to an apologetic gesture. But beneath his composure simmered anger. His butler was usually efficient in carrying out his strict instructions. Crawley would need to explain himself if he wanted to keep his position. 'Well, no matter about the letter.' Jack smoothed the matter over. 'At least you are here with me now.'

'What brought you urgently back to Croxley Grange?' Dawn looked at Sarah. She appeared in good health and very content. She was laughing while playing pat-a-cake with Lily. She was soon to be a bride and had the face and figure of an adult—her fine lemon gown clung to her

curves—yet her behaviour seemed rather imma-
ture. It was hard to imagine the young woman
as a viscountess. Difficult as it was for Dawn
to endure, she realised Sarah needed somebody
like Jack to protect her from life's cruelties. The
thought was reinforced when Dawn's flitting
gaze alighted on a fellow across the road, stationed in the bakery doorway. He was dressed
in a seafarer's reefer jacket and peaked leather
cap and appeared to be watching Sarah. Aware
he was under observation, he turned and strolled
off along the street, eating a bun.

'You believed I'd gone away without leaving
you word, didn't you? Don't you trust me even
a little bit, Dawn?' Jack narrowed his eyes on
the sailor.

'What was I supposed to think?' Dawn shielded
her guilty blush by dipping her bonnet brim. 'The
vicar called on me the following day to collect
Lily and take her to Essex. He knew you had already returned there whereas I did not. I imagined
you had left quickly because you wanted a clean
break to protect our names.' The memory of what
they'd done to risk their reputations played over
slowly in her head, turning the pink in her cheeks
to fiery red. Had they been disturbed a few minutes later she might have been partially disrobed
instead of just doing up buttons. The vicar might

have burst in and seen her naked body and the very idea of it made her insides squirm in mortification. 'I understood why you deemed it best to put some distance between us. I still do…more than ever now. While I am, alas, forced to remain in Essex, we should avoid one another.'

'Hush…no more,' Jack growled, stepping closer to her and blocking her from view behind his muscular physique. He raised a discreet hand to stroke her face. 'This will come right for everybody, Dawn. If there is any justice at all in life it has to. Just give me some time to make it so.'

Over his shoulder Dawn spotted the ladies who'd been gossiping about him earlier. She discreetly moved away, hoping that any curious townsfolk believed them to be just people enjoying a polite chat while shading from the afternoon sun. She had her grandchild with her and Lord Sterling was accompanied by his future wife so there was no reason why onlookers should believe differently. And now she had come to her senses there need be no deceit in such an assumption.

'Did Mansfield bring you into town this afternoon?' Jack gazed along the street as though believing he might spot their nemesis.

'No… I brought myself and his new housekeeper in his dog cart. Mrs Broome is ordering groceries this afternoon. I need to have those loaded on shortly.'

Jack smiled wryly. 'So you can handle the reins, can you?'

'Very well, actually,' she said with mock boastfulness. 'Not that I drive in London. I don't have a vehicle of my own.'

'We can change that. You can have anything you want. Just name it.'

Their eyes tangled in contest. Oh, she knew as Lord Sterling's mistress she'd have the sort of pampered life she'd never previously tasted. A life that many women of straitened circumstances would adore to be offered. She tore her eyes free of his hold before her new good intentions wavered. 'What I want is to always have Lily in my life and living in London with me. If you could give me that, sir, I would be happy indeed and ask for nothing more.'

'Is that the only reason you came back here? To ensure your granddaughter was properly cared for? You weren't missing me or worried about me even just a little bit after believing I'd disappeared without a word?'

'After what you overcame in Tangier I'm sure you can take care of yourself,' Dawn said on a smile.

'And I can take care of you. And Lily. Trust me on it.'

'And you must take care of Sarah,' Dawn said bluntly. 'Your future wife is your priority, sir.'

'Surely you realise you have no reason to feel jealous now that you have met her?'

Dawn avoided his eyes. She *had* felt twinges of jealousy and felt ashamed because of it. 'You told Sarah about me and Lily. Why?'

'Sarah asked what I'd been doing in London and who I'd seen.'

'And what did you say?'

'I said I'd seen a good friend and her little granddaughter. I said I hoped to go back and see you both again soon.'

So she had been right. His fiancée hadn't a clue that Mrs Fenton might be a rival. Sarah and Lily were approaching, having seen their fill of what the toyshop window had to offer.

'What emergency brought you back here?' Dawn speedily asked.

'I received a message that Sarah couldn't be found. Villains are known to haunt the area and her chaperon was in a panic about a kidnapping as the local smugglers have committed similar crimes for ransoms. It was a false alarm, thank the Lord; Sarah was safe and well at home when I arrived. Her chaperon is supposed to accompany her when she goes out walking in the grounds, but Sarah admitted she purposely gave her the slip. Apparently she has made a friend and likes him very much. They talk about fishing.' Jack smiled. 'She used to go sea fishing with her father in Tangier.'

Dawn was surprised that Jack appeared to have recovered from such a fright, considering Sarah's history. Nobody would blame him for being angry at her for acting silly and defiant. But there was no more time to discuss the intrigue. 'Little wonder you rushed back here!' was all she managed to blurt out before Sarah and Lily arrived beneath the tree.

'Can Lily come for tea, please, this afternoon?'

'That would be nice,' Jack said with a smile.

'Thank you, but perhaps another time,' Dawn hastily interjected. 'I still have my shopping to do.' Mrs Broome would think she'd been forgotten if she didn't meet up with her soon.

'Tomorrow?' Jack suggested. 'Come to the Grange in the afternoon to have a picnic in the garden.'

Sarah approvingly clapped her hands and Lily joined in, copying her new friend.

'Very well, tomorrow,' Dawn agreed. She couldn't deny her granddaughter an outing that she was already looking forward to. Taking Lily's hand, she stepped away. 'Now I must get on before the shops close.'

Jack helped Sarah aboard the curricle, then turned to Dawn. 'Tomorrow then. I'll send a carriage at three o'clock.'

Dawn walked back along the High Street in the direction of the drapery, quite slowly because Lily was complaining of feeling tired. She was still aware of him…knew exactly when the curricle was approaching. As it passed by Sarah turned to wave a hand. Dawn waved back as did Lily. But her eyes were on the broad back of the driver as the vehicle gained speed and disappeared from view. She knew that she was on his mind as he was on hers. But what good would wishing do them?

He'd said he'd bring it right…but how *could* it all end well for everybody? With a sigh beneath her breath Dawn forced herself to concentrate on the mundanities that needed attention. She had Lily's vests to buy and if the grocery order was ready she must have it loaded on to the cart. In the distance she could see Mrs Broome standing by the pony, having a gossip to somebody. About to speed up in that direction, Dawn hesitated because she had spotted somebody else she knew and had wanted to speak to earlier. Mrs Grove was sitting on a bench outside the local tavern and beside her was the sailor Dawn had noticed by the bakery. Dawn was curious to know who the fellow was and perhaps find out the reason for him staring at Sarah.

To save Lily's legs Dawn scooped the child into her arms and quickened her pace towards the tavern.

'Mrs Fenton! Oh, it's so nice to see you. I thought I spotted you across the road and have been loitering about hoping to bump into you. I never thought the day would come that you'd return to this place.' Mrs Grove looked thankful that Dawn had taken time to speak to her. She struggled to her feet, using her stick. 'And how is this little one?' The woman raised a wrinkly hand to cup the child's soft cheek. 'Miss Lily's looking very bonny.'

'We're both well, thank you. How have you been, Mrs Grove?' Dawn asked as the sailor also got to his feet, his cap tucked beneath an arm.

'I've a touch of lumbago, but mustn't grumble.' Noticing Mrs Fenton glancing at her companion, she tutted. 'Oh, where are my manners? This is my late brother-in-law's boy, William. He's on a visit to his old auntie, aren't you?' She patted his sleeve. 'William's a sea captain. He's got his own boat now and is doing good trade.'

The woman looked proud. 'Fine prospects has William. His parents would be pleased as punch for him. God rest them both. He's stopping with me as he's ashore for a while.' She gave her quiet nephew a nudge. 'Really you've come home to do a bit of fishing, haven't you, William? He takes his boat out from Wivenhoe and catches us some plump mackerel to cook for supper and plenty left to sell in the market.'

William was gazing at Lily rather intently and Dawn instinctively drew her granddaughter closer to her skirt.

'I must be off now, Aunt Grove.' William began to rotate his cap in his hands. 'I promised to meet a chum and have a drink with him. I'll be back before supper time.' He executed a neat bow. 'I'm pleased to meet you, ma'am.'

'It's nice to meet you, William,' Dawn answered, watching him disappear inside the tavern doorway. She believed she'd just discovered the identity of Sarah's friend...the person the young woman had risked trouble for and who shared her enthusiasm for fishing. Dawn wondered if Jack also knew about William Grove. She believed he did. Jack would have made it his business to find out. William appeared to be some years older than Sarah and not an obvious choice of friend for a young woman to have.

'I'm glad I've seen you. I have something for you.' Mrs Grove's tone had changed and she was wearing such a grim expression that Dawn forgot all about the woman's nephew.

'What is it?' Dawn frowned.

'It's a letter. If you accompany me home, I'll give it to you. I live just over there.' Mrs Grove jabbed her walking stick at a row of cottages adjacent to the Green.

Dawn had the impression the woman didn't want to discuss any more of this business out in the open. They set off, Mrs Grove walking quite briskly with the aid of her stick.

Once inside the spick and span, if spartanly furnished, cottage, Mrs Grove turned to Dawn to ask politely, 'Would you like some tea, Mrs Fenton?'

'Thank you, no. I'm already late getting back. I got talking to somebody.'

'I saw you with the Viscount and Miss Snow.' Mrs Grove smiled. 'She seems too young to be getting wed to a grand man such as he…if you get my drift.'

'I do…yes,' Dawn said, but was determined not to be drawn into gossip about Jack.

'William has spoken to the young lady. He met her out walking in the meadow. He thinks her very friendly and nice.' Mrs Grove sighed.

'Well, no matter about that. This is what I wanted to give to you.' She opened a drawer in the dresser and took out a letter. 'I found it in among Mrs Mansfield's things. I was going to give it to the master. But I didn't.' She gave Dawn a significant look. 'If his wife had wanted him to know of it, she wouldn't have hidden it in among her chemises, is my thinking.' She held out the sealed parchment addressed to Dawn. 'I'm glad I've seen you. William promised that he would safely deliver the letter when next he visited the city, but now he won't need to.'

Dawn felt her mouth drying as she looked at the message from beyond the grave. What had Eleanor wanted her, but not her husband, to know? She immediately recalled the bruises on her stepdaughter's arms and Mansfield's explanation that his wife had got those falling over. Dawn slipped the letter out of sight in a pocket. 'Thank you for carrying out Eleanor's final wish.' Dawn's voice had turned husky with emotion.

Mrs Grove nodded. 'That's how I saw it, too. Now you take yourself and the little 'un back to London, soon as you can.' Mrs Grove smiled at Lily. 'She looks to be blossoming in your care, but she won't if she stays with him.'

Dawn knew that was true, but simply said,

'We must get going. Mrs Broome is waiting for us by the dog cart.'

'Does *he* know you've driven it?' Mrs Grove raised her eyebrows.

'No…the vicar had gone out so I couldn't tell him I intended to borrow it.'

'Mrs Mansfield drove herself once without his permission. He didn't like it. She never took the cart out again.' Mrs Grove pursed her lips. 'Go on now. With any luck you'll beat him back and he won't know. God bless you both.'

Once outside the cottage Dawn waved to Mrs Broome to let the woman know she was at last on her way. Dawn realised that helping herself to the vicar's dog cart without asking permission might be seen as a liberty. But why should she twiddle her thumbs sitting indoors on a fine afternoon, or tire Lily out from a long walk when there was no need for any of it? She wasn't his poor bullied wife and neither was she frightened of him. Thoughts of Eleanor caused her to curl her fingers about the letter in her pocket. She was impatient to read it, but knew she must wait and seek the privacy of her bedchamber before opening it.

Chapter Fifteen

'Ah, there you are, my dear. I have been waiting for you to return.'

Dawn whipped about in surprise on hearing the vicar addressing his daughter with unusual fondness. He approached them in the dim corridor and she realised it was *her* he was looking at, not Lily. She wasn't fooled by his faux amity, or that smile that barely warmed his eyes. Before he could accuse her of appropriating his pony and cart she declared, 'We have been shopping in town. As the vehicle was idle I borrowed it; it's too far for Lily to walk. We have brought back the provisions that were needed rather than wait for a delivery. I didn't think you'd mind.' That was untrue, she realised. She had known he *would* mind but if she and Lily had to live in this house they wouldn't be prisoners in it, too.

She could tell that she'd taken the wind from

his sails with her bold confession. But he gave a shrug, maintaining a mild expression.

'As you say, on this occasion I did not need the cart myself. Another time I might have done so and thus your behaviour would have greatly inconvenienced me.' Peter glanced at the housekeeper who was in the process of unbuttoning Lily's coat. 'Mrs Broome may take the child to the kitchen for some refreshment. If you would come to the study, Mrs Fenton, I should like to talk to you.'

Dawn's fingers instinctively tightened on the letter in her pocket. But he couldn't possibly know about that. Much as she wanted to hurry upstairs to read it she murmured her agreement to a meeting. 'I will be along in a moment. I am thirsty and would like a drink.' As he disappeared into his study she let out a breath that she hadn't realised she'd been holding in. There was something about the vicar's manner that she found increasingly disquieting.

Mrs Broome led Lily towards the kitchen and Dawn followed, untying her bonnet. Though she had no wish to go and find out what Peter wanted, Dawn knew she must in case it was favourable news. There was a chance he had got fed up with having his daughter around and wanted Dawn to take the little girl away. She had noticed him scowling yesterday when Lily fell over and started howling. His daughter was a tomboy and as there was no swing to play on in the vicarage's garden she liked to race around the pathways, chasing the kittens instead.

'Kittens...' On entering the kitchen a disappointed Lily had immediately rushed to the empty basket.

Mrs Broome shut the back door that had been ajar. 'I'm sure I left that bolted before I went out. The master must've been down here and forgotten to close it. Be it on his head then if the mice get at the oats before the cats come back.'

Dawn drank her glass of lemonade, then, leaving Lily in Mrs Broome's capable hands, went back upstairs to the study. She stood outside for a moment, crossing her fingers that fate would be kind. She longed to hear that the vicar—irritated by his boisterous little daughter's company—wanted them both gone. She tapped on the door and was summoned inside.

'Please make yourself comfortable.' Peter indicated a chair while sailing to and fro with his hands clasped behind his back.

'Thank you, but I won't tarry. Lily is quite tired from her outing and would benefit from a short nap before her tea.' Another fib. Dawn wouldn't let Lily sleep this close to her bedtime and risk a restless night.

'As you wish,' Peter replied stiffly and ceased perambulating. 'I will get straight down to things then. I have decided the child needs a proper routine. She must be permanently settled with a woman prepared to give her a mother's care and attention.'

Dawn's heart soared. Had her dream come true? Did he mean that Lily could always live with her? 'I agree, sir, and I believe Lily will continue to benefit from living in London with me.'

'I am grateful to you for your interim assistance, but I want a formal arrangement in the future. The child is young and will in time forget the female who gave her birth and believe the person who is with her is her mother.'

Dawn took a step closer to him, her optimism already waning. 'Your daughter is sadly now without her mama, but she has me. *I* love her as a mother would.'

'But you are not Mrs Mansfield, are you?'

Dawn stared at him in mounting disbelief. Surely he wasn't implying he was already considering taking another wife? But as he crossed his arms over his chest, staring challengingly, she realised he indeed meant to remarry. 'Eleanor is barely laid to rest a few months, sir,' she gasped. 'You surely cannot be thinking of replacing her, before even a proper period of mourning has passed?'

'I miss my wife, of course, but life must go on.' He sighed. 'We are not fashionable people here, my dear. Etiquette is of little consequence in Wivenhoe. We country folk believe a child needs a mother and it is my duty to find one for her.'

Dawn made a shocked little noise, almost like a laugh. 'It seems you have given the matter some thought, sir. Have you a lady in mind?' She wondered who on earth would be foolish enough to tie herself to him. Of course, he was able to conceal the worst of his character, as he was doing now with his oily smiles and soft voice, but she wasn't taken in by it.

'You have a natural fondness for her, Mrs Fenton, and as you are a widow and I am a widower…'

Dawn froze in shock before revulsion shaped her features. She snapped herself to attention, noting anger glinting in his eyes as he read her reaction to his proposal. 'I must stop you, sir, before you say something that I would find utterly distasteful,' she rattled off. 'If you wish to remarry with indecent haste, of course it is your own business, but please understand that I would never welcome you approaching me. Neither do I believe that Lily is in need of a stepmother when she has a grandmother to care for her.'

Peter cocked his head, resting his chin on a fist. 'Perhaps I have startled you with the news that I find you pleasing enough to wed,' he said. 'I know it is an odd situation. You were married to my father-in-law. But we are not blood kin so there is nothing improper in what I suggest. We are of a similar age and I believe we would have some compatibility...'

Dawn watched his eyes crawling to her bosom and his tongue snaking between his teeth to wet his lips. Biliousness rolled in her stomach and she felt an urge to flee his presence. But she didn't. She straightened her shoulders and stood her ground. 'Unfortunately, I believe the opposite to be true and can only impress on you that I would never want you to repeat what you have just said to me.' She barely paused before adding with admirable aplomb, 'Now if you will excuse me. I must take Lily upstairs.' Though her limbs felt palsied she approached the door quite nimbly. Before she could exit the room Mrs Broome entered it.

'There is a gentleman caller, sir. He said the matter is urgent.'

'Can't you see I'm busy? If it's a parishioner, send him away,' Peter barked with obvious frustration at the interruption.

'It is Lord Sterling, sir.' Mrs Broome's tone held a caution.

'And I have no intention of going away no matter how busy you are.' Jack pushed the door open wider and strode past the housekeeper into the study.

Dawn stared at him with a mingling of astonishment and relief. She certainly hadn't been expecting to see him again so soon. She wanted to launch herself into his arms and beg him to spirit her away from this foul place. But her happiness at being granted the unexpected gift of his company was ebbing away, transforming to anxiety. He was enraged about something, although managing to contain his temper.

'Oh, my extreme apologies, my lord. You are indeed welcome to call at any time.' Peter's bowing and scraping prevented him immediately noticing his visitor's menacing demeanour. Straightening his back, he flicked impatiently at Mrs Broome to dismiss her. 'I did obey your summons, Lord Sterling, the moment I returned from London.' He sounded earnest, believing the Viscount tetchy from imagining he'd been ignored. 'Your servant said you were otherwise engaged, but I certainly intended calling again tomorrow.'

'Well, now you have no need to,' Jack enunciated through his teeth. He looked at Dawn and his features softened a little.

Peter intercepted that look and it caused a subtle smile to writhe on his mean lips. One of Dawn's attractions for him—and there were many—was that she had this influential fellow in the palm of her hand. Peter was confident that she would marry him rather than risk losing contact with the grandchild she adored. When she were under *his* thumb he would be able to manipulate Lord Sterling through his mistress. Peter wouldn't object to a peer of the realm bedding his wife when such sweet benefits were to be had from the liaison. Sin, for its own sake, he wouldn't abide in others and believed such fornicators needed to be severely punished.

'We were just conversing about the child's welfare,' Peter explained Dawn's presence in his study. He wanted her gone in case she alerted the Viscount, before time, to having a rival. 'The matter is trifling and can wait until later. You may leave us, Mrs Fenton.'

'Mrs Fenton will stay. She should hear what I have to say.'

'Very well…if you wish, my lord. I know you are close friends.'

Jack was aware of the sly inflection in Mansfield's remark, but paid it little heed. He was more intent on employing a blazing look to reassure Dawn that she had no reason to fret. Whatever transpired here this afternoon, he still intended to put everything right as he had promised to do. Her spontaneous pleasure at his arrival had shone from her beautiful green eyes just minutes ago. Now it had dimmed; she was watchful, anticipating bad news. And in a moment he would upset her by disclosing why he'd come. Yet this matter had to be dealt with.

'A servant of mine has arrived from London bringing a strange and perturbing message.' Jack turned his attention to the vicar, his gaze dark with contempt. 'Before you returned here, you called at my Bruton Square residence and were given the letter I had left for you in my absence.'

In case he *were* ever accused of stealing the missing *billet doux* Peter had prepared a response. His sweating brow had nevertheless betrayed his nervousness and that he'd an idea of what had brought the Viscount here with a face like thunder.

Jack's mouth took on a sardonic slant as a row of glistening droplets began sprouting on the fellow's face. Half an hour ago his butler's comprehensive report of domestic issues had been handed to him. In it Crawley had stated that Mrs Fenton's letter had disappeared and although a thorough search had been made, it hadn't been found. The butler had gone on to state that he suspected the Reverend Peter Mansfield had taken it from the hall table. Initially Jack had found it hard to believe that the vicar would have the audacity to do such a thing. No such qualms remained. He was convinced of the fellow's guilt.

'While you were at my house you stole a letter that was addressed to Mrs Fenton.' Jack's eyes resembled shards of black ice. He extended a hand. 'Give it to me now.'

Dawn's letter had been quickly written, yet contained explicit references to his desire for the woman he loved. The fact that this weasel had read his private thoughts made Jack feel like abandoning caution and knocking Mansfield to the ground. He turned away for a moment to control himself although his fists remained balled at his sides.

'I... How dare you accuse me of theft!' Peter blustered. 'I would never knowingly take anything that didn't belong to me.'

Dawn's eyes widened in disgust as she noticed

Peter's flabby jowls turning florid. He wasn't ashamed of what he'd done, just of being found out. She recalled how smug he'd seemed when taunting her that the Viscount had left town without contacting her. Knowing the opposite to be true had amused him!

'Give me the letter or I will search your pockets, then tear this room apart until I find it.' Jack's threat was issued with such ferocity that the vicar took some rapid backward steps, believing himself about to be attacked. He had banked on His Lordship's butler concealing the matter to cover his dereliction of duty.

'I, in fact, received *two* letters from your man-servant,' Peter announced haughtily. 'I had quit the house by the time I realised his error. One parchment was stuck to the other with wax,' he continued with his fluent lies.

'Then why did you not return it the moment you discovered the mistake?' Jack demanded.

'I was on my way to see Mrs Fenton and thus was aware I could do you a good turn by delivering the note.'

'And yet she has never received it,' Jack drawled in a voice of steel.

'We spoke mostly of important arrangements for the child, as I recall. Minor matters slipped my mind, sir.' Peter's voice became breathy as the Viscount continued stalking him.

'Well, this matter hasn't slipped my mind.' Jack thrust a beckoning hand beneath the vicar's nose.

Peter dragged open a drawer in his desk and retrieved the parchment, tossing it to the edge of the mahogany top.

Dawn had been listening to proceedings without offering her own comment, though she had felt like adding her condemnation to Jack's. Now she did. She pounced on the parchment bearing her name, turning it in a hand. 'It's been opened.' Her eyes sparked with disgust. 'How dare you take my letter then read it!'

Jack had turned his back on Mansfield and was staring bleakly at Dawn. 'You cannot remain in this godforsaken place.'

A look of torment was in her eyes as they tangled with his. How she wanted to beg him to wait while she packed her things…and her granddaughter's, too. She knew that he wanted her to go now with him and never come back. But she couldn't! Lily's father had other ideas for his child. Dawn realised now as never before that Peter Mansfield would use his little girl as a bargaining chip. Whether it be his intention to marry her, or to wheedle favours from the lord of the manor, the vicar would exploit her love for Lily to try to get his own vile way.

'I'm sure Mrs Fenton will not abandon the child and go with you.' Peter's smug comment verified Dawn's fears and shattered the throbbing silence in the room.

'Then let Lily come, too.' Jack whipped about, his eyes narrowed to slits between which blazed his hatred. He knew the damnable fellow had a point and the upper hand. 'You still lack a proper nursemaid and Mrs Fenton has made an excellent job of caring for your daughter.'

'Has she indeed?' Peter purred. 'The child's moral character is of equal importance to her good health. I'm not sure that Mrs Fenton is the person to groom her in that respect.' The glance he cast Dawn's way made an explicit insult unnecessary.

Jack strode towards him. 'What the devil do you mean by saying that?'

'I believe you, of all people, know what I mean, sir.' Peter cocked his head to an insolent angle.

Jack's hand shot upward, aiming for the vicar's throat, but Dawn wedged herself between them, pushing Jack away. 'It doesn't matter,' she croaked. 'Please...just leave now. You must go—I'm sorry, but you must.'

Jack gave a harsh laugh from behind a hand that covered his snarling mouth. 'What is it you want, Mansfield? Money? How much?'

'My lord...how vulgar to mention the root of all evil to a man of the cloth.' Peter looked gleeful. A moment ago the Viscount had had him on the back foot. Now positions were reversed. The fellow really was besotted with Dawn and would do anything to assist her in keeping her granddaughter.

Jack understood, too, that the balance of power had shifted. He could do what he was itching to do and thrash his opponent, thus making matters worse for Dawn and Lily while they remained beneath the vicar's roof. Or he could control his temper and bide his time in the hope of exacting revenge in the future. He knew in his heart there was just one option open to him.

Dawn's small fingers encircled his muscular forearm and she urged Jack towards the door, blinking back her tears. He raised a hand to warm her small cold fingers in a comforting caress. She wouldn't leave the child behind whatever he said. And oddly he didn't want her to. Her goodness and selflessness just made her more adorable.

'Come to the Grange tomorrow afternoon for tea as planned. We will talk then.'

'How nice…' Peter said brightly, having heard their quiet discourse. 'An invitation to tea. I shall look forward to it. We can discuss those matters you have for me, my lord. And I believe I have thought of some requests to make also.'

Jack sent a look of loathing over a shoulder. 'Indeed…do come, Mansfield. I have much to say to you.' With a last lingering look Dawn's way, he strode into the corridor.

Dawn wanted to leave the room as well, but she didn't. She had something to impress on Peter Mansfield. And she launched into it immediately. 'You may threaten what you will, but I shall never agree to marry you. If you find another woman willing to be your wife, I will step aside and allow Lily's stepmother to care for her.'

'Marriage is not necessary between us any more than it is necessary between you and your Viscount.' Peter had dropped any sham of courtesy now the man he wanted to impress had gone. He stalked around her rigidly held figure, looking her up and down. 'You are a whore, my dear, I knew that even before I read Sterling's letter. You are no better than those harlots who infest the dockside taverns, lifting their skirts for sailors.'

He touched a finger to her cheek and Dawn shrank away as though that stubby digit was poisonous. 'Don't ever think to again lay one finger on me,' she spat, her green eyes afire. 'For indeed you will regret it.' A moment later she had swept from the room, her heart beating so furiously she felt she might faint.

Chapter Sixteen

Dawn was resting fully clothed on her bed with Jack's letter spread on her pillow. She had read it so many times now that she knew the paragraphs off by heart. Yet the need to feast her eyes on his passionate words was undeniable. Picking up the parchment, she angled it towards a candle's flame, savouring it one final time before carefully folding it and slipping the paper into her pocket.

There was nothing contained in his sloping black script to indicate the nature of the calamity that had taken him back to Essex. Dawn was glad that Mansfield remained ignorant of Sarah's folly. But the knowledge that he was aware of Jack's feelings for her made Dawn feel horribly violated. The vicar now had the means to hurt Sarah Snow by revealing her future husband was in love with another woman. But at least he no longer had the letter in his possession to bandy about as proof. The Reverend Peter Mansfield was a disgrace to his profession; he could call her any name he liked, but he wouldn't cow her or make her feel ashamed. She was determined to remain strong for his daughter's sake as well as her own.

She glanced at Lily, asleep beside her in the bed. Dawn often let her granddaughter stay overnight with her if the child seemed lonely in the nursery and fretful for her mother. Earlier, she'd had supper with Lily in the parlour as was their usual routine. She never ate a formal meal in the dining room with the vicar and thankfully he no longer requested that she do so. Carefully, so as not to disturb Lily, she got up, tucking the blanket snugly about the child. The rumpus earlier had left Dawn feeling on edge, unable to concentrate. She had been looking forward to their visit to the Grange tomorrow...but Mansfield was to accompany them now, spoiling the treat. She went to the window and gazed in the direction of Jack's magnificent house. The uncurtained windows of the Grange were ablaze with twinkling light and she knew he would have had every sconce lit. He was sending her a signal to comfort and impress on her that he was close by should she need to run to him.

A sudden sound of spitting gravel outside made Dawn shrink back and conceal herself. From behind an edge of brocade she glimpsed the pony and cart turning into the drive. A figure dressed in a billowing black cassock jumped down and Mansfield hurried towards the entrance. Dawn felt a modicum of relief that he would soon be off out again. If he were home for the evening, he would have stabled the animal.

Taking a seat at the dressing table, she began to unpin her hair. She was untangling the thick chestnut tresses with her brush when a floorboard creaked on the landing, bringing her swiftly to her feet. She put down her brush and sped noiselessly to the door. The timbers squeaked again, then she saw the handle slowly turning. She had already locked her door, leaving the key in the hole to thwart Peter entering with his own key. Nevertheless, she glided to the dressing table and picked up the heavy candlestick just in case he attempted to force entry to assault her. If he did, she'd have no compunction in swinging the brass at him with all her might. The memory of the lust in his eyes when he'd looked her over in his study was making her feel queasy.

Dawn was sure she could hear his heavy breathing, or was that just her blood hissing through her veins and thudding in her ears? Minutes ticked by like hours as she strained to listen for a sign of him withdrawing. But there was nothing other than Lily's faint snores and sighs to disturb the quiet. Dawn realised he'd gone from the house when the pony whinnied softly. She put down her makeshift weapon and stepped to the window, keeping herself out of sight. The vicar was fastening a lantern to the side of the dog cart, then he climbed aboard and turned the vehicle on crunching gravel. The pony picked up speed along the lane, the lamp swinging to shed a dappling glow on the dark hedgerow.

Her pent-up breath was slowly exhaled, but her relief was short-lived. She'd glimpsed something else that was alarming her. Another figure, on horseback this time, had hove into view. He was approaching so slowly that Dawn guessed it wasn't his intention to catch up with the vicar, still visible in the distance. It wasn't Jack; Dawn knew that straight away and felt a stab of disappointment. How she longed to see him! This man's frame wasn't as tall or broad. As horse and rider came to a standstill, merging with the shadows cast by the hedge, Dawn realised the fellow was taking pains to conceal himself so he might follow the cart unobserved.

As he spurred his horse forward a shaft of

weak moonlight escaped the cloud, gleaming on his leather cap brim and enlightening Dawn to his identity. She'd met William Grove just that afternoon when she'd stopped to speak to his aunt.

Mrs Grove! Dawn's hand flew to her mouth in consternation, and she spun away from the window. With the earlier commotion with Jack and the vicar, and the theft of her love letter filling her mind, she had forgotten about her meeting with the old housekeeper and the other note she had received. Both messages had come into her possession belatedly. Dawn had intended to read Eleanor's the moment she was on her own.

With a pang of guilt Dawn relit the candle, eager to right her wrong. She retrieved her pelisse from the wardrobe, laying it on the bed, then dug in the pocket. Settling down at the dressing table, she placed the parchment on the marble surface, feeling daunted about opening the precious yet eerie communication from her dead stepdaughter. But she sensed Eleanor was at her shoulder, urging her to hurry up. Dawn snapped the seal and, having unfolded the letter, started to read.

'Why… What is it, m'm?' Startled to wakefulness, Mrs Broome struggled upright on her pallet. Moments before, Dawn had quietly rapped on the door of the attic bedchamber. Receiving no answer, she had entered to gently shake the housekeeper awake.

'I'm sorry to disturb you, but I must go out, Mrs Broome,' Dawn rattled off. 'It is a matter of some gravity. Would you keep a watchful eye on Lily for me, please, until I return?'

The housekeeper scrambled to her feet, sensing danger. 'What is it, m'm? Are villains upon us?' The housekeeper knuckled sleep from her eyes. 'Is the master aware of it?'

'I… I can't explain right now. But the master mustn't know of this,' Dawn said, trying to keep her voice level. Oh, there was villainy and the master *was* aware of it! The Reverend Peter Mansfield was the greatest villain of them all. But Dawn knew she must keep what she knew about him from the housekeeper. The truth might make the woman swoon or fall into hysterics and Dawn desperately needed her to stay calm. 'The vicar has gone out, but if he returns before I do, I'm sure he will go straight to his chamber and not bother you. If you would go to my room and lock the door until I return, Lily is sound asleep in my bed.'

Mrs Broome pulled on her night rail, tying the belt. 'There's something about this place that's not right.' She gave Dawn a fierce look, gripping her arms to emphasise her point. 'Trouble's afoot. I knew that the moment the handsome Viscount turned up with murder in his eyes. And the more I get to know the vicar the less I like what I've done, coming to this place.' She shook her head sorrowfully. 'I found the kittens...drowned in the well.'

Dawn covered her horrified gasp with her fingers. The housekeeper had guessed who was responsible for that barbaric act. And so had Dawn! Mansfield had paid her back for taking his cart in a most cruel way: by hurting two defenceless creatures and also Lily who had loved playing with them.

'God bless you and take care of you out there,' Mrs Broome whispered. 'I know you wouldn't be risking the night unless something bad made you do it. You'll tell me more in time, I expect. But for now, know that you can rely on me, Mrs Fenton. No harm will come to that little one while I've breath in my body, that I promise.'

'Thank you.' Dawn gave the woman a spontaneous hug of gratitude. A moment later she was heading towards the door.

On the lower landing they quietly parted company, Dawn descending to the hallway and Mrs Broome hurrying in the direction of Dawn's bedchamber.

* * *

A flapping sound had Dawn frozen to the spot and she backed against a tree, hands searching behind for the trunk's wide girth to hide behind. She held her breath, anticipating another such warning signal reaching her ears that she was being stalked. There was silence, apart from the night-time scurrying of small creatures in the undergrowth. A rustling overhead made her snap up her face and squint at a canopy of swaying leaves. An owl hooted somewhere nearby, making her start and stuff a fist to her mouth to stifle a shriek. Then a white blur burst through its cover, swooping low and close. Dawn squeezed shut her eyes, unsure whether to giggle or groan at what had given her such a fright. An owl! She pushed herself away from the bole of the tree and started to run again. She'd dodged through another hundred yards of woodland in the direction of Croxley Grange when she spotted a bobbing light dotting yellow into the pitch of the night. Then it was joined by another and her insides knotted in trepidation. She sought more sturdy wood to dart behind as she heard leaves being trampled. No beast was responsible for that noise. A gruff masculine laugh, then another, higher pitched, and heavy twig-cracking footsteps alerted her to the fact there were at least two men approaching. But they weren't following her; they had no idea of her presence and she must keep it that way. She didn't dare contemplate what would be her fate should she be caught.

Dawn pulled her dark cloak up high about her throat, to cover the flag of her pale bodice. The men passed within yards of her, kegs slung over their shoulders, lamps in their hands. Their conversation was still indistinct...intentionally muted. She twisted herself around the scraping bark to continue watching them as they carried on their laborious way, wondering why she thought she recognised one of them. A moment later it came to her that he had been the fellow talking to Peter Mansfield at the Cockerel on the day she first travelled to Essex. It seemed such a long time ago since she'd made that journey that had ended in tragedy.

When she judged the smugglers to be far enough in the distance she stepped out from her hidey hole...primed to make a dash for it. But she was unceremoniously dragged back. A hand was fastened over her mouth before she could take a lungful of air to scream. She squirmed to liberate herself, simultaneously trying to bite her captor's muffling fingers.

A pair of strong arms yanked her back against

a muscular torso that felt familiar. A mingling scent of tobacco and musky verbena that had wafted to her nostrils also held a pleasant redolence.

'Hush…be still, sweetheart,' Jack murmured against her small ear, trailing his lips on her cheek to soothe her. 'There are more of them coming.' Lifting her feet from the ground, he took them both swiftly and silently backwards into the shadows cast by the boughs of a tree.

Dawn felt such overwhelming relief at being with him that tears started to her eyes, blurring her vision. She roughly cuffed them away. The vital, shocking news contained in her stepdaughter's letter that had caused her to brave the dark this evening, was again at the forefront of her mind. She desperately wanted to garble it all out, unburdening herself. But that difficult conversation must wait until the coast was clear. And what an unbelievable tale she had to tell!

To convey feelings she couldn't express, she simply pressed her spine trustingly against him as he imprisoned her about the waist. Had he not been so fortuitously right here she would have been seized by the smugglers about to burst into view. Jack pointed a finger to indicate where they were. She had been on her way towards that very copse when he stopped her headlong flight to the Grange.

* * *

She could hear them now: a rumble of low voices and clopping hooves. More lights became visible, a string of them this time, and marching feet heralded an imminent sighting of a caravan of free traders and beasts of burden. Jack's warm breath was on her temple a second before his lips traced a wordless reassurance that she was safe and protected. She tightened her fingers on the hands clasping her midriff. She felt quite calm now…and if the worst happened and they were discovered she would battle to protect him as she knew he would fight for her.

The flowing robes of the Reverend Peter Mansfield emerged from the trees as the vicar led his cohorts into view, holding on to his pony's bridle and steadying the large barrels slung over the animals' haunches. Just a glimpse of that hated individual had made Dawn tense and glance up wide-eyed over her shoulder at Jack.

Half-a-dozen smugglers and horses filed forth, both men and beasts laden with contraband. She wasn't surprised to see Peter in the company of criminals. He was their ringleader, she knew that about him from Eleanor's letter, and much more besides.

Although it seemed that hours passed while they stood like statues, in just five minutes the convoy had gone and the only sound was the music made by nocturnal creatures bringing the woodland back to life. Momentarily Dawn felt webbed in serenity, resting in Jack's embrace with the darkness enveloping them. He, too, felt the entrancement and didn't immediately turn her to face him but rocked her gently in his arms as though to apologise in advance for the scolding he was about to deliver.

'You little fool! Had you been caught spying on that motley crew, Dawn…' He abruptly swung away from her, thrusting his fingers through his hair, unable to describe her likely treatment at the hands of those miscreants. He knew only too well what young women endured at the hands of their captors. Yet Sarah was happy again and Jack couldn't claim credit for making her so. But he knew who he had to thank for doing it. He turned back to face Dawn, attempting to control his anguish as he said, 'What in God's name were you thinking of, risking your life like this?'

'You're risking your life, too!' Dawn retorted. 'After what you went through in Tangier I would've thought you'd learned your lesson about tangling with cut-throats.' She was genuinely concerned for his safety…but it seemed he wasn't.

A flash of white teeth in his dark visage, and a grunt, told her he'd given a soundless laugh. The brace of duck's-foot pistols he'd got from his pockets, ready to defend them, were slipped back whence they came. 'A run-in with villagers dabbling in free trading isn't the same as battling professional brigands, Dawn.' He touched her face in thanks for her concern. 'You've no need to worry about me, I promise. That incarceration, and the months that followed tracking those barbarians, taught me a lot about how to toughen up and survive. I'll never again be the easy fellow I once was.'

'I know,' Dawn murmured. And indeed she did know that Jack Valance, the man she had fallen in love with years ago, no longer existed. The guns he'd handled with casual skilfulness had seemed to form an extension to his swift hands. The looks she'd slanted up at intervals at him had shown her a perilous glitter in his eyes. Oh, he knew how to survive and to kill, she suspected. And yet…sometimes she caught glimpses of the old Jack when he was kind to Lily or she caught him watching her with an expression that sent her spinning back through the years. And there was no doubt that this hardened Viscount appealed to her, too. Far too much when he had a fiancée waiting for him at home.

Thinking of Sarah always stabbed a pain beneath her ribs, making her feel horribly guilty for sinking to jealousy. Yet she found it hard to control. She moved away from him, with a quiet warning. 'Don't underestimate the vicar's wickedness. I've found out he is a devil.'

'Has another calamity taken place at the vicarage?' Jack approached her, drawing her closer as he saw a sparkle of tears on her lashes.

'Yes… No…not in the way you mean,' Dawn badly explained. 'I've left Lily with the housekeeper and was on my way to Croxley Grange to find you. I fear Lily is in danger. I must take her away from there, Jack.' She gazed at him, her eyes large and frightened. 'I'm sorry to draw you into this again, but I need your help.'

'You can have it. Anything you need you only have to ask.' He paused, then admitted, 'I wasn't out tonight stalking smugglers. I was on my way to speak to you.' He cupped her face in his hands, turning it up to his. 'I intended climbing up to your bedchamber window and making plans for you to escape that damnable man once and for all. If I'd known he was from home, I would have brought a carriage to get you quickly out of the house tonight. He'll accompany you tomorrow and eavesdrop on everything we say.'

'Indeed, he does do that,' Dawn admitted on a

sigh. 'He even spies on me talking to the house-keeper.'

'I want you and Lily to stay at my house as my guests and damn the consequences. I'll deal with him. Let him sue for the return of his daughter; I'll put the best barrister in the land on to him. Mansfield isn't fit to rear a dog.'

'Indeed, he isn't!' Dawn agreed vehemently.

'He and his gang are responsible for the deaths of Revenue men shot on the beaches. Once evidence is gathered and a case is made against him, he will face gaol if he doesn't swing. Until that happens you and Lily must stay away from him.'

'I didn't know he'd killed Revenue men as well!' Dawn covered her mouth with a shaky hand, feeling overwhelmed with fear for Lily. 'He is indeed a murderer and I have the proof of it. Oh… I must quickly go back to my grand-daughter in case that monster returns and finds me gone. She isn't safe with him. He hates her. I know he does.' She tried to pull free of Jack's arms to run back the way she'd come, but he restrained her, giving her a little shake to calm her.

'Hush…he won't harm his daughter.'

'She's not his daughter.' Dawn gazed up wild-eyed at Jack. 'That's what I was coming to tell you. Lily's father was a man called Ben

Grove, the nephew of the retired housekeeper. Peter Mansfield found out about Eleanor's lover and killed him in a jealous rage. He *knows* that Lily isn't his child, but has maintained the sham rather than be known as a cuckold and a criminal.'

Jack's dismay on learning that was limited to a blasphemy ejected through his teeth. He knew that without a bond of blood as meagre protection, the child would indeed be in peril from such a brute. 'Are you quite certain?' he asked calmly. Who has told you all of this?'

'Eleanor. She concealed a letter addressed to me in her room. After her death it was discovered by the housekeeper. I thank the lord her message eventually got to me.' Dawn quickly recounted her meeting with Mrs Grove earlier that day. 'I'm sure Mrs Grove is unaware Lily is kin of hers. Perhaps she has had her suspicions over the years while working at the vicarage. But she is a God-fearing woman and was dedicated to serving Eleanor. She told me months ago when Eleanor was still alive that her mistress was unhappy and that the vicar was the cause of that unhappiness. I didn't give the matter enough thought at the time.' Dawn gave a regretful shake of the head.

'If Ben Grove's murder is proven the vicar

will face a noose, and his vestments won't save him. I've heard of Ben Grove. He ran his own smuggling ring in Kent. He has a brother named William.'

Dawn was about to say that she'd met William earlier that day and not only that, he'd been loitering outside the vicarage not two hours since. But she didn't get the chance. Jack took her hand and urged her in the direction of the vicarage.

'Come… With any luck we will beat the fiend back and get Lily away from there. Mansfield and his tub men will be busy at the churchyard secreting their booty for many hours yet.'

Dawn skipped to keep up with his long stride and when he broke into a trot she jerked her hand free of his to gather her hampering skirts from her feet. Gamely she kept pace with him though she knew he limited his speed to accommodate her. By the time the looming outline of the vicarage was visible her lungs were burning and she was glad she'd kept quiet and conserved her energy for the race to rescue Lily before the vicar returned home.

Chapter Seventeen

The Reverend Peter Mansfield's nocturnal business had kept him out until just before first light and thus he had risen later than usual. On entering the dining room to have his breakfast, he had been enraged and astonished in equal part to hear from Mrs Broome that, notwithstanding her presence, he was alone in the vicarage. At first he'd believed that the woman must be raving and had barked that at her. But his housekeeper wasn't a meek mouse like her predecessor. Planting her hands on her hips, she had insisted that Mrs Fenton and her granddaughter had gone with Lord Sterling before midnight and she'd not been told when they would return.

Having stomped up the stairs to satisfy himself it was a fallacy, he instead found that his housekeeper had spoken the truth. The nursery and bedchamber were empty but for the clothes that had been left behind. He'd found it hard to believe that Viscount Sterling would risk a charge of abducting the child with his paramour, therefore had reached the conclusion that the man had intended to return his doxy to her own bed, but had got delayed in the matter.

Forgoing his kippers, Peter had immediately set out for Croxley Grange to discover what in damnation was going on. To his surprise, he hadn't been fobbed off with excuses, but had been granted an immediate audience.

For some ten minutes now he had been kicking his heels amid ancient tomes soaring ceilingwards behind leaded glass. Peter darted bitter glances hither and thither; undeniable proof surrounded him of his opponent's wealth and exalted status. The library's heavy oak furniture and hide upholstery was of the finest quality, the rug carpeting the polished boards butter soft beneath his restless feet. Contrarily, Peter was exasperated that he was unable to fully appreciate this opulence now the meeting with His Lordship must take place under a cloud. He heard the door being opened and ceased prowling to adopt a pained expression and a puffed-out chest.

'I'm sorry to call so early, my lord,' Peter began saying in a tone of weary stoicism as the master of the house strolled in his direction. 'But I have been given some alarming news by my housekeeper. I believe that my daughter has been brought here without my permission. I have come to collect her and take her home.' While delivering his grievance, Peter had eyed the distinguished-looking fellow from silvery fair head to expensively shod foot, greatly resenting his rival for being such a damnably fine figure of a man.

Jack moved a languid hand. 'I've been expecting you, Mansfield.'

Peter had hoped for an immediate apology. But Sterling didn't look or sound sorry, or guilty. Yet the man obviously knew what he'd done was wrong or he wouldn't have acted under cover of darkness. 'I know that you and Mrs Fenton have a liking for one another and how you go on is your own business.' Peter paused to curl a scornful lip. 'But the child is my concern and that woman had no right removing her from her bed at dead of night in order that you and she might...' The obscenity was swallowed before it could roll off his tongue. 'Enjoy one another's company,' he finished stiffly.

'We do and I'm glad you understand that,' Jack replied smoothly though this pantomime of manners was making his guts roil. What he really wanted to do was beat the wretch to the ground for his devilry. But Jack knew he couldn't start a fight when so much was at stake. And he wouldn't, although he'd felt sick to his stomach on reading Eleanor Mansfield's letter. Dawn had produced it rather than relate its heart-rending contents in full. By the time he handed it back Jack was thanking his lucky stars that he hadn't delayed putting into action his plan to bring Dawn and her granddaughter to Croxley Grange. He had encountered many wicked people in his life, but he found it particularly despicable that Mansfield had sunk to concealing his depravity behind the respectable façade of his marriage and his church.

'Understand this, too, Mansfield,' he said. 'Mrs Fenton and her granddaughter are my house guests for the foreseeable future. And as that is all you need to know at present, I see no reason to detain you.' Jack thrust his hands into his pockets to prevent using them to drag the vicar out of his house by the scruff of the neck.

Peter put a finger to his lips, frowning contemplatively. It suited him to retain this man's patronage and for that he must appear docile... until the time was right to get even. He could curb his wrath at having been summarily dismissed as though he were the butcher's boy. But something else was incensing him that was harder to control. Peter was certain that the Viscount had not long since risen from a warm bed, with Dawn in it, and that was stoking his jealousy. He was berating himself for not having kicked down her door and tumbled her himself. A hint that he'd been first between her thighs last night would have wiped the arrogance from her lover's handsome features. He could see Sterling was impatient for him to leave; his tall figure was stationed close to the door as though in readiness to show him out.

'Mrs Fenton may reside wherever she wishes, but the child will return to the vicarage with me.' Peter peered earnestly over a steeple of his fingers. 'Beg pardon, but before I take the girl home, my lord, I should like to speak to Mrs Fenton. We have unfinished business to conduct.' He still hoped to coerce Dawn to marry him and he knew to do that he needed his late wife's bastard in his custody. Dawn would do anything to keep the child with her...even give up this illustrious fellow.

'She can't presently see you. If you have a message, I'll relay it.'

'I'm afraid what I have to say is of a personal nature, my lord. I really must see her and the child this instant.' Peter crossed his arms over his chest. 'I don't mind waiting while Mrs

Fenton makes herself presentable.' His mouth twitched slyly.

'I thought I made myself clear. Mrs Fenton has no desire to speak to you and her granddaughter is asleep. If you wish to write a note, you may do so and I will deliver it.' Jack opened a drawer in the table and withdrew paper. He skimmed that, and the inkstand, over the leather table top, gesturing at them.

Outside the library door, Dawn frowned and put her ear closer to the timber panel. The sudden silence within was as worrying to her as had been the preceding hostile conversation. Her fingers began creeping towards the doorknob, but she withdrew them. She had promised to wait for Jack to return and relate the gist of his conversation with the vicar. He would be expecting to find her where he had left her: at breakfast. When the butler had entered the dining room to announce their foe's arrival, Dawn had shot up from the table and offered to speak to him. Jack had sensibly argued that he was more likely to rid them of Mansfield without a fuss. But a need to know what was happening had got the better of her. A few minutes after he'd quit the dining room she had been unable to stop herself following him.

A little after sunrise Jack had slipped a message beneath her door, requesting they talk downstairs. Comfortable as the bed had been she hadn't slept and had felt certain that he hadn't got any rest either to be up so early. They had a daunting task in front of them and needed private time to discuss how to bring Mansfield to justice.

Though hungry, Dawn had been too preoccupied to do more than move scrambled eggs on her plate and nibble at toast. Jack had done justice to the savoury assortment laid out before him on a chalk-white cloth. As she'd watched him eating heartily, her mind had travelled back to that snowy sojourn at the inn, cherishing it again as a good time even though it seemed so long ago and had been the start of the troubles enmeshing them.

Much had happened yesterday between taking the dog cart to town and ending the day sleeping in a silk-sheeted four-poster bed. On their return to the vicarage to collect Lily Mrs Broome had assured them the master hadn't been back. Lily had unprotestingly got dressed in warm clothes, then let Jack carry her out into the darkness. From the start she'd seemed to enjoy the adventure and had obeyed her grandma's whispers to be still and quiet in this game they were playing. During her second trek through the woods

Dawn had constantly squinted into shadows to locate lurking dangers. Though on high alert, she had felt quite safe, her hand snug in Jack's as they headed for the sanctuary of his house.

Lily was still sound asleep, in the care of a maid charged to let Mrs Fenton know the moment the child stirred. Apparently Sarah's routine was to take her hot chocolate in bed and emerge from her chamber just before noon. Jack had wryly added that she would be surprised and delighted to see they had turned up in good time for their picnic.

The quiet from within the library stretched, making Dawn anxious as to what was going on. They needed Mansfield to go away and give Jack time to present their evidence against him to the authorities. Jack had wisely pointed out that they mustn't reveal their hand to the vicar too soon. If he suspected he was about to be arrested and exposed as a murderer, he would flee or concoct a defence. Though Dawn wished never again in her life to clap eyes on the Reverend Peter Mansfield, she didn't want him to just disappear. Peace would only be secured when he was apprehended and there was no chance of him returning to wreak revenge on them.

The sound of conversation broke into Dawn's frantic reflections and she ceased her fidgeting to press closer to the door. She had condemned the vicar for eavesdropping, yet she didn't feel guilty employing the same underhand tactic.

'I really must insist on taking my child home, my lord. Please inform Mrs Fenton of my intention… I'm sure she will wish to accompany me.' Peter had been mulling matters over in his mind while pretending to compose a note. His intuition that trouble was afoot had strengthened. He had successfully masterminded a smuggling ring for more than a decade and could smell when something wasn't right. Before he quit this place he was determined to discover what it was. He crumpled the parchment and dropped it into his pocket. It was time to use his ace. 'Mrs Fenton is to become a proper mother to my daughter in name and deed. It is a convenient arrangement that will not intrude on our lives. But we shall marry and I am surprised that you, her particular friend, seem unaware of it. Or perhaps you do know, but are confident it will make no difference to your…closeness to her. Indeed, I would not put an end to it, never fear.' Peter tossed that in, hoping to please the fellow.

'You're lying—Mrs Fenton would never agree to be your wife under any circumstances,' Jack snarled. 'Now, I've had enough of asking you nicely to quit my house.' He took a threatening step in Mansfield's direction, sending the man scuttling behind the library table.

Jack resented that worming doubt that was at the back of his mind, niggling away. But the more he tried to shut it out, the deeper it burrowed. Dawn saw herself as Lily's mother, the vicar was right in that. Why hadn't she told him of Mansfield's proposal? Had she been considering accepting it before reading Eleanor's letter and discovering the man was steeped in devilry and corruption? Had she felt cornered into marrying for duty, as he had?

But Jack knew he couldn't go ahead with his wedding. No matter what solemn death bed vows had been made, there was no honour in having a barren shell of a marriage and a wife he would only ever fondly consider to be his ward. Somehow promises would have to be picked apart and rearranged in a proper order. And he had a feeling that his fiancée might be as relieved as he was to be released from the shackles her father had wound about them both when liberating them from their Arab captors.

'Bring Mrs Fenton here and ask her if you do not believe me,' Peter blustered, continuing to retreat from the athletic man stalking him. 'Just yesterday we discussed her becoming Mrs Mansfield and a proper mother to the child.'

'How dare you imply that I agreed to be your wife!' Outraged at Peter's claims, Dawn could no longer stay outside, holding her tongue. 'Only a fraction of what you have just said is true and you know it.' She sent an appealing glance at Jack, hoping her vivid green gaze would speak for her. She would have told him about it, given more time. Since Mansfield's proposal her concentration and energy had been taken up with safeguarding Lily. The proposal had been nothing to her. It still seemed of little significance. But she could tell that the troublemaker intended to exploit the smidgeon of truth in his report to drive a wedge between them. And a spark of some raw emotion was blackening Jack's eyes.

Mansfield intercepted the intense look passing between the couple and gleefully rubbed salt into the wound. 'It should be *I* withdrawing from our arrangement, madam, considering the circumstances in which I find you. A ménage à trois with the Viscount and his future wife might suit you, but I have decided it doesn't suit my daughter. I will not allow the child's mind to be infected with such blatant immorality.'

Jack gave a sardonic grunt of laughter. 'And this from the vicar who frequents bawdy houses.'

Peter pursed his lips and loosened his collar from his ruddy throat. 'You are little better than a harlot and the child requires better. My daughter will be sent to Scotland. My aunt was a governess and knows how to handle children.'

'She's not your daughter and God only knows I'm glad of that! Better born out of wedlock than be the devil's spawn!' The moment she let fly with that Dawn realised she had been stupidly reckless, allowing herself to be goaded by threats and insults. She had disclosed far too much…and from Peter's stiff, white features she realised her knowledge of the truth had indeed shocked him. Then a crafty gleam entered his eyes.

'What madness is this?' He licked his lips, his eyes darting from one to the other of them as he started to sidle towards the door.

'You heard what was said, Mansfield. And you know it to be true, don't you?' Jack approached him, grabbing his shoulder and tightening his grip when the vicar would have wrenched free.

'You've no proof of anything of the sort,' Mansfield hissed. 'And whoever has been spreading such wicked lies will be punished.' He glowered up at Jack from his inferior height. 'Unhand me, sir and let me pass this instant.' Peter knew he needed to instantly escape to lick his wounds while deciding what to do next. The game might not yet be up—only Eleanor and her lover could damn him with the truth and they couldn't bear witness and betray him now. But any further hope of extracting cash from Sterling—ostensibly as donations to the church, but to be diverted to Peter's illegal enterprise—had come to nought. His Lordship was no ally and there was no profit to be had in continuing to bow and scrape to him. 'Unhand me, I say,' Peter shrilled as his struggles to free himself failed. 'I will fetch the magistrate and have you arrested for what you have done!'

Jack snorted a grim laugh. 'Strange…you have taken words from my mouth, Mansfield.' He didn't elaborate and sent Dawn a look.

Dawn understood the caution. She still felt horribly foolish and guilty at having let the cat out of the bag.

Jack shoved the vicar away from him. 'Remove yourself from my house, or I will have you ejected.'

'Indeed, I shall, sir.' Peter had stumbled against the library table, but brushed himself down in a display of righteous outrage. 'You have not heard the last of this. I will discover who has spread such lies about me and indeed they shall regret it. As will you when I return with the authorities to take my daughter home.'

Jack followed him out into the hallway, dogging his footsteps towards the great oaken doors.

He gestured his butler away as the man sprang to open up. Jack did so himself, though he restrained himself from hurrying the vicar down the steps with the toe of his boot.

Dawn had been pacing, agitatedly waiting for his return, and the moment the door opened she sped to him, plunging her arms about his waist. 'I'm so sorry, Jack,' she keened. 'I know I shouldn't have said what I did. But I was so angry...'

'Hush. Never mind. It would have come out sooner or later. I almost lost my temper with him and knocked him down. That would have aroused his suspicions as well,' he ruefully admitted. 'Nothing is yet lost. He looked guilty as hell, but he believes we have no proof and as long as we let him think that...' He tailed off and dried her damp cheeks with sweeps of his thumbs. 'Now there's no time to lose. I must take that proof we have to the magistrate and get Mansfield behind bars before he bolts for cover.'

Dawn withdrew Eleanor's letter from her pocket and gladly handed it over. 'I honestly did not accept his proposal,' she said, looking up with tear-bright green eyes. 'And not for one minute did I have any intention of doing so.'

'I know. But why didn't you tell me about it?'

'I... So much was going on...and telling you

he asked me to marry him didn't seem important.' Dawn knew that it sounded like a poor excuse and she could tell from his tight expression that Jack thought so, too.

'It would've been important to me,' Jack said quietly, pocketing Eleanor's letter. 'Before I set off for town I'll make sure all the men on the estate are instructed to block Mansfield's entry should he come back in my absence. You will be quite safe. But stay in the house, out of sight.'

Chapter Eighteen

'I know you are older than I am, but I think we might get on well, Mrs Fenton. So may I talk to you as though you were my friend?'

'Yes, of course, if you would like to.' With a last lingering look at the empty horizon, Dawn came away from the rain-spattered window and sat down on the velvet sofa beside Sarah.

They were ensconced with Lily in a spacious parlour that overlooked the sweeping drive at the front of the house. Sarah had proudly shown her into the pink-hued room known as the rose salon. It was one of the few reception rooms that had been redecorated. A goodly part of the vast mansion was still in a bad state, but Sarah had said she was confident all the rooms would look as splendid as this one and that she would always consider the rose salon a favourite place.

Sarah had arrived downstairs accompanied by her chaperon—a rather stern-looking woman. Sarah had been delighted to see she had guests and had sent the chaperon away, giving the woman the rest of the day to herself. Then Sarah had taken pains to ensure that her guests were comfortable and had all they wanted in the way of refreshment. She had directed the hovering servants to bring more tea and food earlier, impressing Dawn with her quiet authority. Sarah might never be a true wife to Jack, but she had qualities to make a husband proud of her. She looked the part of a budding society lady, too, dressed in an elegant morning gown of sprigged muslin with her Titian locks stylishly curled. By comparison Dawn felt rather dowdy in her plain cotton dress with her thick brunette hair swept into a simple chignon.

Last night she and Lily had retired soon after arriving at the Grange. Jack had sent a maid to attend to their needs. Nightclothes had been laid out for them and warm lavender-scented washing water provided. Lily had become overexcited, preventing Dawn from carrying on poring over matters with Jack. She had known that further conversation must wait until morning. Softly she had crooned lullabies to her granddaughter until eventually Lily had settled down to sleep. And so had Dawn, although her own rest had been fitful during the few hours remaining until daybreak.

The moment she'd heard the sound of paper scratching against her bedroom floorboards she'd risen, thankful to abandon further hope of sleep. Dressing without assistance didn't bother her. She was used to having few servants around her: her late husband had been a man of modest means and when still beneath her spendthrift father's roof his circumstances had rarely allowed her the luxury of her own maid.

Dawn had speedily pulled on her crumpled clothes, then sped downstairs. She had wished Jack didn't look quite so dapper when she saw him stationed in the hallway, waiting for her. Wounded vanity had soon been forgotten the moment she'd been manoeuvred into an alcove, out of sight of the footmen, to be given a lingering good-morning kiss.

At some time she would have to return to collect their belongings from the vicarage...then hopefully onward to London with Lily safe at her side. But before any of that could take place she needed confirmation that the Reverend Peter Mansfield was under lock and key.

Quite fortuitously the day had come on to rain so no explanations had been needed as to why they couldn't picnic in the gardens as planned.

Dawn was glad she'd not had to frighten her young hostess with the news that a dangerous fellow might be lurking in the grounds. Dawn had been keeping a vigil for the vicar as well as for Jack's return while gazing into a dreary vista. She was optimistic that Mansfield wouldn't return and, if he did, he'd never get past the patrolling manservants. Of course, Peter had cohorts to call on if he was determined to come with a mob to seek revenge. But that wouldn't be yet; he wouldn't reveal his true colours until the final scene was played out.

As it wasn't possible to have an al fresco lunch, a spread of cakes and sweet and savoury pastries had been laid out on a sideboard so they could enjoy an indoor feast. Also within easy reach were board games and playing cards should they fancy indulging in those pastimes.

Sarah had produced some tin soldiers when Lily told her that her friend Bernard had a set and she'd liked playing with them. The toys had belonged to her late father, Sarah had explained, and were a precious memento of him. She had ranged the redcoats on the floor and had kindly joined in a game with Lily before leaving the child to play alone. Now Lily, too, had grown bored. Sated with cake and lemonade, the child had curled up on a sofa with a thumb in her mouth and her eyelids fluttering low.

'I'm quite worried about telling anybody my secret…' Sarah had spoken following a lengthy, contemplative quiet. 'It will come as a great surprise, but it isn't fair to put it off any longer. So I suppose I must speak out.'

'I can be trusted with secrets.' Dawn gave the younger woman her full attention, feeling rather rude to have been absorbed in inner wrangling when Sarah obviously wanted to get something off her chest. She gave her companion's fingers a little squeeze. But her eyes were once more with the view beyond the casement, her ears straining for a sound of hooves on gravel, heralding Jack's return. Hours had passed since he'd gone on horseback to speak to the magistrate. What was keeping him? Had Mansfield and his gang ambushed him…attacked him?

Dawn calmed herself down. Her imagination was running riot; she must simply be patient. Jack and the magistrate might be closeted for many hours, deciding what to do about Mansfield's various crimes.

'*I* can be trusted with secrets, too.' Sarah gave an impish smile. 'If you tell me something, then I will feel it only fair to confide in you in return. So what I would know from you, Mrs Fenton, is: why did you come here with Jack on foot through the woods and stay overnight?'

'Did Lily say that she slept upstairs?' Dawn had hoped no explanation on their early arrival would be needed as Sarah had risen late.

'She told me Jack carried her here and you all played a game hiding in the dark.' Sarah frowned. 'But I doubt it was a game, was it?'

'No...it wasn't a game,' Dawn replied honestly. 'I had noticed somebody loitering suspiciously outside the vicarage. I wasn't sure if he was up to no good and felt rather uneasy.' She paused to think carefully how to word the rest. If she stirred Sarah's interest too deeply in the matter, she'd face a barrage of questions. 'The vicar had gone out for the evening, but luckily Jack turned up. We agreed it would be sensible to go to Croxley Grange rather than stay at the vicarage...just to put our minds at rest.' Thankfully Dawn hadn't needed to reveal too much and neither had she lied.

'The fellow you saw might have been a smuggler.' Sarah sounded matter of fact.

'Who told you about those people?' Dawn was sure Jack wouldn't have brought the subject up.

'A good friend of mine told me all about the free trading that goes on in these parts.' Sarah chuckled. 'There... I have started revealing a little bit of my secret.' She cocked her head. 'You like Jack, don't you, Mrs Fenton, and so does Lily. She told me so.'

'Yes... I like him very much. He is a good man, I think.'

'Oh, he is!' Sarah readily agreed. 'My father said he was the finest fellow he ever knew. Papa only trusted Jack to care for me when he was no longer able to.'

Dawn wasn't sure whether to stop Sarah revealing more, or to beg the girl to tell her everything. Jack might not like her prying into his life behind his back, but there was so much she yearned to know about those missing years spent battling with mercenaries—both friend and foe. And she wanted to know about Jack's relationship with Sarah. They had spent years in each other's orbit and Dawn envied the girl the time she'd had with Jack...time that should have been hers.

Sarah suddenly launched into, 'The secret I have to tell you is that, though I adore Jack, I intend to break off my engagement.' She frowned. 'It makes me sound flighty. But I'm not. I never really wanted to marry him; I was being a dutiful daughter when I went along with it. You see, my papa rescued me from pirates and was mortally injured in the doing of it. It was my fault he died.' She sniffed back tears. 'I'd been disobedient, going to the seashore when he'd told me to stay indoors in case the brigands raided the coast. They did that day and it was the worse for us both.'

'Hush…' Dawn put a comforting arm about the girl's slumped shoulders. 'Jack told me all about it. Please don't say any more and upset yourself.' Though she spoke gently, she felt stunned by what she'd heard. Was Jack *not* to be married after all?

'Please let me talk about it,' Sarah piped up. 'I need to; Jack always avoids the subject, thinking bad memories will make me ill. But the pain won't go away if I bottle it up.'

Dawn could only agree with that brave logic.

'Papa fretted over who would care for me in the future when he knew he was dying,' Sarah resumed her tale. 'He got quite a bee in his bonnet and Jack and I just wanted to calm him down so he could pass away peacefully. My father put us both under a dreadful obligation, but especially Jack, asking the poor man to sign the marriage contract in his own blood. A blood pact! So medieval.' Sarah tutted and rolled her eyes. 'I haven't told Jack yet that I can't marry him. But when he comes home, I shall.' Sarah sat back, folding her arms over her middle. 'I've fallen in love, you see. Jack knows about William Grove. He thinks we are just friends, but I want to marry him.'

'I met William yesterday when in town,' Dawn said. 'I know his aunt as she used to work at the vicarage. I thought he seemed nice.' Dawn had reeled that off as Sarah fell quiet. Indeed, she had thought William a polite young fellow and his aunt had had good things to say about him. But what on earth would Jack's opinion be of Sarah's bombshell news that she intended to jilt him to wed a sailor?

'You liked him…really?' Sarah demanded in an animated way, then clapped her hands at Dawn's nod. 'You must tell Jack you like William. He will listen to you as you are good friends. At first Jack tried to stop me seeing William, but I said I'd never forgive him if he did.' She frowned. 'He wants to protect me, but I won't be wrapped in cotton wool or spied on by nursemaids. I like my freedom and when they won't let me have it I give them the slip. She grinned cheekily. 'I use the small side door in the back hall to go outside. One of the footmen meets his sweetheart by the stables and slips out that way, too, I've seen him. He keeps a key hidden under the vase.'

Dawn didn't know what to say. She didn't

want Jack to think she'd had a hand in persuading his fiancée to jilt him. Before she could consider an appropriate reply Sarah carried on blithely.

'I know it will be a relief to Jack when I set him free. I know he'd sooner be a bachelor again. But he is an honourable gentleman and will find it difficult to go back on his word to my father, so he might object.'

'I expect he will understand... He wouldn't want to make you unhappy,' Dawn murmured the first platitude that came into her head. A burgeoning joy was swelling in her chest...a glimmer of hope that she and Jack might soon be a proper couple and not need to hide how they felt about one another.

'Jack is very kind and generous to me and very handsome. I just don't like him in the way a wife should like a husband in order to have children. He is nearly as old as my papa.' Sarah sighed. 'I'm glad he will have somebody as kind as you to turn to when I jilt him. Actually, as you're a widow, I hope he marries you instead of her. You're much nicer than *she* is,' Sarah whispered conspiratorially, 'He thinks I don't know he has a special friend. He takes Pauline to the opera and the theatre. When *I'm* with him, though, she's lucky to receive a nod in passing if we bump into her. Oh, I didn't mean to make you blush.' Sarah looked apologetic. 'I thought you'd be aware of Jack's popularity with the ladies.' She sighed. '*I'm* not very ladylike, am I, talking about such things?'

Dawn felt as though she'd been dealt a physical blow. But she managed a mild reply. 'I think you're a nice young lady, Sarah. And I'm glad you like me best out of Jack's friends.' She got up and approached the sideboard to look at the food while composing herself.

All the recent dramas that she and Jack had battled together, and the closeness they'd shared while protecting and nurturing Lily, had made her forget about Jack's mistress. Just because *she'd* forgotten about her didn't mean that Jack had. Was Pauline the blonde woman he'd been with on Regent Street? Or had he an attachment to another woman as well? Dawn knew he regretted as bitterly as she did that they had not married years ago. But that was then. What of now?

She had taken for granted that *she* was the only love in his life...the one woman he would choose to be his wife. He'd told her he wanted her and that she had his heart, but he had never actually said that he still wished to marry her.

Sarah came up behind Dawn and gave her a

hug. 'I'm so glad you've met William. I know he must like you as much as I do.'

'Does he feel the same way about you and want to marry you?' Dawn asked, pinning a smile to her lips as she turned about.

'Oh, yes.' Sarah's eyes sparkled as she dwelled on her beau. 'William told me I'm the most beautiful girl he's ever met. He told me so again after I admitted that bad things had happened to me in Tangier. He said that made no difference to how he felt about me, but he would sail to Tangier in his boat and kill every pirate he found.' Sarah giggled and flipped a hand. 'I told him there was no need to as they'd all gone now. He believes I deserve to be rich and well cared for as a viscountess, though my wedding will break his heart.' Sarah's eyes held a fiercely possessive glint when she added, 'But I shan't let another girl mend his heart. *I* want him and we *shall* get married.' Sarah sounded stubborn. She skipped to the window, gazing out. 'Sometimes he comes and stops in the field over there just to catch a glimpse of me.' She gazed up at the drizzle. 'I don't suppose he'll come today, though.'

Dawn joined Sarah at the window. A short while ago she'd stood here and yearned for Jack to thunder into view on his horse. Now she felt reluctant to see him until she'd worked out what to say to him. For his part, what would he say? How would he take his fiancée's rejection? Would his conscience allow him to break that blood pact with Sarah's father?

And if he did, what then? Dawn wished now she had demanded some answers about his other women. Failing to do so might have made it seem that she'd tolerate his dalliances because he'd not made any effort to hide the fact he had lady friends in his life. In fact, he'd approached her while out shopping with one of them. If they were to be together, Dawn would want him exclusively to herself. There would be no compromise on that. She was too staid… too conventional, she realised. Her modest upbringing and her convenient marriage had taught her nothing of glamour or worldliness…nothing much of the needs and wants of men either. And Jack had now moved even further away from her into an elevated social circle where wealth and pedigree often mattered more than morals did.

She loved him with every fibre of her being, yet had never properly told him so. Neither had he spoken those three vital words to her. An obstacle had always blocked their path to being a proper couple and what point would there have been in pledging love and fidelity when such promises might prove impossible to keep? Perhaps fate had been kind, not cruel, preventing her baring her soul and putting her heart and pride in jeopardy. She hadn't long to wait now to know for sure what sort of man Jack Valance was. Next week he would in all probability be free and able to make an unforced choice. So which woman, if any, would he pick to marry?

Peter Mansfield had been crouching down, removing flint from the graveyard wall, when he spied Viscount Sterling, long riding coat flying out behind him, riding hell for leather in the direction of the town. Hastily Peter shoved inside the hidey hole the message alerting his smuggler colleagues to dangers closing in on them, then rammed home the loose stones to hide the scrap of paper. It seemed he'd penned the warning not a moment too soon. He'd a nasty suspicion that Sterling was on his way to the court to tell tales. And if he were, then Dawn Fenton or the Viscount must have turned up something to use as proof against him. Leaping upright, Peter hoisted his cassock from his feet and dashed in the direction of the dog cart stationed on the lane. Scrambling aboard, he used the reins, determined to follow at a distance and discover what Sterling was up to. He hunched forward as the vehicle picked up speed, his narrowed eyes fixed on a blur of horse and rider up ahead, his mind ferreting for an explanation as to how he could have been betrayed.

Something had obviously come to light, but what the devil could it be? His wife was dead; her lover was dead. But Ben Grove's brother had come ashore, perhaps to wreak mischief. Peter had spotted William Grove on the High Street, but the fellow hadn't shown any obvious interest in him. Besides, if William had guessed, or been told by his brother, about his affair with Eleanor, it was only hearsay now the adulterers were gone. The dead couldn't speak.

As Eleanor's husband, and a pillar of the community, the Reverend Peter Mansfield would deny everything and display his outrage at the slur on his wife's memory. Still he was growing increasingly anxious. He had a cargo of contraband buried in tombs in the churchyard and another due to cross the Channel very soon. He didn't want dragoons or Revenue men snooping around at such a crucial time. With that thought nagging at him, he swung an agitated look over the countryside for pursuers, then spurred the tired old mare to a faster pace.

Once he knew what Sterling was about he'd return and gather his men together. He had a plan of his own.

Chapter Nineteen

Was the vicar under arrest? Was Jack safe? Would she soon be going home to London with her beloved granddaughter? Dawn knew if she didn't soon receive some answers to these questions, uncertainty would drive her mad.

She took another turn about the room, taking care to be quiet. She didn't want to wake the rose salon's other occupants. Sarah had curled up at the opposite end of the long sofa to where Lily was softly snoring. The patter of rain on glass and the crackle and hiss of logs in the grate were somnolent sounds and Dawn could understand how the girls had been lulled into slumber. Dawn would have liked to catch up on some sleep, too, but her restlessness had denied her a blissful snooze, ensconced in a fireside armchair.

For the umpteenth time she gazed out of the window, her eyes immediately drawn to the long empty drive stretching into the distance. The rain had stopped; a glimmer of weak sun had put a silver halo about the clouds and a glitter on the wet green grass.

Her flitting eyes returned to a thicket where she'd noticed a dark shadow beneath low branches. Her heart leapt to her mouth and she prayed that Mansfield wasn't skulking about. She squinted, making out the shape of a horse and rider. Thankfully it wasn't the vicar and she expelled a pent-up breath. She'd recognised William Grove's silhouette from his peaked cap. Perhaps realising he was under observation, he urged the horse further beneath the dripping leaves.

So…he had braved the weather and come to be close to his love. Dawn glanced over her shoulder at Sarah, her cheek pillowed on her hands as she napped. Dawn didn't know whether to wake her and let her know William was close by. She decided not to. Jack wouldn't want Sarah to go outside and, besides, she looked so content. But Dawn was far from content…

On impulse she whipped noiselessly towards the door. Once in the corridor she hurried in the direction of the exit that Sarah had told her she used when sneaking out to meet William. Dawn didn't want him to disappear before she'd had a chance to speak to him. She took the key from under the vase, unlocked the door, then closed it noiselessly behind her. She found herself standing on the gravel of a quadrangle. Swiftly she got her bearings, then set off at a trot towards the west. The puddled path soaked her shoes and her skin collected dew from the damp atmosphere as she hurried on, but she barely felt the discomfort.

William was Lily's uncle. Her granddaughter had a close blood relative…the only one left to her that Dawn was aware of. She desperately wanted to know if William was also aware of it, or if he knew how his brother had died. William had taken unusual notice of Lily when they'd met in town, as though searching for a resemblance. Now she dwelled on it, Dawn knew there *was* a family likeness. Lily's colouring and neat features were similar to her uncle's, although fortunately her mother had also been fair.

Fired by a compulsion to have some answers, Dawn put on a spurt. William had spotted her approaching and was making ready to turn the horse and leave. 'Oh, please wait, I should like to speak to you, sir. Don't go.'

He doffed his hat politely, then hesitated before dismounting and tucking the cap beneath his arm. 'Good day to you, Mrs Fenton.'

'Good day to you, sir,' she replied a trifle breathlessly after her dash.

'The rain has stopped at last,' he blurted out, obviously seeking some small talk as a prelude to escaping.

'Yes, thank goodness it has... Are you hoping to speak to Sarah this afternoon?'

His complexion, weather-beaten from seafaring, became ruddier beneath his tan. But her comment had stopped him in his tracks as she'd hoped it would. 'I... Yes, it would be nice to see her, m'm. Sometimes we chat if Miss Snow is out walking.'

'I know, she told me.' Dawn wanted to gain his trust and find out what she could, then quickly return to the house before she was missed. 'Forgive me, I know we are barely acquainted, but there is no time for niceties. Something extraordinary has come to light and I find I must speak plainly and rather indelicately. Were you aware that your brother and Eleanor Mansfield were lovers and that Lily is your niece?'

His eyes widened on her. 'Who told you that, ma'am?' he demanded in a low, husky voice.

'Eleanor,' Dawn replied bluntly. 'How did you find out?' She hadn't needed to wait for his reply; she could read his knowledge in his wary expression. Months ago Mrs Grove had told her of the miserable atmosphere at the vicarage, and hinted at dark deeds going on. Had the woman guessed her nephew had sired Lily and been murdered by the vicar? Or had she just been warning Dawn against straying outside after dark and encountering the smugglers?

In her letter Eleanor had made it clear she'd never confided in a soul about any of it, for fear they, too, might be in peril from the devil she'd married. She had wanted to flee to Ben Grove and take Lily with her, she'd written, but Mansfield had pre-empted them, killing Ben before the lovers could humiliate him. Thereafter Eleanor had been kept as a virtual prisoner in her own home, constantly anxious for her own and Lily's safety. She had been forced to submit to her husband's demands to provide an heir and had fallen pregnant. The vicar had thus lost his son through his own stupidity by refusing to call the doctor to Eleanor. A harsh justice indeed for the innocents concerned.

Dawn was determined the vicar wouldn't thwart *her* in carrying out her stepdaughter's final wish. Lily must be protected from the sadistic bully at all cost and she must pick William's brains for any small thing that might help her in the doing of it.

'Did your aunt guess the truth about the affair

during her time as housekeeper at the vicarage and tell you of her suspicions?' Dawn prompted William for an answer.

William shook his head, looking grave. 'I don't think my aunt knew about the affair or that the child was related to her. My brother lived in the next village and didn't see much of Mrs Grove. They didn't get on—she disapproved of the way he earned his living.' Sibling loyalty prevented him condemning his dead brother, although William had also wished Ben had followed another path.

'I know he was a free trader... Eleanor let on about that in her letter,' Dawn said.

'My aunt suspected the vicar of being involved in smuggling from noticing what went on around the church at night time. But she avoids speaking of any of it. Most folk round here plead ignorance if questioned by Revenue men for fear of reprisals.' William paused before admitting, 'I was close to Ben and could tell he was troubled. I nagged him until eventually he told me all of it. He predicted it would end badly with Mansfield and it did.' William rubbed his chin with his hand, looking thoughtful. 'I'm surprised that Mrs Mansfield confided in you. They took pains to keep the matter secret to protect the child from being branded a bastard. Ben would have done anything for Eleanor and their daughter. He said he'd die for them.' William frowned as though unsure whether to continue. But too much had been aired now not to conclude the sorry tale prised from his brother a short while before he was murdered. 'The vicar had discovered the affair. He'd followed Eleanor to a cottage where they'd meet and threatened my brother with a pistol before dragging his wife home. After that she vowed never to meet Ben again, but secretly they planned to run away together. Mansfield found out…he is a cunning wretch.' William's mouth tightened into a bitter line. 'He made sure she couldn't cheat on him again.'

'You suspect he murdered your brother, don't you?' Dawn whispered.

'I know he did.' William gave harsh laugh. 'The vicar recruits his colleagues from the Kent area so folk round here can't betray him or say for sure he is a criminal. But Ben knew; he ran his own gang and thus was Mansfield's business rival as well. He knew Mansfield would want him permanently out of the way to kill two birds with one stone. The villain managed to protect his reputation as a husband and a smuggling lord within the fraternity. And it seems he has got away with it.'

'He hasn't got away with it!' Dawn shook William's arm in comfort as she saw the sheen in his eyes. 'He will be punished, I promise. Viscount Sterling knows about all of this. He left hours ago to report everything we know to the magistrate and put in motion the vicar's arrest.' Dawn's eyes swerved to the drive and she willed Jack to appear. He should hear what William had to say. Lily's uncle could also bear witness against Mansfield and relate what Ben Grove had said before he was silenced.

'But without any hard proof...' William sighed disconsolately.

'I have proof.' Dawn again closed her fingers on his arm in comfort and reassurance. 'Before she died, Eleanor wrote me a letter that has only just come into my possession. It is a damning report of the vicar's crimes and of his hatred for Lily. Eleanor fretted for her daughter's safety from the moment Mansfield wrung the truth of Lily's parentage from her. I am also greatly worried for my granddaughter. The vicar is cruelly cold to her.'

'Lily's my kin and he'll not harm her.' William ejected the vow through his teeth. 'I should have killed Mansfield last night. I had the chance. I've been wanting to do it since my brother's murder. But now...' He tailed off into silence.

'I saw you outside the vicarage,' Dawn

blurted. 'I watched you following his cart from my window.'

'I had a clear shot at him… I should have taken it.'

'I'm glad you didn't,' Dawn said earnestly. 'You are all the true family Lily has left. She will love to get to know you as she grows. You mustn't risk imprisonment or worse for the likes of Mansfield.' Dawn could see his agony in his features. He was torn between avenging his brother and keeping on the straight and narrow. But she imagined that he hadn't taken that shot and had kept on the right side of the law for Sarah's sake rather than for the niece he barely knew.

'Has Sarah told you about us?' William bashfully lowered his eyes. 'I won't ever come back and bother her if that's what she wants. I'll stay away if she tells me to, I swear. I'd never do anything to hurt her.'

A sound of rapid footsteps made them both twist about to see the young lady herself trotting towards them. Sarah had her pretty skirts rather high about her calves to keep the muslin from gathering wet from the grass. She uninhibitedly launched herself at William to give him a hug.

'I'm so glad you came. I'm glad you've met my new friend. Mrs Fenton and her granddaughter have had a picnic with us today…indoors as it has been such foul weather. Now the sun is coming out we can all take a walk towards the parterre…'

William gently disengaged himself, holding her at arm's length with a look of faint embarrassment on his face. 'It's nice to see you, Sarah, but you should not be quite so familiar with me when…'

'Oh, I have told Mrs Fenton that I love you and intend to marry you,' she interjected airily. 'And when Jack gets home I shall tell him, too.'

'I must speak to him as well when you do,' William said.

'Where is Lily, Sarah?' Dawn interrupted rather shrilly, taking a few paces towards the house. She had been frantically looking to and fro while the couple talked. 'Is she still asleep?'

'No. She woke me up and wanted to find you. I spied you through the window talking to William so I brought her outside.'

'Where is she, then?' Dawn had started to swing glances to and fro, desperate for a sight of her granddaughter.

'Oh, she is quite all right. The Reverend Peter Mansfield turned up to take her home. He claimed to be her papa. Lily said he was and she took his hand when he held it out to her.'

Sarah frowned, sensing her companions' agitation. 'What is it? Have I done something wrong?'

Dawn gave an anguished cry and started to run in the direction of the house, then veered aside, flying headlong towards the avenue of trees that wound towards Croxley Grange. Jack had at last galloped into view.

'Hush…' Jack rocked Dawn in his arms in an attempt to comfort her. 'I will bring Lily back safely, I swear,' he said hoarsely. A second later his lips touched the curve of her tear-wet cheek to seal that solemn vow.

'But you just said the magistrate has already sent for the dragoons to arrest Mansfield…they might already have done so.' Dawn clutched the front of his coat in despair. 'What then has become of Lily? What has he done with her? Is she already…?' Unable to finish expressing her tormenting thoughts on her little granddaughter's fate, Dawn turned away, covering her face with her quivering fingers.

'It is too soon for the dragoons to have arrived from the garrison,' Jack soothed, turning her again to face him.

When he had first spotted Dawn outside, racing to meet him over the wet grass, he had immediately known something bad had happened.

Vaulting from his horse, he'd sprinted to meet her, barely able to understand a word of her hysterical report. Once inside the house Dawn had forced herself to calm down. A corner of her mind had retained enough sense to know that if they were to beat Mansfield at his own game they must strive to be as cool and crafty as he was.

Jack knew he must go immediately to search for the child. Time was of the essence in bringing Lily back; but where to start looking? Now Mansfield knew the game was up he'd hardly be holed up at the vicarage.

'A message, my lord. A boy from the village delivered it.' The butler had entered the room at speed. The servants had been primed for a calamity to occur from the moment their master told them to be on the alert for the vicar's unwelcome return.

Jack snatched at the note, praying he held in his hand Mansfield's terms for releasing the little girl. He'd give the fiend every penny he had if he'd just let her go. He also inwardly vowed to hound the villain across continents if that's what it took to bring him to justice. Jack's eyes raced over the single pencilled sentence.

'He has offered to exchange Lily for the letter Eleanor wrote to you.' Jack paused. 'He's found out about that, then, and doubtless wants to destroy his wife's testament. But that won't save him from a noose. The magistrate has read it and knows the catalogue of his crimes.'

'Peter doesn't know that, though!' Dawn pounced on a glimmer of hope. 'If the dragoons have not yet caught up with him, we surely have a little time to try to negotiate?'

'We do indeed…and must use it.' Jack's attention was drawn to the couple stationed in a corner of the room as a loud sob was heard. Sarah was being comforted by William. The poor girl had been distraught on learning that the man Lily believed to be her father was, in fact, a villain who might harm the child.

'I don't blame Sarah for letting the vicar take Lily.' Dawn dabbed at her bloodshot eyes. 'Nobody but us would have acted differently when he approached, demanding to take Lily home.'

'I must assist you in bringing Lily back, my lord.' The moment he noticed the Viscount's eyes on him William quit Sarah's side to approach him. He'd spoken quite forcefully and knew it wasn't the only time he'd overstepped the mark with this man. But a conversation…perhaps a bad argument…about Sarah's future would have to wait.

'Mansfield is a dangerous man and doesn't

work alone,' Jack warned William of the risks he faced in offering to pitch in.

'So am I a dangerous man when needs must and my niece is in peril,' William answered gravely. He needed no telling that the Reverend Peter Mansfield was a monster when his brother lay dead in Wivenhoe churchyard.

Jack cupped Dawn's face in his hands. 'Stay here inside the house. She'll soon be home, I promise.'

Dawn was half-aware of William watching their interaction, of a dawning intelligence entering his eyes before he diplomatically averted his gaze.

A moment later Jack was striding from the room with William at his heels. The younger man glanced at Sarah, giving her an encouraging smile. She sniffed and blew him a kiss from her trembling fingertips as he closed the door.

Dawn watched from the window, a comforting arm about Sarah as the two riders thundered off over the turf and were soon lost from sight. She closed her eyes, praying for their safety and her beloved granddaughter's, too.

'I'm so sorry, Mrs Fenton,' Sarah gasped out for the second time in a few minutes.

'None of this is your fault and you must not blame yourself. Why don't you go upstairs and rest? You will feel calmer.' Dawn steered the girl to the door. Her suggestion hadn't been wholly altruistic: Dawn wanted to be alone to deal with the muddle of emotions curdling her stomach. Once Sarah had left she eyed the black clouds gathering again overhead. The sunny interlude hadn't lasted long. But a drizzle wouldn't stop her going out. She knew she must defy Jack's edict. She couldn't simply stay where she was. The two people she cared most about in the world were in peril and she wouldn't...couldn't sit still and wait for news when every second might count in rescuing Lily.

If there was no sign of Mansfield at the vicarage and the dog cart was idle she would commandeer it and search for her granddaughter. She couldn't put from her mind that Mansfield intended to double-cross them. For speed of getaway the vicar was sure to be on horseback, or he might have gone to ground. She believed that he had concealed Lily, too. He wouldn't want to be burdened with a child while scheming with his gang on his next move. Dawn stuffed a fist to her mouth to stifle a sob at the thought of Lily, cold and frightened and alone. It was too much to bear. She bolted noiselessly to the door and was soon hurrying upstairs to collect her cloak.

Chapter Twenty

'Why… Mrs Fenton! I wasn't expecting to see you. I feared it might be *him* back again.' Mrs Grove had opened the door of her cottage and peeked nervously through an aperture. She tugged the door fully open, beckoning her wan-faced visitor inside.

'I'm sorry to bother you, but something terrible has happened.' Dawn realised there was no point in beating about the bush; when the dragoons appeared in town the scandal would spread anyway. Mrs Grove had suspected somebody unpleasant had called on her and Dawn could guess his identity. Nevertheless she asked the question.

'Yes, the vicar came here earlier,' Mrs Grove confirmed. 'And if I'd known the reason for his visit I'd not have let him in,' she added darkly.

'What did he want with you?' Dawn anticipated hearing more bad news.

'He was asking questions about his wife and
none too politely. I believed you must have told
him I'd given you that letter.' The woman regretfully shook her head. 'It was only afterwards I
realised he'd been fishing for information, but by
then it was too late. I'd told him what I'd found
among Mrs Mansfield's belongings and that I'd
given the letter to you.' Mrs Grove pulled back
a sleeve to display a bruise. 'The brute had me
by the arm the whole time.'

Dawn embraced the woman in comfort. 'I've
come to ask if you know any of that devil's secret hideaways. He has kidnapped Lily and I believe will take her to a local cottage. I pray he
won't harm her.'

'Kidnapped his own child? Harm his own
child?' Mrs Grove parroted in a daze. She sank
on to a chair, crossing herself.

'The vicar isn't Lily's father. Eleanor wrote
that letter because she wanted me to know the
truth and protect Lily from Mansfield. She told
me dreadful things about the man she'd married.'
Dawn kneeled on the rug beside Mrs Grove's
chair, looking solemnly into the woman's face.
'Lily is Ben Grove's daughter…kin of yours, too.
And the vicar found out the truth of it.'

Mrs Grove crossed herself again, falling against the chair back as though she might swoon in amazement. 'I saw Mrs Mansfield with Ben once,' she finally gabbled out. 'They were down by the stream, but I thought them just acquaintances. Ben kept his distance from me after I told him his parents would be ashamed of him. He associated with rogues. I never saw him call on Mrs Mansfield at the house while I worked there.'

Dawn pounced on a small clue she'd just been given. 'You said they were by a stream. Is there a cottage in the vicinity? Eleanor would rendezvous with your nephew at a cottage, but she didn't pinpoint its location in her letter.'

'There *is* a cottage…if you could call it such, it's such a tumbledown affair. But the garden is still nice. Mrs Mansfield said she went over that way to pick flowers. She would come back with posies of poppies and put them in vases by the windows…' she glanced at Dawn with an enlightened expression '…a signal to Ben, I expect.'

'Where is this cottage?' Dawn asked excitedly.

'You'd need to head towards the windmill, then take the lane that leads to the farmhouse.

It was a fine thatched dwelling in its time, but a fire destroyed half of it.'

'I know it.' Dawn sprang to her feet. She had seen that building with blackened timbers exposed to the elements. She'd seen the poppies, too, growing wild in the garden.

'It's not a night to be out alone, my dear, if the vicar's up to no good.' Mrs Grove grasped Dawn's arm, giving it a warning shake. 'You should wait here with me and when William gets back we can send him to fetch help. You've confirmed my fears that the vicar isn't a character to cross. I worked for him for many a long year, but kept my place and kept my distance. I always wondered if that man dabbled in the same bad business as my nephew Ben. I saw lights at dead of night at the church when no decent body would be up there.'

'Mansfield *is* a smuggler, but I don't have time to explain how I came by that knowledge,' Dawn said. 'Viscount Sterling and your nephew William are on their way to try to negotiate with him to free Lily.' A cold shiver passed over Dawn. 'But now I've had time to think about it, I fear that Mansfield has tricked them and sent them on a wild goose chase.'

Dawn suddenly decided. 'I must go; there's no time to lose. William will explain everything to you in due course, I'm sure.' She rushed outside and quickly climbed aboard the cart.

Yanking up her cloak's hood, she set the cart in motion, praying that she wasn't sending *herself* on a wild goose chase. But it seemed the sort of cruel thing that Mansfield would delight in doing: abandoning Lily in the place where she had been illegitimately conceived.

The drizzle was back and dusk had almost fallen when Dawn used the reins to halt the mare outside the dilapidated cottage. There was no discernible light or sound in the building. All that reached her ears was the rushing of the stream close by as it fell away into the valley.

She jumped down and bolted to the door, immediately entering when it creaked open. The smell of musty charcoal assaulted her nostrils and trepidation soured her stomach as she proceeded into the dim interior. Squinting, she carefully advanced by touch, urgently calling out her granddaughter's name.

'She can't hear you...the sweet little thing is fast asleep, courtesy of the laudanum I gave her.'

Dawn froze at the sound of that hateful sarcasm, then pivoted about to find a shadowy male figure blocking out the pale moonlight filtering through the open door. He'd given up masquerading as a godly man and his silhouette displayed he now wore breeches and a jacket.

Fury conquered her shock and she stepped closer to Mansfield, fists balled at her sides. 'Where is Lily? Let me see her at once, you vile beast.' Dawn's voice was shaking with loathing.

'All in good time...' he purred, kicking shut the door, then advancing on her. 'She is safe... for now.' He struck a match and it illuminated his vicious smirk as he jerked a nod at another room.

Dawn made to rush in that direction, but he discarded the light and grabbed both her arms, hauling her back against his body.

'First things first, my dear,' he hissed into her ear. 'You must pay for things you want. We have business to attend to, you and I. You have caused me much trouble from the start and it is time you made amends for it.'

She fought him in earnest as his hands fondled her buttocks, making her squirm in disgust. But Dawn wasn't strong enough to break his grip. In frustration she stamped hard on his foot and received a slap for her pains. 'That is just the start,' he snarled as she gasped and pressed a hand to her smarting cheek.

Keeping a cool head would be imperative if she were to outwit him. She wasn't cowed by his violence; she simply despised him all the more.

A piece of loose timber might have fallen from the charred roof and be easy enough for her to wield to defend herself. Talking to him seemed a good place to start while her eyes grew accustomed to the dark, enabling her to locate such a likely weapon. The more she knew of his scheming, the better it would be. 'You didn't want Eleanor's letter, did you? That note you sent bartering for it was a red herring,' she declared.

'Of course I didn't want that harlot's letter. What good would that do me?' he scoffed. 'I want you, my dear, and now I have you. You are worth ten times what a scrap of paper is, or the child is.'

'How dare you call my stepdaughter names?' Dawn retorted. 'Little wonder the poor woman sought comfort elsewhere. How wretched she must have felt married to a vile bully like you. Yet even that small happiness you took from her, murdering the man who had loved her before she could leave you and make her life with him.' Dawn's voice rang out. She hoped that Lily would wake and start to cry. She was desperate for a sign that her granddaughter was still breathing. 'You may try to flee, but you'll be apprehended and will face trial. The dragoons are already on their way.'

'I guessed as much and suspect I have you

to thank for that.' He snaked a hand out to grab her, but Dawn glimpsed it, slapping it away and making him chuckle nastily. 'There's nowhere for you to escape to and you'll make it easier on yourself by coming willingly to me.'

'You would add violation to your crimes, would you?' Dawn elevated her chin. She wouldn't let him see her fright, though the idea of what he had in mind for her had started her limbs trembling and her stomach rolling. Yet she knew even that she would bear if only he would allow her to take Lily safely home afterwards. But how could she trust the word of such a devil?

'My crimes are not proven and never will be. I shall claim the child as mine and a father cannot kidnap his own offspring. A dying woman's hysterical ravings, penned when she was not of sound mind, won't be believed by a court. Eleanor was delirious at the end...the doctor will verify it.' He barked a triumphant laugh. 'I guessed you might know the details of her sordid fornication and know about their love nest. I guessed, too, you would come, in your infuriatingly meddling way, to save their bastard,' he mocked. '*Your* lover meanwhile forlornly kicks his heels waiting for me to show up at White Ridge, the fool. I had posted a lookout and received word that he rode off in that direction. A message reached me that you had also emerged from the Grange and taken a different route towards town. I knew there was a good chance you would follow the clues here and so have been waiting for you, my dear.'

He sounded so horribly full of himself that Dawn felt like charging at him and pummelling him just for that. But she held her temper and let him crow.

'I doubt your Viscount cares more for the brat than I do, but we both have a lust for you. I'll wager that fellow will do anything to have you back in his bed. But first you can taste mine. Not that it is much of a bed, I'm afraid,' he chortled. 'No feather mattress here, just a blanket on the ground but perhaps by the time I'm done with you, you'll have learnt to like a rough ride as well as I do…' He sprang forward, trapping her against the wall and forcing his mouth down spitefully on hers.

Dawn twisted her face away and lashed out at him, making him laugh nastily.

'Fight away… I'll enjoy taming you.' He ripped open the front of her bodice, exposing her chemise. 'The Viscount seemed smitten. To get you back I believe he'll see me safely out of the country with a tidy sum in my pocket,' he panted.

'You couldn't be more wrong, Mansfield.' Jack had burst in through the door, taking the vicar by surprise and sending him flying with a savage punch to the head. 'I'll see you safely to a gallows, though.'

With a grunt of mingling rage and pain Mansfield steadied himself against the wall. For a moment it seemed he might surrender, but one of his hands dived into a pocket and he lunged forward with a knife.

Jack dodged the blade, swiping Mansfield's feet from under him in an efficient, brutal kick. In a second he had dropped to the ground to wedge a knee against the villain's throat and wrench the hilt of the dagger from Mansfield's fingers. He drew forth his duck's-foot pistol, levelling it at his opponent's head.

'It's safe to go to comfort Lily,' Jack said softly to Dawn, though his eyes never left Mansfield's squirming form. 'William got in through the open window and is in the back room with his niece. We saw her curled up on a blanket.'

Dawn needed no second telling. Gulping back a sob, she darted into the room to find William cradling Lily in his arms. Tears were blurring her vision as she gazed upon her granddaughter's dear face and gently touched the child's cold cheek and matted hair.

'She is well enough considering what the poor mite's been through.' William kept his voice low for fear of disturbing Lily. He transferred his precious burden into Dawn's arms so she might ease her grief by cuddling the child. 'She has been drugged, but stirred a moment ago as though she might soon recover.' He indicated the medicine bottle by his foot, then sent it over with his foot, spilling the laudanum on to the floor. 'Come, let us leave this confounded place.' Having relieved Dawn's trembling arms of Lily's weight, he placed a comforting hand on her shoulder, guiding her through the gloom.

They joined Jack to find him hauling Mansfield to his feet now he had bound the devil's hands together behind his back with his belt. Jack felt relief surging through him as he saw the child stretch before again becoming still. But his eyes soon returned watchfully to his prisoner.

'You must go with William,' Jack told Dawn. 'He will take you to Dr Wilson so he can examine Lily. Then if she is well enough to travel William will see you both safely back to London in the morning with my transport and servants as escort. There is nothing more to fear, I swear.'

'I will willingly do that, sir, you may trust me on it.' William readily accepted his mission.

'I will take this one myself direct to the garrison at Colchester and see him with my own eyes under lock and key. As soon as I can I will join you in London.'

'How devoted you sound, my lord... How long will that last, I wonder with that snivelling brat around?' Mansfield sneered. The bluster had gone from him; he sounded bitter now he'd accepted his defeat.

For a moment Dawn's eyes merged with Jack's through the shadows, then William took her elbow. 'Take care, Jack,' was all she whispered before going out into the darkness.

William quickly placed Lily on the cart seat, then assisted Dawn on to the vehicle before tying his horse behind. They set off swiftly once Lily seemed comfortably settled with her head on Dawn's lap.

As soon as she felt composed enough to hold a conversation Dawn blurted out, 'Thank you so much for all you have done and thank the lord you knew of this place and rescued us in time. Did your brother tell you where he would meet Eleanor?'

William shook his head, looking bashful. 'It is the Viscount you should thank for your salvation. I guessed nothing of the double-cross. But he knew from the start it was a ruse. He said Mansfield would have a lookout stationed close by to report to him, so we played the game. We rode for barely a half mile before heading towards the beach, thinking he might be making his escape to France with Lily. Instead we found his cohorts hiding there. They scattered rather than tangle with Lord Sterling, though we had little interest in them. The Viscount thought my aunt might have some clues to help us locate Mansfield, so we headed there next. She told us you'd not long left her and where you were headed in your search for Lily.'

Dawn stroked her granddaughter's face as she whimpered. William glanced in concern at his niece, putting the old mare to a faster pace. 'Not far to go now to the doctor's house. She is a fine sturdy child...' His voice tailed off as if that were all the reassurance he could honestly give. He concentrated his eyes on the dark road ahead.

'Yes, she is strong and she will be fine,' Dawn said calmly, willing it to be true, for the alternative were too horrible to contemplate. 'Nothing will ever again hurt you, I swear,' she whispered to her granddaughter.

Chapter Twenty-One

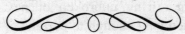

'It seems so outlandish a tale that it is hard to believe it can really be true.' Emma's expression displayed a mingling of amazement and admiration that her friend had been embroiled in, and survived, such a ghastly drama.

'I know what you mean, but unfortunately it did all happen,' Dawn replied on a rueful sigh, glad to have finished reporting the extent of Peter Mansfield's wickedness.

'Poor little Lily! Yet she is so lucky that you have stepped up to care for her. And thank the lord she has completely recovered. I'm sure I would have ended up in a jangle of nerves if even half of it had happened to Bernie. Yet you seem your usual calm self,' Emma marvelled.

'I blubbed most of the way home to London and William, bless him, played with Lily so she wouldn't notice my distress.' Dawn admitted that it *had* all caught up with her. She wouldn't feel wholly content until Jack arrived safely in London and confirmed that Peter Mansfield was finally behind bars, due to stand trial for his crimes.

She had been back at home for several days following a tiring, unbroken journey. William had tarried long enough to partake of the meal she'd pressed on him before he set back on the road to Essex. Dawn had tried to persuade him to rest overnight in London, but he'd politely declined that hospitality. He'd admitted to being eager to return to see Sarah and sort out their futures, although he wouldn't be drawn into saying much about his love. Dawn had warmed to him even more for his discretion. Lily's uncle was a good man, a man to be trusted, and she hoped to see him again soon and had told him so as they'd parted.

Polly had eagerly welcomed her mistress home, glad to be done with her lonely life caretaking the house. Dawn had kept from her maid the catalogue of woes that had befallen them, in case the poor girl fainted dead away. She'd pleased Polly by telling her Lily's father would never be back to bother them. With a twinkle in her eyes her maid had said she hoped the Viscount might again knock on the door, though, and very soon.

So did Dawn hope that…with all her heart… despite knowing there were difficult subjects to broach when he did turn up. Once she had answers to her questions she might have a better idea of what the future held for her. So many disasters had befallen since their reunion on Regent Street, that there had been scant opportunity for them to *really* get to know one another again as a couple.

Since returning to town Dawn had been thinking long and hard about their relationship. She had concluded that she had neglected Jack and their romance to the point that it might wither. She had also forlornly concluded that if he had a woman in his life who provided things she didn't, such as an uncomplicated liaison and her full attention, she couldn't blame him for going to her. Yet if he did so, it would break her heart and leave her miserable and jealous.

He had once told her that he hadn't paid a call on her to play with her granddaughter when she said Lily would appreciate seeing him. Then during his next visit he had shown her explicitly what he did need when with her. The memory of that raw passion still had the power to send exquisite shivers racing through her, yet it reinforced her concern that he'd prefer a lover with no strings attached.

Now the battle for Lily had been won, perhaps he might decide to retreat to a woman who didn't have a child as an obstacle to adult pleasures. Jack was a kind and decent gentleman, but he was also a virile man with natural desires. She'd greedily accepted his assistance in safeguarding Lily, but in return had been a distracted companion and an absent lover.

Though Dawn wanted to put every memory of Mansfield from her head, some of his spiteful taunts had stuck in her mind…possibly because she wondered if they contained a grain of truth. *'I doubt your Viscount cares more for the brat than I do, but we both have a lust for you… How devoted you sound, my lord…how long will that last, I wonder, with that snivelling brat around?'*

Jack understood her granddaughter would always remain her priority, but that didn't mean he had to accept such an arrangement when alternatives were open to him.

Having Lily constantly in the background might finally grow to irritate him. He might choose to marry Pauline and to sire children of his own…if he didn't still feel beholden to Sarah's father and intend to keep the vow he'd made.

Or would the uncomplicated life of a bachelor beckon?

'How extraordinary and wonderful that Lily has an uncle. I'm sure he will want to visit Lily as she grows.' Emma's observation brought an abrupt end to Dawn's poignant inner turmoil.

'William said he will always want to keep in touch with us both, wherever the future takes him,' she replied. 'I hope that life treats him well. William Grove is a fine young man and deserves to be happy.'

'So do you deserve to be happy, Dawn, yet I fear that loving Lily alone might not be enough to fulfil you. And why should it when you are a lovely young woman in the prime of her life?' Emma glanced at the door as her husband entered, then a moment later another gentleman followed him into the cosy salon. 'Look...someone has just turned up who might prove to you one way or another whether I'm right.'

Emma was now quite big with child and Dawn helped her friend to struggle up from the sofa to greet Lance. It wasn't until Dawn was also on her feet that she noticed the Earl wasn't alone. Her heartbeat accelerated in elation and an excited fluttering stirred in her belly as her gaze was captured by a pair of warm grey eyes. The children had been kneeling on the rug, ranging tin soldiers and commencing battle by knocking over casualties among the cavalry. But both youngsters were soon scrambling over soldiers in their eagerness to greet the newcomers. With a little shriek of delight Lily dashed to grab Jack's legs in welcome.

Dawn's recent theories were still at the forefront of her mind. Hastily she disentangled two small arms from a pair of elegantly breeched knees. Her granddaughter behaved with Jack in the same way that Bernie did with his papa: with boisterous familiarity. The poor child, famished of a father's care and attention all her young life, had found a substitute in this man. But Jack wasn't Lily's father or her kin in any shape or form. Dawn wasn't even sure how to describe *her* relationship with him. They'd become close friends, but she knew they both wanted more than that. The stumbling block might be that they needed different things from one another and neither of them could compromise.

'How are you, Dawn?' Jack gained his full height, having crouched down to say hello to Lily. 'You look very well.' A pair of low-lidded eyes roved her face before travelling over the curves beneath her lavender gown.

'I am very well, thank you.'

So he still desired her…that was plain to her

despite his attempt at discretion. But knowing he wanted to touch her wouldn't put her demons to rest. Now he was here with her, the musky male scent of him drugging her senses, she knew being his mistress would never be enough for her. She needed so much more than a twilight life with Jack Valance. As her granddaughter grew older and bolder she might ask about his nocturnal visits and Dawn couldn't lie to create a fake morality. Innocent Lily shouldn't be raised in a household where a man and a woman shared a bed out of wedlock and neighbours whispered behind their hands about them. Mansfield had raised a valid point when throwing that in her face.

So she must be prepared to stand strong… and alone if necessary. The quiet between them stretched. 'More importantly…how are you, sir, after tangling with that fiend?' Dawn rattled off, then immediately regretted having sounded too formal. A ruefulness shaped his mouth as he casually spread his hands.

'As you see, no harm done.' He watched Lily skip back to Bernie and resume their game. 'It's wonderful to see your granddaughter in good health. William arrived back in Essex on the day I was leaving. He did tell me that the doctor had said she'd suffered no lasting ill from the laudanum. It was a great relief to have that news.'

'Indeed, it was. How is Sarah?' Dawn was desperate to know what had happened between them all. From Jack's expression she gleaned he understood her meaning. Thus a serious conversation must have taken place before he travelled to London.

'Sarah is well and happy.' Jack glanced at the children as a squabble over the soldiers broke out. 'There's much I have to tell you. I called at your house, but your maid said you'd gone off in the Houndsmeres' carriage.'

'Emma invited us to tea. Lily loves playing with Bernie. I hope letting her do things she likes will keep any bad memories at bay for her.'

'I hope so, too,' Jack said gently. 'Have you time to talk…somewhere private?' He glanced at the window, frowning at the dark clouds, threatening rain. 'A walk in the fresh air might not be a good idea, though.'

'We could go back to my home,' Dawn blurted out, then blushed, hoping she'd not sounded vulgarly eager. She was too aware of how handsome and appealingly virile he was, she realised. Thoughts of his mouth and hands on her body in her shady fire-lit parlour rushed into her head… to be followed by an unwanted memory of Mansfield turning up and putting an abrupt end to her sensual bliss. An image of his leering countenance dominated her mind, dampening her mood, but Jack appeared quite unaffected by having dealt with the brute for her. Lord Sterling was a flintier character to the mild-mannered gentleman she had fallen in love with years ago. Yet he was still everything she'd always yearned for in a man…in a husband. But even if he wasn't quite so perfect she'd still want him by her side because she loved him.

'I imagine it's not yet Lily's bedtime,' he said wryly. 'There might be a better opportunity for a private interlude here, while your granddaughter is playing with Bernard.'

Dawn winced. So she had been right; he saw Lily as an impediment even to an adult conversation. 'Emma said earlier that she would like Lily to stay overnight… Actually, she asked us both to stay overnight…' Dawn felt herself growing warm beneath the speculative look he had immediately turned on her.

'Are you intending to take up that offer?' he asked.

'No… I shall go home but…but Lily may remain here, if she says she would like to.' Dawn raised her eyes to meet his sultry regard. He was thinking she was offering him a night of passion.

Was she? If he gave her answers she didn't like later, would she snatch at those crumbs from his table anyway, just to make him stay? So much for standing strong and alone, she mocked herself. Her resolution not to be his mistress could crumble before they'd even kissed.

'I would very much like to go home with you, Dawn.' He gave her a thoughtful half-amused smile.

'I shall just say goodbye to Lily and Emma then,' she rattled off, before she could change her mind. The idea of leaving her granddaughter behind was already niggling at her. They hadn't spent a single night apart since Lily lost her mother.

'Are you missing your granddaughter and regretting not bringing her home?'

'No… Honestly, I was not thinking of that. I know she is in the best hands.' Dawn stirred herself from her soulful reverie.

'What were you thinking of, then?'

She stood up from the sofa and started to approach Jack, stationed with his back to the sideboard with a glass of cognac in his hand. The pull of attraction was too great to resist it any longer, but she stayed just out of arm's length. The longing to touch and be touched was a constant throb low in her belly, but she ached for answers, too.

They had travelled in the curricle, in amicable quiet, to her home. There had been no need to hasten into conversation during the short journey; they both knew they had hours in front of them to settle down and debate everything. But now, with drinks distributed and small talk done, the time for getting down to brass tacks had arrived.

And Dawn realised she didn't know where to start, or indeed *if* she wanted to start. She had been impatient for their reunion and bursting with things to ask him when the moment eventually came. But keeping the status quo and basking in the quiet, candle-lit atmosphere with him, while wishing it never to end, was very tempting. She wanted Jack Valance to herself with no distraction from female rivals or evil vicars…or even small children…intruding on their precious time. Electrifying the space separating them was his unspoken demand she move closer. But if she ceded to it, he would reach for her. She would be transported by kisses and caresses to that magical place where worries didn't exist and it was just the two of them. But tomorrow would come…and put paid to the fantasy.

Putting off a crucial talk wouldn't help one bit.

She had responsibilities now that she wouldn't shirk. Her beloved granddaughter was dependent upon her and, with or without Jack by her side, she must accept all that entailed.

'What were you thinking of, Dawn?' he asked huskily, placing down his glass and closing the gap between them.

'You…' she said softly. 'I was thinking of you and of the debt I can never repay you. You saved Lily's life, mine, too, I suspect: I doubt that Mansfield would ever have let me bear witness against him.'

Jack took her hands to tug her closer so barely an inch separated their bodies. 'There is no need for you to feel obligated in any way. You surely know that I would do it all again and most willingly to keep you both safe. As for Mansfield, he is where he can't hurt you. I shan't waste another second of my life on him. And please don't you think of him either.'

'Lily knew him as her father for several years. It troubles me that she might ask about him at some time if a memory of her mama and the vicarage surfaces.'

'If that comes to pass, we will find a way to deal with it.' Jack pressed his lips to her brow to soothe her. 'Don't torture yourself with what might never be. Lily is young and will have many wonderful times ahead of her to obliterate any bad memories from her mind.'

Dawn nodded, though frowning still. She wanted it to be so, but it was too soon for her to be completely free of Mansfield's dark shadow.

'A court will decide his punishment. A noose, deportation…whatever the outcome of his trial you may rest assured he will spend whatever days remain to him incarcerated and in chains.' Jack offered up more reassurance, aware of her lingering uncertainty. 'You will never see him again, I promise. I know it is hard for you to forget what he did, but no more of him…please?'

Dawn made an effort to eject Mansfield from her mind. He had presented her with such danger and heartache, but Jack was right, she shouldn't allow his malevolence to blight another single second of her future.

She knew Jack was watching her for a sign she felt more at ease and she gave him the smile he'd been waiting for. It was a bittersweet pain knowing he meant everything to her while simultaneously fearing their remaining time together could be short. To drive that possibility away, she slipped her arms about his neck, grazing her body on his solid physique in silent demand that he tell her all she wanted to know without the need for her to ask. Once the questions were out there would be no going back. The die would be cast for both of them.

Jack moved his hands seductively over the contours of her back, moulding her against him. The moment his breath stroked behind her ear, sending delightful shivers streaking through her veins, her lids fluttered low over her eyes. A sigh escaped her as his lips glided towards hers and covered them. His mouth was hot and hard, hungry for her, and as he ground their hips together she felt the rock-like urgency of his desire. His tongue tip caressed the silk of her lower lip, inserting between her pearly teeth to tangle with hers. 'God... I've missed you, missed this. It seems like an age since we've even been alone together...' he whispered against her cheek before again slanting his mouth over hers with an ardour that stole strength from her limbs.

His long fingers twined into her hair, loosening pins so thick chestnut tresses coated his hand before tumbling to sway against her shoulders.

Dawn arched her back, exposing a creamy column of throat that was immediately lavished with scorching kisses. With a groan Jack swung her up into his arms and carried her to the sofa, depositing her gently before following her down, his mouth swooping on hers.

The earthy sensation heating her feminine

core was making her squirm her hips against
the knee he'd wedged between her thighs. She
clasped his head, sinking her small fingers into
strands of silvery-fair hair while trying to block
from her mind that what happened next would
determine not only her future but her granddaughter's, too.

Lily deserved to have a fond father figure as
she grew. A man who didn't just sneak into the
house when she was abed. Dawn wanted *this*
man to fill that paternal role and she knew that,
young as she was, Lily had instinctively cho-
sen him, too. But if he would not…would Dawn
again settle for a marriage of convenience with
a pleasant fellow for her granddaughter's sake?
Could she again endure all the disappointment
for herself that such a union brought with it?

His fingers were at her bodice, undoing buttons, his ravening mouth tantalising the achingly
sensitive skin he was exposing. But the thought
wouldn't go away that they should talk before
she fell completely beneath his spell. There
would be no point in refusing to be his mistress
once the deed was done. And once it was done…
it wouldn't be enough. If she found out at some
time that he was to be somebody else's husband
she would feel cheated and bitter. Better to part

as friends, quickly and with her pride and her reputation intact…

'You said earlier you had much to tell me,' Dawn gasped out, clasping his abrasive chin to stop his mouth doing its wicked work. She gazed into his sleepy eyes. 'It isn't just Mansfield we need to talk about, is it, Jack?' she said hoarsely.

The ironic slant to his mouth displayed he was frustrated she'd withdrawn from him. In consolation she brushed a kiss against his cheek, then rested her forehead on his shoulder. 'Sarah confided in me that she loved William and intended to jilt you.'

'I know she confided in you…she told me.'

'Why haven't you mentioned it to me, then?' Dawn searched his eyes.

With a sour laugh he was on his feet and a moment later had walked away.

Dawn sat upright, fumbling at her button hooks. 'Would you have told me you'd been jilted?' she asked quietly.

'Of course I would have told you. But not right now. I've not been with you…*really* been with you, in a long while. Can you blame me for wanting some time for us before the hubbub starts again?'

Dawn stood up, a chill starting to replace the sensual heat that had almost stolen her reason.

'No… I don't blame you. But don't blame me either for wanting to know to what hubbub you refer. Do you mean Lily?'

'No…'

'I think you do. You find my granddaughter's presence annoying.'

He picked up his glass and shot back the cognac in one swallow. 'Why ask me a question, then tell me you know the answer better than I do?'

'Don't be clever with me. Just tell me the truth, Jack.' Dawn attempted to keep a note of pleading from her voice.

'I always tell you the truth. But if you want to concentrate on other people rather snatch the opportunity to have some time just for us for a change, so be it.' An oath beneath his breath was smoothly followed by, 'Let's start with Sarah, then. Yes, she jilted me and I'm glad for her and for me that she did so. I had already decided that I couldn't go ahead and marry her. But…coward that I am… I'm glad she spoke first and saved me the job of possibly humiliating her with a rejection.'

'You're not a coward,' Dawn said huskily. 'You're the bravest man I know. And it was a sweet thought to consider her pride before your own. So…will you allow her and William to get married?' Dawn took a step closer to him.

'I've given them both my blessing. If her father were still alive, I hope he would approve of my decision.' Jack toyed with the empty glass on the sideboard. 'Before he died Snow told me his abiding wish was to know that his daughter would be safe and happy with a kind husband. He believed the fact that she was badly compromised would prevent a decent gentleman marrying her.' Jack frowned at the memory of that solemn conversation. 'He believed I owed it to him to always protect her. He was right. But I believe I've upheld my end of the deal by letting Sarah go to William Grove. She tells me he is the only person who can make her happy. He is a gentleman…one of the best…and quite capable of keeping her as safe as his wife as I would were I to marry her. In fact, she is safer with him. She told me if I refused to let her go she would keep running away to find William until I did.'

Dawn gave a wry smile. 'You are a good man…a wise man to have found the logic in it. You have nothing to regret in acting compassionately.'

'I'm a good man, am I?' he mocked. 'So why don't you trust me, Dawn?'

'I do…of course, I do. What do you mean by saying that?'

'You do, do you? Yet you believe I'll abandon you once I have had my wicked way. That's the truth of it, isn't it?'

'I didn't say that…' she choked out.

'You didn't need to, sweet, I can see it in your face.'

After an indignant moment she demanded, 'Well…will you leave me?' She challengingly elevated her chin. 'You've never actually made it clear where I stand with you. Yet I have plainly refused to be your mistress. If, indeed, you still want me as such.'

'Why would I not want you?' he queried silkily.

Dawn took a breath before throwing caution to the wind. 'Sarah told me something else: she knew you would be glad to be jilted. She believed you'd sooner marry Pauline instead.' Dawn's eyes blazed accusingly at him. 'If that is your intention, then maybe you'll have no need of a mistress…especially one burdened with a small child. A decent gentleman would honour his vows and stay true to his wife.'

'Is that it?'

'Is that *what*?' Dawn cried, infuriated by his cool, faintly amused, demeanour.

'You're jealous of a woman from my past? I haven't visited her in ages and have no intention of doing so again. Our relationship was over the moment I saw you on Regent Street. I took her home that day and haven't seen her since.'

Dawn sank her small teeth into her lower lip and gazed at him, wondering.

'That's why I say you don't trust me, Dawn,' he said and gave a mirthless grunt of laughter. 'You believe me to be lying, don't you?'

'If you had been open and told me about her, perhaps I wouldn't have doubts,' Dawn retorted.

'You want me to discuss my mistresses with you?'

Dawn snapped her eyes to his. *'Mistresses?'* she echoed waspishly. 'How many have you got?'

'Now? Not a single one...believe me, I'd know if I had because I'm sorely in need of some female attention,' he muttered sourly.

'Some female attention?' Again, Dawn sharply returned to him some of his own words. 'Well, don't let me detain you, sir. Go and find it,' she said icily and turned her back on him.

He tipped up his head to smile ruefully at the ceiling. 'It was badly phrased. I'm in desperate need of you, Dawn. I want your attention. And well you know it.'

She spun back to face him. 'And for how long would I be your mistress before my devotion to Lily made other female attention seem preferable to "snatching time for us" as you call it?'

'The fact that you bring that up makes me wonder if you really like me or know me at all,' Jack said quietly.

'The fact that you promised to give me carriages and anything I want in return for sharing a bed with you shows how little you know me! I don't want any of it,' she said heatedly, tears glistening in her eyes.

'What do you want, Dawn?' he asked quietly.

'Jack Valance…' she murmured after a tense pause. 'Not a viscount, not a fortune, not a mansion…just you and what you promised me years ago.'

'What makes you think that I've gone back on that promise? I told you that you had my heart. Do you believe me lying about that, too?' He came closer to slide a hand over her tear-wet cheek. 'Give me something. Have I got your heart? Have you room for me in there as well as for Lily?' He dropped his head, looking bashful. 'I'm not complaining, I swear. I understand how you feel about her…how you love her. She is a dear little thing. And you are wonderful to care for her the way you do. She's the luckiest child to have you in her life.'

Dawn started to shake her head, grinding her forehead against his shoulder. 'She's not lucky at all to have a grandmother like me. If I'd been less selfish, her mama might still be alive to love and care for her.' Dawn looked up at Jack through blurry vision. 'At times I feel so guilty,' she said in choked tones. 'I *owe* it to Eleanor to care for her daughter and love Lily as she did. And it is an easier task than ever I would have thought it could be.' Dawn paused to compose herself and Jack allowed her those silent moments, simply caressing her gently. 'Before all of this horrible time I would visit my stepfamily perhaps a few times a year and gladly return home afterwards, feeling I had done my duty. In truth I found it tiresome to be a grandma at my young age… vanity no doubt played a part.' Dawn hesitated, feeling ashamed of what she must admit to; it still gnawed at her conscience, making her feel wretched. 'I should have gone earlier this time to see them. A week earlier when I was supposed to. But I was happy with my friends and found a reason to stay in London to enjoy myself. During that missing week Eleanor became gravely ill. By the time I turned up and got the doctor to her my stepdaughter was beyond saving.' Dawn tried to stop a sob from escaping, making herself hiccough. 'I can't put from my head that Lily's mother might not have died if the doctor had just been brought earlier to attend to her. It's my fault she suffered so. She lost her life because I wasn't there when I was most needed. I will make it up to Lily, I swear...'

That was all Jack could bear to hear. He hugged Dawn, rocking her gently against the strength of his body. 'Don't ever say that it's your fault. It isn't, I swear to you, it is not. Mansfield is to blame for the tragedy. The responsibility was his to care for his wife and her daughter. Nobody could have guessed the extent of his evil nature or his neglect. The local magistrate was astonished to hear that such an upright chap, as he termed Mansfield, was so arrantly corrupt.'

'But I never liked him... I should have guessed at his fiendish nature and might have done so had I paid more visits and more attention.'

Jack enclosed her face between his palms and gazed into her eyes. 'Listen to me... Mansfield was the root of all the trouble. Nobody else could have averted what happened; not you, not William.' Jack eased Dawn back from him and placed his lips against hers. 'You are the most wonderful woman any child...any man could have in his life,' he said huskily. 'I want you in my life, always, as my wife and the mother of my children. God willing, we will have some brothers and sisters for Lily to mother as she grows. She *will* be happy…and so will you, Dawn, I'll make it so, I promise, if you'll only say you'll marry me.'

Dawn closed her eyes, a feeling of peace rippling through her as he, in one anguished-sounding speech, put all her demons to rest. At that moment she loved him more than she thought it possible, but she felt too enervated to tell him so. She slipped her arms about his waist, resting against him, and he allowed her that quiet time without badgering her for an answer.

'Say you love me,' she whispered.

'I love you… I've always loved you. Through some long hard years I've loved you and will carry on doing so until the end of my days. Thoughts of you kept me going in that confounded gaol…'

Now it was Dawn's turn to comfort. She tightened her arms about him and rubbed together their cheeks. 'No more thoughts of that…it is in the past…nothing can hurt you now.'

'You can…if you don't say you love me and will be my wife.'

'I think you know that I would adore to

be your wife and I've always loved you, Jack Valance…even when I was married to my husband I couldn't forget you…'

'Don't speak of him…please.' Jack stopped her reminiscence of Thomas Fenton by brushing a thumb on her lips. 'I know he treated you well…and I'm glad. But don't speak of him—those years he had with you should have been mine.'

'No more jealousies…for either of us.' Dawn placed a comforting kiss on his cheek. 'I have already forgotten Pauline,' she teased. 'Now it *is* just us…alone together in the peace and quiet. No hubbub…'

He chuckled. 'And the hubbub to which I referred, and which I assure you will soon start, is Sarah's wedding. She has plans for a lavish celebration despite her future husband looking quite startled by the idea of marrying amid society in Mayfair.'

'And will you indulge her?' Dawn asked simply.

'Yes…of course…if it is still her wish after William has done his best to persuade her a quieter affair might be just as nice. Whatever they decide, I believe I can make William happy, too, by putting him at the helm of a trader docked at Liverpool. We have already briefly spoken of it…'

'You can't separate the newlyweds so soon…' Dawn sounded scandalised.

'Sarah will go with him,' Jack explained. 'She's already made that clear. She's a good sailor and a seafaring husband is just what she needs. She would accompany her father on his voyages.'

'Good for her,' Dawn said simply.

'And now enough of others,' Jack said, his voice sultry and his eyes slipping over her with passionate intensity. 'Will you marry me, Dawn? Will you let me finally keep that promise I made to you to come back and make you my wife?' He gave her a sweet seductive kiss, adding with wry persuasion, 'We can marry tomorrow if you like…or this evening if you wish it to be sooner. I got a special licence this afternoon.'

'You are very sure of yourself, sir, and of me.' She suddenly became shy and serious. 'Of course I will marry you, Jack. I was beginning to think you might never ask.' Then flirtatiously teased him, 'But tomorrow would suit me very well. I think I might like to be your one-night mistress.'

'I think I might like that, too…' he said wolf-ishly. 'One night…' He glanced at the fading

light beyond the window. 'And it's still young…
plenty of time yet.' He suddenly swung her into
his arms. 'You know one night doesn't mean one
time, don't you?'

Dawn slipped her arms about his neck, kissed
him full on the mouth with bold abandonment.
'You told me once you never sleep well… I'm
going to make sure that tonight you do, Jack Valance. You will be quite exhausted by dawn…'

* * * * *

COMING SOON!

We really hope you enjoyed reading this book. If you're looking for more romance, be sure to head to the shops when new books are available on

Thursday 3rd October

MILLS & BOON

Coming next month

A MIDSUMMER KNIGHT'S KISS
Elisabeth Hobbes

'It smells wonderful,' he said, cupping the rose in the palm of his hand and bringing it to his nose.

'May I?' Rowenna asked.

This time Robbie did not hold the flower out at arm's length, but kept it where it was so he could smell it at the same time. Rowenna leaned in towards him. She rested one hand on Robbie's shoulder. The other took hold of his wrist to steady it as she had done when she smelled the lavender. She buried her nose in the petals and took a slow, deep breath, then sighed with pleasure, closing her eyes and inhaling again. Her face was close to Robbie's, tilted a little to one side, with only the flower between them. He could count the individual eyelashes that seemed to reach all the way up to her arched brows. Her lips were the same deep shade as the rose he held, almost as soft as the velvety petals, but much fuller and more enticing.

'Beautiful.' He sighed.

'It's so strong it makes me feel lightheaded,' Rowenna said.

She opened her eyes and looked at him over the top of the flower, the long lashes widening to frame eyes that were now heavy with sensuality. Her lips curved into a wide smile and Robbie's heart began to beat faster.

He was starting to feel lightheaded himself, but that was nothing to do with the scent of the rose. Lightheaded, and more than a little reckless.

'I don't mean the flower,' he murmured.

He folded his hand over the rose and lowered it, noticing in the back of his mind that his hand was trembling. He bent his head down a little more until he was close enough that his mouth was next to Rowenna's. Close enough that he could feel the softness of her cheek against his. Close enough to whisper and be perfectly certain that no one else who might venture to this part of the garden would be able to hear the words that were meant only for her ears.

'I mean you.'

And he kissed her.

Continue reading
A MIDSUMMER KNIGHT'S KISS
Elisabeth Hobbes

www.millsandboon.co.uk

LET'S TALK

Romance

For exclusive extracts, competitions
and special offers, find us online:

- facebook.com/millsandboon
- @MillsandBoon
- @MillsandBoonUK

Get in touch on 01413 063232

For all the latest titles coming soon, visit
millsandboon.co.uk/nextmonth